I0783284

L.M. Pampuro

Maximum PANIC

LM Pampuro

L.M. Pampuro

Maximum Panic
Copyright 2025 by L.M. Pampuro

This book is a work of fiction.
Names, characters, locations, and events are either a product of the author's imagination, fictitious or used fictitiously.
Any resemblance to any event, locale or person, living or dead, is purely coincidental.

This story is a product of human imagination – not artificial intelligence.
This book is from the imagination of the author, L.M. Patarini. A.I. was used for spelling corrections and comma additions only.

All rights reserved. No part of this book may be used or reproduced by any means, graphic, electronic, or mechanical, including photocopying, recording, taping, or by any information storage retrieval system without written permission of the publisher except in the case of brief quotations embodied in critical articles and reviews.

Cover design by the LMPatarini group

PAPERBACK ISBN: 979-8-9884171-3-2
E-BOOK ISBN: 979-8-9884171-2-5

Maximum Panic

L.M. Pampuro

Maximum Panic

L.M. Pampuro

Maximum Panic

Getting caught up quickly...
Zack and Maxi were first introduced in *Maximum Mayhem* (2012) as Zack investigated a scam that Maxi had no idea she was involved in. Now the crazy part here is that Maxi had a crush on Zack in high school yet in a cruel twist of fate, he ended up friends and colleagues with her brother Pete, the golden child of the family.

Maximum Mayhem brought the two together during trying circumstances of betrayal, false friendships, and both Maxi and her ex-husband getting shot. (He dies—she did not).

The story ended with the possibility of a couple ship between Maxi and Zack.

Fast forward five years later to *Maximum Trouble* where while vacationing in Aruba, Maxi and her family get caught up in a crazed psycho's attempt to take over the island and seek revenge on the United States government.

(A little far-fetched yet at one time Venezuela sought the ABC islands, Aruba, Curacao, and Bonaire, back from the Dutch so maybe not entirely off).

Maxi and her family spend a horrific time dodging drug lords and double agents trying to survive as others around them parish. Zack is deployed as part of the team to rescue the family and others.

L.M. Pampuro

This time Zack gets shot yet obviously survives because this final book in the trilogy, *Maximum Devotion*, finds Zack and Maxi living in Northern Vermont while Ric, Maxi's son, is in college.

So, here is your short catch up. If you'd like more details about Maxi and Zack's relationship, please read *Maximum Mayhem* and *Maximum Trouble*, though this is not necessary to understand this plot.

A note from the author: If my massage therapist at the time, an avid reader, hadn't said that Maxi and Zack needed more time together and a better ending, the second nor this book wouldn't have existed.

So, I thank you Eileen Waldman, for the love of my characters and the motivation to do right by both. I hope you enjoy this one as much as the last two.

Peace.

Maximum Panic

L.M. Pampuro

RIC

Wheezing noises from the other side of the bed awakened him from a fitful sleep. The mattress shook as the person next to him struggled to breathe. Ric rolled in the opposite direction of the noise, up onto his hip. The sunlight that sparkled through thin gray curtains blasted against his half-open eyes. Each haggard breath to his left added a pounding pressure in his skull. He tried to bring his focus to the framed yellowed magazine photos of the ocean, each set in a straight line across a paneled wall.

Behind him a loud hacking cough was followed by a sucking sound with a gurgle of phlegm. He struggled to release his legs from the tangled thin blanket. Once freed, he stretched both legs over the side of the bed. On the opposite side of the mattress, stringy blonde hair semi-covered the face of a girl, her age hidden. Her exposed arm had needle tracks around the elbow. Ric held both of his arms out in front to examine his skin.

"No holes," he whispered as his hands rubbed down his biceps and forearms.

Ever so gently, Ric pushed down on the bare mattress to move his body without disturbing the rest of the bed. A lacy bra, tank top, and jean shorts lay scattered across the worn carpet. With his clothes nowhere to be found he moved aside a long curtain that separated the bedroom from the rest of the space. Just on the other side, in a semi-folded pile, lay his pants and shirt. He stepped into his pants and felt his empty pockets.

"Crap," he said at the same moment his hand moved to cover his mouth. As he walked along the carpet, worn down in spots to the metal underneath, the hacking breaths continued. Ric tried to move aside piles of magazines, newspapers, and dirty dishes that covered the bench seating and a table at the opposite end of the cramped space.

Under the table, kicked into the far corner, his phone lay, screen flickering. He reached for it and when he pulled into view, a few bars of battery remained. Now seated on the floor, he could see his hemp wallet just outside another folded door. The wallet lay spread open, and Ric saw all his credit cards were missing from their spot, in the fold behind his Vermont driver's license. None of the cash remained, including the emergency 50-dollar bill that he'd hidden inside the flap.

He peeked back behind a folding door that closed with a magnet built into its side, only to be slapped with the stench of urine and vinegar. With the curtain open, he could see from front to back. When a quick search around the kitchen sink and stove failed to locate his cash and cards, he moved in a slow turn to see every surface, windowsills, stove, and sink covered with empty beer cans and soda bottles, dishes with the remains of food along with the empty takeout containers that the food originated from.

Ric maneuvered around the piles of garbage to the exit without disturbing any of the mess. Once outside, the scorching sun temporarily blinded his sight. He stumbled down a few metal stairs, missing the last and falling on the hard ground.

With a quick jump back to his feet, he turned to see that the trailer was an old Airstream parked in the middle of an expansive valley. A weathered grey barn, the only other structure, off in the distance across a yellowed field. The peaks of the majestic Rockies circled.

How the hell did I get out here? For one moment he considered waking the stranger inside to try and get a ride back to camp. A quick flicker to the tracks on her arms sent that thought away.

Instead, he walked around the back of the trailer to relieve himself. "Man, my piss smells better than that entire trailer," he mumbled as he zipped up. The sound of a combustible engine out front broke into his thoughts. As he leaned his body around the side of the trailer, a massive man, shotgun in hand, came into view. Ric spied that he had stepped out of a beat-up, rusty Ford pick-up and he walked heavy stomping on the hard ground in a path to the trailer, which shifted under the man's weight as he entered.

"Susanna!" the man called. "Susanna, darling." There was a brief silence then screaming.

"Get that fucking gun away from me!"

"Awe darlin', aren't you lying there naked just waiting for me. Didn't you miss your old boy?"

The trailer shifted then started to gently rock. When sure that both parties were distracted, Ric took off in a sprint in the direction of the truck. Much to his delight, a set of keys hung in the ignition. A turn of the keys and the truck's engine snarled to life. Ric crammed the stick shift into reverse, swung the truck bed in a circle, and stomped down on the gas.

Shouts and a gunshot came from behind, and a bullet pinged off the side mirror. He followed the dust-covered trail until he came to a group of granite rocks that rose up to the sky in front of him. To his right and left, dirt roads led away from the trailer, without any signage. "Of course, there isn't an effing road out here," He slammed his fist against the steering wheel as if pain would help his plight. He looked in the rearview mirror to see the girl from the bed outside, next to the towering man, who waved his arms in the air and jumped up and down. The gun now nowhere in sight.

He held his phone out the window. The device showed only one faded bar and the red indicator of a battery dying. He looked in both directions before opting for a left-hand turn. "I'm probably screwed either way."

He drove as close to the rocky edge as possible without scraping against the hard surface. A boulder or two along the edge marked the space where guard rails would exist on a more frequently traveled road. Space, a mountain range, and a cloudless sky made a view that any artist would want to recreate. On a normal day Ric would have pulled over to take in the sight.

The truck lurched from side to side. Ric tightened his grip to fight with the steering wheel to stay on the road. His shoulder bounced against the metal frame of the door. The throbbing in his shoulder matched the one in his hand. The passenger door screeched as metal grazed along the granite cliff. The other lane's lack of guard rails and drop into the air gave Ric no alternative—he had to cuddle the cliff. He drove as fast as he dared, cringing as the truck's tires bounced through every rut, pothole, and plot of asphalt.

Around a curve, up on the hill a cellphone tower disguised as a pine tree brought signs of civilization. Little puffs of smoke floated up over a valley that lay straight ahead. Ric was so captivated by the view; he didn't see a substantial rut in the trail. The truck jerking motion kept his hands clung tight to the steering wheel as he tried to keep from slipping off the road.

The needle on the gas tank dropped above the E. He moved the shifter out of gear and slid down a steep incline riding the brakes. The smell of burnt metal seeped in from a hole in the rusted floor and gray smoke slithered up into the cab. Around a sharp bend, a small western town appeared like an abandoned old cowboy movie set. He rolled the truck into an empty parking space along the street and jumped out, leaving the keys resting in the ignition.

After a few deep breaths, Ric turned his attention to his dying cellphone. The red battery light had stopped blinking. "Fuck," he muttered as he tried the power button. When no life came into the phone, he put it back in his pocket. Off in the distance, he saw a sign for a gas station with a general store that had an open flag swinging in the breeze on a pole by the road.

Ric started to walk along the sidewalk. He passed a closed Italian restaurant named Doug's with its dining room full of white and red checkered tablecloths, a few unmarked buildings, and a United States post office.

Nothing here felt familiar. He opted to enter the federal building. A grey-haired woman with a warm smile greeted him. "Hi there," she said. "What can I do you for?"

"I'm looking for an Uber back to Pride Ridge?" His voice rose at the end as if he'd asked a question.

"No Ubers out here," the woman laughed. "And Pride Ridge's about an hour drive. They sometimes send the shuttle down around five for folks to go to Doug's. Best Italian in the Rockies."

Ric nodded. She continued, "I can call up and see if they can send one down earlier. It may cost you, though."

"That's okay," Ric said. His mind went to his empty wallet. "I just need to get back to camp."

"How'd ya get here?" she asked as she dialed. Ric opened his mouth to answer and was silenced with a raised index finger. "Sully, this Marge over in Cross Creek. I got one of your guests here. Says he needs a ride back." She glanced over at Ric. "Uh ha. Yep. Got it. Thanks, Sully." Marge nodded her head as she listened. "Today is your lucky day. Sully said that he had a guy on his way to drop off some mail here. So, he's going to get a hold of him and let you ride back in the truck." Marge let out a laugh, "He'll probably charge you for a shuttle ride so tip the heck out of his guy, okay."

"Thank you so much," Ric said. "Do you know when he'll be here?"

"Sully said he was on his way, so that could be any time between now and an hour. There's a coffee bar two buildings down, and you can get a decent sandwich at the gas station. Of course, you are welcome to wait here too." Marge gestured at an empty wooden table with two chairs. "Just seat yourself over there."

***

Ric awoke with a start at the sound of a door opening. A huge figure, outlined in sunlight, cast a vast shadow. A massive hand gave a tip of a cowboy hat in his direction. Ric returned the gesture with a chin nod. "Hey Marge," the man spoke, "I just got back from Susanna's place. That wreck of a husband claimed his truck was stolen, yet there it was—"

"Parked in front of the saloon?" Marge interrupted.

"Yep, parked in front of the saloon. The only thing is Hawk insists some college boy took off in it this morning." The man glanced over at Ric. "You know anything about that?"

"Haven't heard a word, though things have been on the slow side today," Marge said. She gave Ric a quick look. "My friend here is waiting on the mountain shuttle. Seems to have gotten himself lost."

Ric began to sweat as the man stared in the direction of where he sat. Ric crossed his arms over the camp's name on his shirt and slid his body against the wall. The angle that he stood allowed a hint of sunlight to highlight the dark patches sewed onto the green uniform, the most prominent patch on his front pocket. The word SHERIFF in yellow, all-in caps.

"Got yourself lost, huh? I gotta ask ya, boy, you weren't out in Hawk's Canyon this morning, were ya?"

"Not that I know of sir."

Ric's answer seemed to satisfy the Sheriff. "Hey, Marge," he said, one hand on the doorknob, "let me know when the shuttle gets here. I want to have a word with the driver."

Ric let out a long breath as the door shut. He could feel little shivers through the silence telling him that Marge was staring. When he turned back in her direction, his eyes met hers.

"Listen, fella, if you took Hawk's truck, you wouldn't be the first. That rust bucket seems to go missing every other day. Now not to speak out of church about a neighbor," Marge shook her head from side to side. "That little wife of his is something else," she laughed. "I guess every town has one and good old Susanna is ours. But, you know, fessing up makes the Sheriff's job a whole lot easier, and he'll probably just give you a fine. You know because it happens so often."

Ric nodded then returned his gaze out the window. He blew out an audible breath. What the fuck had he gotten himself into? Last he remembered, a few of the guys were heading into town. Was it this town? "Shit," he mumbled as he sat and stared.

A white pick-up with Pride Ridge written in script on the door parked outside the post office. The Sheriff's mass blocked most of his view. Outside the window, lanky arms in flannel gestured beyond the Sheriff's biceps.

The Sheriff stepped to the side, and a kid about Ric's age walked through the door. Tall, long-limbed with a fluff of brown hair tied back into a messy ponytail. He gave Ric a nod and a peace sign as he heaved a white canvas bag onto the counter.

"Marge, you get more beautiful every day," the kid exclaimed.

"You just say that because driving out here keeps you away from mucking the stalls."

"Touche'" the boy answered. Then, he turned his attention to Ric, "And are you, my passenger?"

Ric stood and extended his hand, "Yes, Ric Malone."

"Well Ric Malone, folks call me Dubs—"

"—no one calls you Dubs," Marge laughed.

"Some people do," Dubs replied. "Anyway, I was going to make a stop on the way back if you aren't in a hurry." When Ric didn't answer, he added, "Just a quick one, I promise."

"Now you listen, Ed," Marge said, "Sully expects you back pronto. Don't go getting my friend in any trouble on one of your adventures."

Dubs stroked his chin. "Okay, back to the camp we go." He grabbed a small sack off the counter. "Thank you, Marge," he added.

"You are welcome, Edward." Marge turned toward Ric. "And it was lovely meeting you, Ric Malone," she said. "Don't forget what I said."

Ric gave a quick nod as he headed out the door. He could hear Dubs behind him mimicking Marge saying, "Sully expects you back. Well, fuck Sully. I mean seriously, the dude's a dick. Why do I do this job?" The conversation with himself lasted into the cab of the truck, followed by "Oh crap."

Ric's eyes followed the direction that Dubs' finger extended. The Sheriff was walking over from across the street, waving his arms in their direction. "Oh, crap indeed," Ric muttered.

The Sheriff approached the truck's passenger's side to block Ric from opening the door. A silver Ford Bronco with emergency lights blaring swerved in front of the truck. "Son, you need to come with me," said the Sheriff. Ric's sweat now soaked through his shirt. He gave a wayward glance at Dub's. "I am so fucked," he whispered under his breath, moving to the side of the truck.

"Why?" Dubs asked the Sheriff. "He's one of the campers from our resort and the kid—"

"—now Ed, this isn't none of your concern."

Ed grabbed Ric's arm. "I'll let Sully know. Get in contact with your buds, man. No worries."

The Sheriff's massive hands moved Ric's arms behind his back. Tight metal circled his wrists. A hand on his back pushed his body into the Bronco. The combined stench of wet dog and unbathed person stench moved into his nostrils. Ric flattened his back against the hard leather seat while trying to wiggle his nose below the collar of his T-shirt to cut off some of the smell.

"You'll get one phone call, son. Better make it a good one," the Sheriff leaned into view from the passenger's seat. Another person in a similar uniform steered a quick U-turn and brought the vehicle to a sudden stop. Ric's body bounced off the back of the driver's seat.

The door opened and the other man in a uniform pulled Ric out of the SUV, catching him right before he stumbled into the sidewalk. Ric looked back to see that the only move the Bronco made was to cross the street and stop in front of a storefront with Sheriff's Office scripted in gold across a large picture window.

"My phone is out of juice," Ric answered. "The number I need is in my contacts."

The Sheriff's laugh bounced off the buildings. "You young ones," he started, "back in my day, we memorized important numbers. Now you all carry those damn phones. Probably should have charged before you went on your spree."

"What spree?" Ric's voice raised up an octave.

"What spree? Son, do you think I am an idiot? We know about the truck and the rest."

"Seriously, what are you talking about?" His heartbeat became audible as panic kicked in. With the other uniformed man holding his arm, Ric walked through a door into a lobby type area. To his left, an open space with two green chairs and a television mounted to the wall in the corner. No sound played, as the Fox News logo blazed in the background. To his right, a swinging door separated the small lobby from a couple metal desks. One faced the television and open area while the other desk faced a series of jail cells.

Ric could make out metal bars and three doors clearly, three jail cells visible to anyone who entered the building.

The Sheriff pointed at the person holding Ric's arm. "Dak, put him in number two." He turned his attention to Ric. "Boy, if you need the facilities, let Dak here know. You will be escorted down the hall. We don't have that fancy plumbing you big city folks get."

"What fancy plumbing? I've never been arrested before—wait, what are you arresting me for?"

"You know what you did," the Sheriff repeated. "When you are ready, you can make that call. Let Dak or me know."

The Dak person jerked the handcuffs so hard that bright red indents dug into Ric's wrists. Ric felt a sting of pain followed by a release of pressure as the steel links loosened their grip. He reached into his back pocket and held his phone up. "Do you have a charger? I need to get the number...." A short shove to the back moved Ric into a cell. He jumped at the loud clank of the door shutting. "If you have a charger, I just need a little juice to access my contacts." The only number committed to memory was his mom's, and he wasn't going to call Maxi. Nope this one needed his stepdad's action.

Neither man answered.

Ric paced the length of his cell, then again asked, "Hey, if I could get a charger, then I can get my parent's number and end this thing." Laughter from the lobby followed his plea. "Assholes," Ric muttered.

"What you say boy?" the Sheriff's voice boomed.

"I said that if you could get a charger for my phone—"

"After that," the Sheriff pressed his face against the bars. "What did you say after that?" he screamed. The volume of the Sheriff's voice sent Ric back against the cement wall.

"I, I, I."

"Yeah—that's what I thought."

Maximum Panic

The Sheriff sauntered into the lobby, hearing him add, "Humph, college boys," A loud grunt was followed by a high-pitched squeaking sound that rushed through Ric's ears.

A bed sat in the corner farthest from the cell door. Ric shuffled over to it and sat, head in hands. *What the fuck!* A snort from the next cell made him jump. A person lay on a cot in the cell to his left. A blanket covered up the person.
"Great another blanket covering another face." Ric stared up at the bars in his only window. The sunlight streaks fading.

ZACK

At the same moment, in two time zones away, Zack Brady, Ric's stepfather, asked the same what the fuck question. He sat, hands folded on his lap, just outside of the United States Senate chambers. Angry voices from protesters just beyond the building spilled into the hall and echoed against the dome. Time moved slowly as he waited to give his testimony.

"Hey Zack, how's it going?" one of the Capitol police stood a few feet away.

"Damned if I know," Zack said. "All they do is go in a circle and argue the same point. I'm getting too old for this shit."

"Yeah, I know what you mean. After the riots, I felt the same."

"But you're still here," Zack noted.

"I am." Trooper Harper rested one hand on the wall as he gave a quick shrug. "Got one in college who wants to work with you guys. Got another finishing up high school, so I got a few years to go. Your kids are grown. What keeps you going?"

"Justice," Zack laughed. "Maxi and I have one in college still, her son Ric, and I'm just not ready yet." Zack looked up at the monitor to see the fist-pumping continue. "But after today, I am not sure this is what I signed up for."

"I know what you mean. They sit in the chamber and debate all day to accomplish nothing. My partner died on January 6th."

"Sorry to hear that."

"Thank you. I want to see those who were at fault held accountable. Twenty, even ten years ago, we wouldn't be having this conversation."

"We live in a messed-up time." The door to the chamber squeaked open. The guard pointed at Zack and waved him in. "Well, here goes nothing," Zack said. He gave an exaggerated eye roll as he stood.

"Good luck, buddy," Trooper Harper extended his hand.

Zack took another moment to button up his suit jacket then made his way down the carpeted aisle of the maple gallery of the United States Senate. He sat down next to his boss. The hum of conversation subsided. The committee chair, a late-aged puff of a man in a suit two sizes too small, clacked the gavel. Zack rose from his chair. "Please state your name and occupation," the Senator from Fremont instructed.

"My name is Zackary Darcy Brady. I am currently a sections chief in the Office of Criminal Cyber Services branch for the United States Federal Bureau of Investigation."

"Where is that located, Mr. Brady?"

"We have offices throughout the United States. My current location is here in the District of Columbia."

"Thank you. Prior to being located here, you were part of our team in New Haven, Connecticut, correct?" The Senator then directed, "New Haven is still part of Connecticut, right?" The aid nodded. The Senator turned back to the gallery. Although his glasses had slipped down his nose, his eyes still bore into Zack.

"Yes, sir."

"Senator is fine."

"Yes, Senator," Zack said. His lips pursed. He stood still and waited while the Senator thumbed through the stack of papers that lay in front of him. The other committee members scrutinized Zack in silence from their perch in the galley. Young men in blue suits took turns whispering in the committee's ears and placing sheets papers in front of their view.

"Oh, here it is," the Senator pulled out a sheet from the pile while his colleagues snickered. "Ah yes, Mr. Brady, you were in New Haven when we had how many states? Was Connecticut separate?"

"Connecticut was part of the original thirteen and still is separate, sir," Zack answered, "At the time the United States was composed of fifty states."

"I don't need a history lesson, son. Just answer my questions. Now while you were in New Haven, did you work with a Spencer Cabot?"

"Spencer Cabot was my immediate supervisor at the New Haven office."

"Ah, yes, it says that here. What type of relationship did you have with Agent Cabot?"

"He was my direct supervisor. I was the senior agent on staff at that time."

"And you were in charge of—"

"I was investigating a series of cybercrimes that targeted our elderly citizens, sir, er Senator. The investigation, OTH—OTN, was closed two years ago. The cyber scammers were located in Florida and brought to trial. This resulted in—"

"—I don't care what the trial resulted in. That is not why we are here." The Senator turned towards one of the blue suits who jumped up at the gesture.

"You asked," Zack mumbled underneath his breath. Finally, he said, "Yes sir," a bit too loud.

The Senator brought his attention back to Zack. "Where was I? Oh yes, tell us about Spencer Cabot."

"Spencer Cabot was my immediate supervisor at the New Haven branch."

"He fired you. Why?"

"A misunderstanding."

"Please elaborate."

Zack sucked in an audible breath. "I received information regarding the situation on Aruba that involved my family members along with several other prominent United States citizens. With that information, I opted to participate in the capture of the drug lord Benedito Arcadio and the freeing of many American hostages."

"Did you disobey a direct order from Spencer Cabot?"

"Yes."

"Was this before or after you solved the OTH-OTN case? And what in blazes do those letters stand for anyway?" The Senator's voice grew.

Zack suppressed a smile. "I had the OTH-OTN case wrapped up at that point. OTH-OTN stands for Over The Hill – On The Net." A wave of quiet laughter swept through the chamber.

"Were you aware of Spencer Cabot's involvement in illegal activities?"

L.M. Pampuro

"No, sir."

The committee chair glanced to his left and then to his right. "Does anyone else have any questions for Mr. Brady? If not, thank you for your time, Mr. Brady. We may ask you back to clarify a few facts."

Zack nodded. "My pleasure, sir." Zack moved to leave the chamber. Another man rose from the back row to follow him out. Zack kept his eyes forward as the other person took long strides to move beside him, "What were they looking for?"

Pete Malone gestured for Zack to follow him into an empty chamber, then took a small device out of his pocket and proceeded to hold the square at arm's length while turning in a circle. After a single rotation, the green indicators remained solid. Pete Malone stopped in front of Zack.

"The Senate president was fishing for something. The fact that he asked about Spencer Cabot, and we know that Cabot worked multiple angles—" Pete said.

"and not all of them in the best interest of the good old USA—"

"Leaves a mark on his existence. I read somewhere that Spencer help our friend the Senator get the western states split—"

"Because splitting the states in two's—"

"And threes in the case of both California and Texas—"

"Gave extra influence in the Senate yet screwed up the House. We know this Pete. So, what's the deal between the Senator and Cabot now?" Zack watched as Pete stood silent with a toothless grin. "Wait, wait, let me guess, frat buddies at Wesleyan?"

"Oh Zack, buddy, I love your cynicism. Yes, college connection yet not Wesleyan this time."

Zack waited. "Are you going to tell me or what?"

"Let's just say that the esteemed Senator from Fremont has similar friends as Spencer. He was fishing to see what you knew and could anything be traced back to him. Those guys on that committee don't give a rat's ass about old people getting conned, but they do care if they can't get re-elected and miss a contribution to their stock portfolios. They are on damage control, my friend."

"So, this is all for a show, and Spencer will have no consequences?"

"I didn't say that. Spencer will be the fall guy and go hang out in one of our cushy country club prisons—"

"--Danbury or Canaan or maybe Cumberland?"

"Exactly. I guess what I am getting at is you were put in a position to take down a lot of people."

"Got it." Zack gave Pete a quick fist pump.

"You should have come to work for me—"

"And go abroad, leave your sister?"

"Both would understand," Pete said. The men laughed. "Okay, maybe not Maxi, but the country would. Step carefully, bro. God only knows what desperate men will do." Pete pushed open the door to an empty hallway. "Tell my sister I said hello."

Zack retrieved his backpack from the security guard then checked to confirm it still contained a cellphone along with an agency-issued 9mm Glock Gann. He quickly made his exit from the US Capitol building at the same moment that his phone chirped with missed calls. Zack decided the twenty-minute walk between here and his office would help him sort out his thoughts as he needed to process what had just happened. He returned the phone to his pack.

The hearing wiped out more than half of his day. Half a day with zero resolution and the possibility he would need to repeat the process. He took in his surroundings as he waited for the light to change. The park on one side was lined with tourists. The sounds of multiple languages floated through the air.

A few blocks away, another set of protesters blocked access to the Federal Communications Commission. Based on the signage, here was another stand against corporate media that would only result in a lot of shouting and little action. A flash from the blazing sun hitting some metal brought Zack's attention back to the present as he moved into the crosswalk.

MAXI

The maples reached high to canopy their leaves over the worn dirt path. The hot Vermont temperature dropped to a cool, dry eighty degrees in the shade. Shadows played off tree trunks and turned the scattered leaves into a floor in motion. The occasional rustle of a scurrying beast broke through the silence, along with the heady scent of moss and pine.

The forest somewhat rested, in the peace of another hazy afternoon positioned within a too-short summer season. The quiet time of year when few ventured this far close to the border with Canada. Winter brought out many blazes along the trail system in whining vehicles, stopping at food huts to rest along the way. The warmer season produced the intermittent backpacker, yet most stayed near the mountain resorts to catch the rewards of great views in exchange for a walk along a narrow, uneven path.

Maxi stood at the edge of her property, sandwiched behind by her private home, while pulled into the tranquil shadows created by a border of towering pines. Her constant companions, a German Shepherd ex-Federal agent, she renamed Jerry after hearing Thunder, the horrendous working name the pup was given, along with his sidekick, a semi-hyper retired bomb-sniffing Labrador she renamed Bobby. Jerry's original sidekick, MaryJane, couldn't handle the Vermont lifestyle because she was a retired airport drug sniffer. The organic marijuana farm next door put the poor pup into a constant state of alert.

L.M. Pampuro

A family in suburban Connecticut was happy to exchange her MaryJane for the ever-hyper Bobby. Like human siblings, the opposites worked well together.

Jerry never left Maxi's side, almost moving along at the same cadence. He slept on a pad at the foot of her bed at night and rose at the same moment she moved. Outdoors, Bobby sprinted ahead, ran around the plants along the side of the trail, and bounced to his own doggie beat. Bobby slept everywhere in the house. Each morning when Maxi ventured downstairs, a new warm spot in the shape of her golden beast would appear on chairs, sofas, rugs, dirty laundry piles, or other spaces throughout the house where the dog had fallen asleep on top.

Maxi and Jerry sauntered along the pathway. The sunlight dazzled, peeking from behind a bush or spreading small circular shapes at their feet. Bobby skittered about after the squirrels, chipmunks, and other creatures who called this area home.

Near the back gate that bordered the property Bobby sat, his bouncing tail kicking up dirt. "Calm down, boy, you will get to swim soon," Maxi said as she punched in a four-digit code. Then, the gate swung open to a buzz with a hard push. Maxi raised one hand above her head to give a quick wave to the security cameras hidden in the trees.

The trail changed from tree-covered to an open field. Bobby's golden coat blended with the blue cohosh, now sporting summer green. The Joe Pye weed had just begun to turn a lovely shape of pink that would soon surround the white buds of the New England Astor.

Maximum Panic

The ferns stood still in command position along the edge, with a slight sway hello as they passed. Faint smells of cow manure swirled between the full blooms of tiny yellow flowers scattered in the middle of bright green single leaves. Her head tilted upward at the vines circling along the tree trunks and over into a patch of pungent wild lavender.

Jerry stopped mid-step to let out a single bark. His panting partner appeared from behind to continue a run of circles around Maxi and Jerry before disappearing into little puffs of dust.

The long blades of overgrown grass brushed Maxi's bare legs. A small sigh escaped. Out here, there were no worries of disease-carrying ticks, like further south in her home state. Here she could enjoy mother nature's touch within her sights without fear of endless rounds of antibiotics.

Across the field, shades of purple, red, and bright yellow peered through the plant life. Maxi turned the corner just as her neighbors, Skye and Rain (short for Rainbow), began dancing in the middle of their organic vegetable field. The two ran around each other in circles holding up some sort of plants in one hand.

Rain dove into Skye's arms. Her laughter stretched across to Maxi. "Max," she shouted as the embrace broke. "Look, beets!" The plant waved in the air.

"Cool beans," Maxi yelled back.

"No cool beets," Rain shouted back.

"We'll have these and special herbs at the stand later," Skye added. "Are you coming by?"

Maxi nodded and gave a wave as she moved out of view. "Should we get some special herbs today?" She asked Jerry. The dog looked up at her like a disapproving mother. "Maybe feed some to Bobby?" Maxi continued.

Jerry gave a single bark in response. "Ah—you are no fun!" She patted behind the dog's ears as he nudged Maxi's hand with his wet nose clearly signaling that he wanted to move in the direction of the stream that bordered the back of the preserve. Maxi and Jerry heard the splash before the water came into view. The German Shepherd hung his head down and shook from side to side.

Maxi's horoscope this morning had said to find solace beyond the shadows. She'd read the piece aloud before turning her attention to her dogs. "What the fridge does that mean?" she'd asked. When neither replied, she had suggested a walk, and both dogs ran to the back door, Bobby barking along the way.

Bobby brought her back to the present with a quick shake of water off his coat. He then turned to show his teeth, panting in a smile, between a few scruffy pine trees. The Labrador let out a loud howl before leaping off all fours back into the stream.

Maxi made herself comfortable on a wooden bench in the shade. Her fingers traced a heart, carved in when the bench was placed there. Two initials, M M + Z B, a reminder that she wasn't alone in this world.

Of course, Maxi knew this. Her parents lived the retiree life between Connecticut and Aruba, while her son, Ric, attended Skidmore College. The fact that Ric did not come home this summer had bugged her, especially with Zack away too. She worried that with all of this state splitting, her son would end up in another country within the center of the original states.

In her heart, she knew that her son needed to find his way, just as she had. And she could understand that an 18 year-old male would be bored silly out in the sticks of Vermont. The Vermont wilderness was beautiful, yet scarcely populated.

Hell, Maxi was bored.

As she pictured her escape, she saw herself in the middle of the vast Saratoga State Park. At under a four-hour drive, she could do a day trip yet an overnight at the Gideon Putnam, dinner downtown, maybe even meet up with Ric and his friends seemed like a better plan. Maybe she could get him to dog sit one afternoon so she could go to the spa. The dogs could hike the trails in the state park or on the trail system. With their training, both animals would be able to keep quiet in a hotel room.

That fantasy would need to wait until her son returned from his stay at Pride Ridge. She had no clue why he would want to visit the Rockies without the snow, yet both he and Zack had pushed for the camp where Ric would help repair parts of the national trail system.

Maxi had argued about waiting a year, after the area settles and he knows where he is actually going. The mid and far western states began splitting up a couple of years ago. At first it was just California, splitting into California, Cabrillo, and Sierra. After the other states watched as the area now had six senators representing D.C., Texas and the Rocky Mountain states joined in on the fun.

Both New York and Maine were denied based on square acreage, yet Ohio, Virginia, and Kansas are pending. Maxi could barely keep track of what state in now where!

Jerry's sharp bark broke through her daydream. The shepherd let out a howl that brought Bobby out of the water; he stood at the edge, head swiveling from side to side. A quick burst of light originated from the opposite bank through the pines. Maxi squatted down to further retreat backward into the shadows. Leaning forward on her knees behind the bench, she peered at the opposite side of the stream through the wooden slats.

A figure emerged from the trees across the stream and stood erect, hands-on-hips. He used hand-held binoculars to scan her side of the stream. Maxi watched as their body moved in slow motion, stopping where Bobby lay in the grass along the edge. The dog popped up before starting to bark. Then, with a great leap forward, the dog splashed back into the water.

The figure turned and held their hands up, palms to sunshine. Bobby swam back towards where Maxi and Jerry hid. The Lab climbed out of the water and shook his long torso to sprinkle liquid and splatter the area. The dog turned twice in a circle before sitting down to face the water. Jerry leaned his mid-section into Maxi's side. He faced in the opposite direction, ears standing in high alert.

A second figure materialized from between two of the trunks. Together they scanned and pointed to the bench Maxi had vacated. Maxi scratched Jerry's ears as she watched the two figures point right to the spot where she was hiding. She positioned her cellphone's lens between the bench slots and snapped twice. Then, crab-style, Maxi moved onto the path, out of sight.

Jerry moved along the edge of the trail as Bobby's bark faded. Maxi smiled when her Lab's training took over and he cut through the brush to meet at the gate to their property. This time, instead of taking the visible path, Maxi walked into a small field of ferns. The non-path lead in a direct line back to the high fence that circled her property.

She ran her hand along the metal until her fingers found a small metal box. The hidden keypad opened another gate, not as noticeable as the first. Maxi and Jerry slipped through the gate, back onto the property with the cameras and alarms while Bobby circled around the organic farm and returned through the front door of the house. The property's security measures fed Maxi's paranoia in small doses.

She again vowed that once Zack returned; they'd have the never-ending retirement conversation again. This crap about the cameras and fencing being for her safety was screwing with her mental state.

She was done. Overdone.

L.M. Pampuro

RIC

Ric sat back on the flimsy mattress. Steel springs from underneath dug into his butt and thighs as he rested his shoulders and head against the cool concrete wall. A lone window with vertical bars allowed warm air to drift in while the stench of old plumbing rose from the corner to dance around his cell. He could see into the outer office where the Sheriff sat, face lit by a computer screen.

Movement from under the blankets in the next cell caught Ric's attention. A curly mass of red hair popped out near the end of the blanket and spilled over the sides of the mattress.

The lanky body of a teenager unfolded from the covers. A boy brought his legs to the floor as he leaned forward to stretch his torso over his thighs. The flimsy blanket fell to the concrete. The boy shook the curls out of his eyes and turned to catch Ric's stare.

Ric noted that he and the boy could be about the same age, but the boy had that look like he was hungover, like someone who maybe partied too much and slept too little. Some of the drinking age seniors at his college had this that made guessing their age part hard.

The boy lifted his arms over his head, releasing a stench of body odor that went beyond anything he had ever smelled. Ric's hand lifted to cover his nose.

"You get used to it." The boy's voice sounded like he smoked a pack a day or had overdone the weed the night before. "They said there's like a shower here, but I probably wouldn't take the chance of using it if they have one."

"Are we still in Fremont or has the state split again?"

"This is Fremont still, at least that's what it said when they brought me in."

"How long have you been here?" Ric said.

The boy shrugged. "Supposedly they called my folks, but good luck reaching them." He swiped his hands under his eyes. "How about you?"

"I don't know, a couple hours, maybe? What did you say about calling parents?"

The stranger motioned Ric to join him closer to the bars that divided their cells. "They," he nodded in the area of the lobby, "will call your parents for bail money – at least that's what they say. I gave them the number after that Sheriff guy brought me in." He looked out then lowered his voice, "My name is Erik."

"Ric."

"Well, Ric, we're both in a bit of a mess here."

"No shit. Tell me why you think so."

"Because I've been here for a while, days, weeks maybe. All I do is sleep and eat," he said. "All I know is that one of my parent's many assistants should have been able to write a freaking check, even if I didn't do anything wrong. Some girl—"

"—picked you up?"

"Exactly. Skinny blonde—"

"—with tracks on her arms?"

"I didn't notice the tracks. I was—"

"Now boys, you know the rules," the Sheriff's booming voice made the other boy jump back, but Ric froze in place. The Sheriff's fat rolls wedged in between the bars on the cell door as he stood just outside, hand resting on his gun. "No making unnecessary noise in here. This ain't no fufu camp like that one in Pride Ridge." He narrowed his eyes at Ric, who opened his mouth to speak, but before he could get a word out, from between the jail cells, a fist connected hard to his shoulder.

"Ow!" Ric said. He looked over to see Erik shaking his head and closing his mouth.

"That's much better. Now you," the Sheriff pointed his finger at Erik, "need to git me another number for your parents cause the one you gave ain't working. And you," the finger now pointed at Ric, "need to git me contact information a.s.a.p."

"Sir," Ric said. "I need to have my phone charged to give you the correct number." He hesitated a minute then added, "because they are both traveling for work. I have the hotel information on my phone."

"Don't people like your parents have secretaries, boy?" the Sheriff asked.

"Actually, no," Ric answered. "My mom is semi-retired, and my dad is off on his own, so both just rely on each other to keep track of where they are. I'm sorry, but the only contact information that is accurate is in my phone."

The Sheriff's lips went to one side as his eyes moved up and down Ric's body. "Seems we have a problem then. Do we look like an electronic supply store?"

Ric took a deep breath. "I have a charger in my room back at the camp. If I just can—"

The Sheriff's laughter interrupted Ric's thought. "If you just can, what, boy?"

"Well, since we need the phone to contact my parents—"

The Sheriff's lips turned down into a sneer. "You," his finger reached through the bars, "are not going back to that fancy schmancy camp!" The big man took in a generous quantity of air. Ric felt the breeze when the Sheriff's lips puffed out the shush of an exhale. "No talking," the Sheriff said. A creak from the lobby chair followed.

Ric caught Erik shaking his head and before he could stop himself, he stood palms up glaring. "What!" came out just above a whisper. Erik turned his attention to the floor and fell backwards on his cot. Ric waited a minute for a response, but none came.

Erik placed his hands over his eyes, stomach rising and falling. Ric stood in the middle of his cell and began to stretch, first folding over from his hips to bring his head against his knees. He then rocked forward to balance on his heels and brought his butt up into the air to point at the ceiling. With a slow movement he sunk his butt down to in between his spread-out legs. He shut his eyes and tried to concentrate on his breathing.

The stretch allowed his brain to quiet so he could escape, at least with his mind. The phone had a faint bar, not enough for a call but maybe for a text. If he could just get it back from the Sheriff. Loud voices from the lobby interrupted his thoughts.

"What do you mean there's no money. You said—"

"—I said not to come here. That is what I said," the Sheriff's voice answered.

"Well, what am I supposed to do? Huh? You promised—"

"—let's go outside." A quick burst of light came into the lobby then the Sheriff's body disappeared with a slam of a door. Ric looked over at Erik, who had moved back under the grungy blanket. Only the top of his curls poked out. The blanket rose in rhythm with the shush sounds from underneath.

Ric stared at the cell door, hoping for a phone charger or better yet, his crazy mother to come looking for him.

MAXI

Maxi paced the length of the house several times as Jerry sat next to the doorway. His head bobbed as he watched both the door and Maxi, like a tennis ball in play. Bobby started to whimper from his perch by the French doors that led out to the fenced in back yard.

Out the kitchen window, off in the distance, movement beyond the trees caught Maxi's attention. Little gaps between pine branches gave way to two human shapes, both far enough off the path to be near the rear property gate.

"Shusssss," Maxi whispered. Her hand absently rubbed against her stomach. The nauseous pit stroked again. "Damn it," she said, as she moved from the kitchen down the short hallway that divided the house in two. One side had three entry arches dividing the open floor plan between the living room, kitchen, and stairway. All ended by the front entry way.

Her fingers hesitated a moment. Bobby let out a low growl. Her fingers found the groove carved into the door frame. She fidgeted around the groove until a clicking sound gave way to a small crack in the wall. Using both hands, Maxi wiggled her fingers inside to position her palms to pull a piece of the wall aside. She sucked in her breath just enough to squeeze through the opening.

Just inside, a series of monitors flickered through images of her property. The images on three out of the four monitors mounted on top of each other on the opposite wall changed, yet the bottom right monitor stayed fixated on her back gate. "I am just being paranoid," she whispered to both dogs. One blocked the doorway while the other was just outside in the hall. She squeezed and released her fingers. "I mean really have no reason to look." She rested her head in one hand while fumbling to open the door further. As she pushed her hip against the frame, one of the monitors beeped. "Of course, I have a reason to look!" The volume made both dogs' jump.

The camera angle on the gate monitor showed the top of two black hoodies. She bent over the control board. Each camera had a knob with a number. "Well, which is which?" She glanced back at the dogs as if they should know the answer. Her hand went to the knob labelled one and pressed down. The top monitor showed an image of her front door and driveway.

Maxi waited for a beat and when the image didn't change, she focused on the other seven knobs. "We want that there." The number seven knob changed the angle of the camera closest to the garage. "Damn it!" Maxi looked back to see the top of one figure pushing against the back gate. Her hand pressed random knobs to freeze the images on the three scrolling monitors. Her hand slammed down on the number one control knob. The rest of the pair's clothing came into view. Black and camouflage covered both bodies along with a scarf across the bottom of their faces. Both carried small black backpacks. She focused on the monitor to see if they had changed their approach.

One rested a shoulder against the gate while the other crouched out of view.

Maximum Panic

All the security cameras were on a digital feed, yet, when the system was installed, Maxi remembered that Zack had shown her a way to take still photos manually.

"Now, how did he do that?" The day Zack taught her about all the new house security additions, she walked behind him and done several epic eyerolls thinking about her husband's new paranoia. "I should have paid more attention." Like, duh," she said to the dogs. Bobby lay at her feet and gave a quiet whimper. Jerry stood at attention by the door.

Underneath the monitors, a well-built two-drawer filing cabinet sat covered in dust. Maxi reached down to open each drawer. The bottom drawer would not open. She jiggled the handle until the top drawer slid open. All arranged in order, a series of folders rested against the backside, while her Ruger LCP Max, a Valentine's Day gift from Zack, along with a few boxes of bullets, seals intact, held the folders in place. She flipped through the first few then stopped to wedge out a file titled *Security System* crammed in the back.

The first page had a note in Zack's handwriting. *When will you ever pay attention when I speak, love?* Maxi held up her middle finger and sucked in a deep breath. "When you retire from your stupid job, and we are planning out our safe, boring life together, love," she said, adding, "asshole," under her breath.

Another whine outside of the room refocused her attention. Bobby had moved to the back of the house. Jerry let loose a low growl that brought her attention back to the monitors. Now on the side camera, one of the figures moved along the perimeter of the fence, a cellphone in hand.

"That can't be good," Maxi said to Jerry, who sat with his back in the doorframe. She flipped through the folder contents quickly, pulling out two pages. *How To Take Stills* and *Emergency Numbers*. The camera instructions appeared pretty simple. She waited until the person walking the fence came to the corner of the property. "To change the camera to focus on one specific area, hit the camera number to stop scanning and then move your cursor to either expand or narrow lens. Sounds easy, right Jer?"

Jerry gave a short huff back in return. Maxi hit the stop button for camera three and then used the curser to focus the lens in from the shoulders up. "Hit the space button. Easy cheesy." The figure looked up to expose their face. She hit space again.

On the monitor, the figure started to finger-point out the hidden camera, and although Maxi couldn't hear, she could see arms flailing. On the bottom of the instructions, in red, she whispered, "System will make a clicking sound at the location of the camera taking the still. Use this option with caution." Maxi glanced over to watch Jerry shaking his doggie head back and forth. "That should have been on the top of the instructions, right?"

Her attention moved back to the monitors. "Oh shit!" The stillness of the trees and vegetation surrounding her property appeared absent from humans. "Damn it." Maxi's stomach started to gurgle as her imagination went into overdrive.

"Zack will fix this." One glance back to the empty monitor upped her heartbeat. The rest of the instructions were a step-by-step guide to downloading the still. After several "dangnabits" and "WTF's," she gave up. Her attention turned to the emergency contact list. Not one name was recognizable.

"Screw this," she said. Both dogs sat facing the back door. Their attention now down the hall. "I'll just text Zack. Should have done that in the first place because I will bet dollars to cookies," at the word cookie, both dogs thumped their tales, "that Zack can do all this crap remotely and he might even know what is going on with these fellas."

Maxi detailed her walk along with the strangers in a quick text, adding *there is a still of one somewhere in the System. He seemed pissed on the monitor that the camera took a picture. Do something, please. Oh, and I love you!* "Okay, boys, what do we do now? Stay locked up in our fortress, or get the heck out of here?" Neither dog answered, of course. "I vote for the latter. Yet we should probably wait for a text back, right? I mean Zack should get back to us pretty quickly based on my text."

The wall calendar had a big black circle around Saturday. Ric was finally coming back from his summer adventure. Her son would be a great diversion from whatever crap hits the house here.

She sent a quick *Can't wait to see you on Saturday!* text to Ric and took the stairs two at a time to pack.

L.M. Pampuro

ZACK

Zack arrived back on the eighth floor at the same time as his old friend, Admiral Donald Atwood. Before Zack could speak, Admiral Atwood motioned for him to follow into an empty office. Zack noted an unfamiliar woman already sat in a large chair behind a turn of the century mahogany desk, the admiral's desk. If this wasn't an intimidation play, the combination of the desk and the woman sitting behind it did the job.

Admiral Atwood took a seat in one of the wing-backed chairs across from this mystery person while both waited for Zack to sit in the other. "Am I being fired?" Zack asked as he sat. Both laughed.

"Zack Brady meet your new team member, Kit Sellers," as Donald spoke Zack rose to shake the woman's hand, only to be waved off. "Kit has been working undercover in the Niza office and will be part of our team moving forward."

Kit interrupted, "where your special talents are needed in a somewhat sensitive investigation."

Zack looked over at Donald. "You know that I promised Maxi—"

"We know. After our last adventure together, I, too, promised your wife," Admiral Atwood held Zack's eyes on the word wife, "and in the case of our problem, I think she would approve." Zack looked over at Kit, who now avoided eye contact.

"Unless it involves family, you will have difficulty convincing Maxi I need to go abroad."

"Who said anything about leaving the country?" Admiral Atwood said.

"All I can tell you, Agent Brady, you have the worst investigation luck."

"Kit, I am not sure what do you mean? I think I'm pretty good at my job."

"Actually, son," Admiral Atwood interrupted, "you are too good. Seems that your old boss Cabot wasn't the only one on the take, and the funnel of cash goes deeper—"

"deeper than the Russians and our old friend Marjorie Lofsmen?"

"Apparently so, Zack." Kit looked at both men. "Let's just get to it, Donald. I have places to be. Zack is a smart person. He probably already knows." She waited for a beat, then continued, "I am always amazed how people are connected; know what I mean?"

"I assume you mean my friend, the Senator from Fremont, and my old boss Spencer Cabot?"

"Yes, Zack, those are two of the connections. You mentioned Marjorie Lofsmen prior."

"I thought Marjorie was rotting in jail for selling American secrets," Zack said. Then, he added, "Of course, if being a useless secretary is a crime, that might get her a few more years." Zack took note that neither person laughed. "Okay, you got me. What about Marjorie Lofsmen?"

Kit cleared her throat before speaking. "First, I want to say that I can't make this shit up. Are you ready for this one? Marjorie Lofsmen's father is our esteemed Senator from Fremont's brother-in-law. That makes Marjorie—"

"His niece. Huh." Zack tilted his head to one side. His fingers massaged the back of his skull as he let this news sink into the room's silence. "So, my investigation—"

"Needs to continue," Kit said. "Yet this will be under different circumstances."

"What kind of circumstances?" Zack observed Admiral Atwood exchange a glance with Kit. "Stop with the silent exchanges and wasting all of our time. Either include me in on what is happening here or let me go back to work."

"We need to make it seem like your investigation has been put on hold."

"Put on hold, you say?" Zack sat up straighter in his chair. "Why?"

"Because the Senator needs to think he has the political power to stop an internal investigation." the Admiral said. "Yet your part will not be on hold the way you are thinking. We are transferring you to another internal investigation team—"

"—been there. Done that. Won't work. I promised Maxi—"

"Agent Brady," Kit said. "Let the Admiral finish."

Zack recoiled at his title use, then rearranged his body to balance his behind at the edge of the chair part way between sitting and beginning to stand. He gestured with his right hand for the conversation to continue.

"Thank you, Kit," Admiral Atwood said. "And, of course, Zack for giving us his time today...." Zack's jaw gave a slight twitch in return. "Zack, we need you because we need someone familiar with floating into a situation and then disappearing. You are good at this."

Zack gave a slight nod.

"We, meaning Internal Investigations, already have proof that some of the money that Marjorie Lofsmen took from the Russians was laundered thru our esteemed Senator's PAC fund."

"So why do you need me?" Zack said.

"Because Lofsmen is out of commission, yet the Senator has raised millions..."

"—close to a billion," Kit chimed in.

"—in untraceable funding. Now you know we keep watch on anyone who received illegal funds or help from abroad?" the Admiral stated. Zack gave a slight nod. "Something is rotten in Niza."

Kit opened a plain manila folder. The first page contained a list of known donors to the Senator's latest campaign. Margorie Lofsmen, along with several others, appeared in bold.

"Are these the folks who contributed through his PAC?" Zack said. "And why are some in bold?"

She pointed to those in bold as she spoke. "The two at the top are already in prison or house arrest for something. The next few are being audited by the IRS. We won't bother with those." Kit flipped the page over to show a list of highlighted names. "Now, these folks, we are in the process of doing an initial electronic audit. Seems that their donations do not match their salaries."

Zack stared at the paper. "What the fucks," slipped out as he read. The names closer to the bottom produced a couple "are you kidding me," comments, before he brought his attention back to the others in the room to asked, "I still don't understand why I am here?"

"Well, you have shit luck, as my grandmother used to say," Admiral Atwood began. "As you can see, this isn't one of our department problems per se, yet some of those names are pretty close to me in the command chain." Atwood pointed to the names of two of his newly retired commanders. "Which is why I am here and suggested you." He waited for a beat, then continued, "I promised Maxi that I wouldn't put you in harm's way again, and I have kept that promise. First, however, I need someone outside internal affairs to help with the investigation. Of course, it helps if this someone already ticked off the Senator." The Admiral let out a low laugh.

"The Senator doesn't appreciate my charm," Zack said. "What do I need to do, and can I take care of this from Vermont?"

Kit Sellers handed over the folder to Zack. "See what you can find out. I don't care where you work, yet know you may have to travel domestically, specifically to Fremont or one of the other split states."

"Fremont, huh? What's there?" he asked as his eyes scanned the list. He pointed to a couple names near the middle. Both Kit and Donald nodded yes. "This is going to be interesting."

"Interesting is a good word, Zack. We already told the folks in Niza to cooperate with you."

Zack thanked both. He walked out the door as Kit Sellers' phone started to buzz. Zack overheard her answer, "This is Eugenie – give me a second to get some privacy."

L.M. Pampuro

In one hand Zack carried the contents of the manilla folder, in the other his cellphone buzzed. He swiped away from Maxi as he stepped into the elevator, certain at this point that no good would come from her communication.

MAXI

Maxi debated between leaving her home and waiting for Zack to get back to her. If she stayed, and the commotion outside continued, the security system would go into automatic lockdown with her stuck inside. "Just like a jail," she said to the dogs. "Do you guys want to go see Ric?" punctuating Ric with a little jump. The dogs stood still, just observing the activity. Her phone swung in her right-hand as she started to chant, "Text me back" with each lift of her arm. Half-way down the hall, the phone vibrated.

Hey love. Sorry for the delayed response. Been in meetings and that Senate thing I told you about lasted a bit longer than I thought. May have a new case that will limit my travels and get me home." Maxi reflected on the last sentence. *I will access the security system from here. Until I get that opportunity, would you please just stay inside? I promise to look as soon as I am done in Atwood's office."*

"Atwood's office," Maxi said. "He must be talking instead of typing." She looked down at Jerry. "Yet this can't be anything good. Donald gets Zack into..." Maxi reread the text again. Formal language said he was in work mode and needed to put his focus there, yet the length told her he rambled that out quickly.

"Crap," Maxi said at the same moment Bobby let out a howl. She ran down the stairs back into the monitor room. On the upper left camera, focused on the back path, one of the two hooded people had one leg over the fence while the other watched from below.

Maxi gazed in horror as the stranger pressed his legs against the gate. His foot slammed against the catch to open the gate.

And kept slamming. She started to count the connections of this stranger's foot to her back gate, "Three. Four. Fuck!"

"It's just a fence," she repeated. "It's a strong fence." All the switches on the lower panel had clear labels, something that Zack did for her in case of an emergency. *Front gate. Back gate. Camera 1 – 10.* "There are ten freaking cameras out there," she said. "Damn. How come I only have eight knobs on the bottom part?"

Next came those labels in red type. *Electricity. Spotlights. Alarm blast. Garage doors.* Her eyes shifted back to *Alarm Blast.* "I wonder if this does what I think it does…" As Maxi reached for the instruction manual, the person on the monitor swung both legs over to her side of the fence.

She hit the *Alarm Blast* switch and followed up with the one labelled *Electricity.* The figure fell to the ground, their body twitching, on the inside of the fence while a horn blasted loud enough to reach Zack in D.C. The second person knelt next to the other, the fence now separated their bodies. Maxi went back to zoom the camera in the area where they lay, hoping she could get a photo of the other one too.

The second person drew a small handgun and shot his companion point blank. "What?!?" Maxi shouted. She dialed Zack's phone only to have it go to voicemail. "Okay, love," she said the word *love* as if describing her dog's feces, "now instead of an intruder, I have what I think is a dead guy back by the fence. I am not sure what I should do."

The alarm hit a higher frequency that sent a screech vibrating throughout the house. The noise drowned out Maxi's voice. Inside the control room, the monitor showed trees and the fern path.

No body.

Nothing. Maxi squeezed her eyes against her palms, took a deep breath, and looked again.

Still no dead body.

"What the hell?" she said. The camera focused on that area revealed an empty spot with a crease in the ferns. Maxi hit the space bar to produce a still image. "I think we need to leave," she addressed the dogs. Both sat side by side at attention, blocking the doorway. She debated on texting Donald Atwood although she hadn't seen the Admiral since their wedding, and prior to that, it was a few years ago after the fiasco in Aruba.

At her and Zack's wedding, Donald had said that if she ever needed anything to get in touch with him and gave her contact information. The fact that his boss voluntarily handed over his private cell number to Maxi surprised Zack as Donald Atwood kept that number for family and a very few close friends. When Donald was out of earshot, Zack immediately advised her to choose her moments of contact carefully as giving out his private line was unusual. Maxi had a clear memory of Zack's agent voice giving her this direction.

Maxi took a breather and tried to compose the text logically.

She spoke as slowly and clearly as possible. *"Hi Donald – This is Maxi Malone, Zack Brady's wife. I just had someone try to break into our property. They followed me and the dogs on our hike. I saw someone get shot yet the body is no longer on the surveillance camera. I texted Zack too, yet he didn't answer me, and well you said at our wedding if I needed anything to - could you or Zack just call me. Thanks! I hope you are well."*

Maxi read back the voice to the text message. "I think I sound calm, almost rational," a manic laugh escaped. "Yes, yes, I do, even after seeing another murder."

She grabbed the small suitcase out of the hall closet. "People just seem to get shot around me," she gave Jerry a quick pet.

Jerry followed her up the stairs. Down below, Bobby had laid his long body across the front door. The dog's ear stood up on high alert.

RIC

Ric wasn't sure of the day, but he knew his mother would be freaking out as he hadn't made the expected weekly phone call. He'd promised to call every Monday evening to tell her that he had survived the weekend. The last time he'd forgotten to call, she'd showed up at his dorm room on Tuesday and waited by his door until he returned from class.

At the time, he'd asked if it would have been easier to call him, and she'd replied that her making the call wasn't part of their deal. Yet crazy mama driving to upstate New York was? He felt his lips curve upward at the thought of his mother busting in the door, pointing her finger into the Sheriff's smug face, and yelling, "You'd better let my son out now or the fire of hell will rain down on you!" Yep, Maxi would take the Sheriff down in one extreme tirade. His mother had a talent if anyone had balls, or a vagina as she liked to say, for putting idiots in their place.

He could tell the Sheriff that the lack of weekly communication would bring in the troops, but he didn't want to give away too much about his life. Something about Erik having a similar experience with a townie girl and how the Sheriff had avoided giving him access to his phone wasn't making sense.

I mean seriously, what about my roommate? Why hasn't anyone from the camp looked for me? Are my roommates in trouble somewhere too? There were too many questions, and information was lacking. His stomach kept jumping and it wasn't the food.

Inside the lobby, the television blared, and a familiar voice cut through the din. "Zackary Darcy Brady. I am currently a sections chief in the Criminal Cyber Services branch office for the United States Federal Bureau of Investigation."

"Wait, what," Ric said, as he moved next to the bars. "Excuse me, please," If he leaned against the wall and the bars at one corner of his cell, Ric could see the deputy, Dak. "Could you tell me what you're watching?"

"Why?" the deputy barked back.

"I watch a lot of CNN and Fox News for school. I'm just curious what case this is?" Ric said.

He heard a chair scratch against the linoleum floor. "Well, at least you watch one good station," The deputy shuffled over to lean one shoulder against his cell door. "I ain't sure what these ones are about. All I know is that our favorite Senator from Fremont is razzing this Yankee boy about something or another."

Ric gave the deputy a nod and waited for him to continue. Instead, Dak returned to his chair. Ric tried to lean as far in the corner as possible, but the screen still evaded his sight line. After trying several positions that involved wedging his shoulder in between the bars while bringing his sight line around the bars, he gave up and said, "Okay, well, thanks."

He heard a mumbled, "My pleasure."

MAXI

Maxi had the small suitcase stuffed with two sets of shorts, tops, undergarments, socks, and a nondescript gray hoodie. The other, heavier duffle bag contained dog food, chew bones, two leashes, water bowls, two feeder Kongs, and Bobby's baby blanket, which the dog wouldn't sleep without.

The wait for Zack or Admiral Atwood to text her back had grown to the point of absurdity. The shooter could still be out there, looking for another way into her property to harm her or the dogs. The fence that bordered had a few gates, not all visible. If they had the means to climb over, they might have some sort of tech detection for entrances.

Maxi's body shook. Waiting wasn't one of her strong characteristics to begin with, yet in this situation, Maxi started to head into save myself and my dogs mode. "We, I," she stuttered, "just need to get out of here." Bobby and Jerry just stared back.

She made certain to exit through the back door, under the deck of her bedroom, out of sight while entering through the garage's side door. The dogs followed in a single file. Inside, her ten-year-old baby blue BMW convertible sat parked next to a hybrid black Ford Explorer with the windows blacked out. She ran her fingers along the side of the Beemer. Briefly, she considered the sports car, top down, wind whipping while she drove those bouncy back roads.

Maxi looked over at the SUV. The SUV screamed cop car, yet the tank proved to be her most sensible choice.

The SUV was her only choice.

Maxi loaded the bags into the far back and opened the side door, the dogs jumped in before she took a seat behind the steering wheel. In the rear-view mirror, both dogs jockeyed for a comfortable position next to the driver's side window.

Instead of following the driveway onto the street, Maxi steered the car along an old dirt road that led to a shrouded exit along the back of the property. She pressed the second button on the mirror, and a gate that blended into the scenery parted to let her pass into the neighboring farm's back access road. When she opened the gate, a tracker located in the back bumper clicked on. The map on the dash camera showed the SUV traveling, for the moment, off-road.

The map also told Maxi that the tracker was working, and if need be, Zack could see her whereabouts. "Huh. If Zack can see us, then any hack could too." Both dogs gave a blast of hot dog breath on the back of her neck. "Do you guys think I should disconnect that thing before our next stop?" When neither dog responded, she continued, "Well, I think that would be a good idea, especially since we haven't heard from Zack or the Admiral." Bobby let out a short bark at the mention of Zack's name.

Once on route 100, Maxi headed south following the winding road, only to slow down when an out-of-state license plate decided to do the low-speed limits through the picturesque towns. After stop-and-go traffic through Stowe, she headed north on the throughway, planning to cross over to New York State in Burlington and head into the Adirondacks.

She stopped at the first commuter lot to let the dogs take a break. The lot appeared full. After circling the perimeter, Maxi chose a space where the SUV would be hidden amongst the other cars. While Bobby and Jerry marked their territory, Maxi slipped her hand along the back bumper until it reached a square object no bigger than her three longest fingers. Digging her nails along the edge, she worked the object loose. A small grey rectangular piece of plastic fell into her palm.

"Well, what do we have here?" Maxi scrutinized the object up close. On the opposite side of the lot, someone had parked a pick-up truck, the bed filled with confederate flags swaying in the breeze. As Maxi got closer, she noted several anti-women bumper stickers covering the tailgate. "Huh. Maybe I shouldn't," she said while walking backward in the direction of her vehicle. "Still tempting."

With a flick of her wrist, the tracker landed inside the truck's bed. Maxi called out to the dogs, who sat at attention on the other side of the car. Once everyone got resettled, she got back on the main drag heading west onto the bridge to New York state.

As she drove, she could feel Jerry's eyes on her. "That was only the one I could find," Maxi reassured Jerry with a quick belly rub. "I know there are other trackers on this car for our safety," she said. Jerry kept his attention out of the window. "I think you two are both doggie chipped even though you both retired," she pointed out. Zack had reassured Maxi that the feds had the option to reactivate the chips, if they wanted, along with noting the electronics did zero harm to the dogs. "Seriously, you two can be tracked by a satellite on Mars," Maxi laughed.

Bobby let out a snore from the backseat. Jerry shook his head, the tags on his collar gave a jingle.

ZACK

Zack slammed the door to Admiral Atwood's office open. The Admiral, along with another man Zack did not recognize, jumped out of their chairs.

"Maxi," Zack said thrusting his phone in Atwood's face.

"I just got one too. We were in the process of attempting to access your security system, yet it looks like you blocked me of access, Zack." The Admiral gave Zack a glare.

Zack nodded at the other man, now hovered over the Admiral's laptop. Atwood dismissed the man with a quick wave of the hand, adding, "Thank you for your help." In return, he received a quick salute. "Computer issues," Atwood explained.

Both waited for the hallway to clear. "Maxi sent this while I was in the meeting with you earlier."

The Admiral read the message on Zack's screen then held out his phone to share what he had received. Zack nodded as he read the contents.

"She's in trouble Donald."

"Did you get the still off your security system?"

"Yes." Said Zack. He flipped through a couple photos on his phone then turned the screen so that the Admiral could see the contents. "I got this still plus the video of two people dragging a third away from my property. I am not sure if the guy being dragged is the one in this photo--"

"Yet I would bet my life that the image on the still is this person," the Admiral said. "He got caught. He was expendable. Have you run the photo through our database?"

"Yes, there is nothing on either face searches." Zack began again, "Maxi left in the SUV—"

"Good choice. At least she is thinking clearly."

"Thinking clearly in Maxi's world. I got a mapped route up until a commuter lot in Burlington. The tracker stops here," Zack points to a map, "but I don't think she is there."

"Why is that?" The admiral sat forward at his desk; eyes focused on the map.

"Because I looked at the satellite photos of the lot, and this is the vehicle that coordinates with the tracker." Zack slid his phone back across the desk.

Atwood burst out with a hardy laugh then covered his mouth with a coughing sound. "I love your wife," Atwood exclaimed.

"So do I," Zack said, "which is why I want her safe. Donald, I don't know what happened at home, but I think I know where she is heading."

"Do share."

"Saratoga. Ric gets home sometime tomorrow. Maxi would feel safer if they were together."

"Mama Bear Syndrome."

"Maxi definitely has that, especially for her only child."

"Zack, most, maybe all mothers have some form of Mama Bear Syndrome. There is a natural instinct to protect their children. Having Ric in her sights gives Maxi the illusion of control while protecting her offspring." Admiral Atwood hesitated before adding,

"You can do the preliminary investigation from anywhere. You should go."

Zack nodded. With the receiver in his ear, Admiral Atwood held up one finger for him to wait. "Any word from Fremont about our friend, yet?" Zack listened to the Admirals side of the conversation closely "Forwarded what you just told me to Zack Brady," Atwood repeated the instructions adding, "yes, I am sure," before hanging up.

"I just sent you the updated information on the Fremont situation."

"Do you think this is all connected?" Zack ran one hand through his hair, a nervous habit he kept trying to stop.

"Maybe," Atwood said. "Maybe not. I just want you to have all the information, and Zack," Zack leaned back into the doorway at the pause, "Be careful."

L.M. Pampuro

RIC

The noise of the cell door closing echoed off the cement walls to wake Ric from a different nightmare. He opened his eyes in time to see Erik's hands behind his back, cuffed, while a hefty, uniformed figure pushed the teen's lanky body out of his cell, into the lobby. The sound of the front door slamming shut jolted him into full awake.

Ric put his hand on top of his twisting stomach.

A new guard squeaked the chair in time with the rhythm of fingers on the keyboard. Ric stood to get a glimpse of which one of his tormentors remained.

"Pow!" said a voice.

Ric jumped back. His knee hit the metal frame of the bed. His body buckled onto the hard mattress. He heard someone giggle. A small face looked up between the bars, mouth covered by two tiny hands.

"Wow, you scared me," said Ric.

"Yeah, you squealed like a girl," the youngster said.

"Well, you scared me like a pro. I'm Ric," Ric said as he sat on the floor near the child. "Who are you?"

"He's someone who is supposed to be reading and not bothering my prisoners," a booming female voice came from the lobby. The child scurried over to the creaky chair. "Now I told you sit—"

"But Mom. When are you going to read to me?"

"Read to you?" Her voice got louder. "Can't you see I am working so we can eat? Read to you. What's the matter with you boy? Read to yourself!"

The kid's voice faded. "And don't you go crying now. You know the rules."

Ric heard a scuffing of feet, a chair sliding across the floor, followed by silence. He looked around the blank walls of his cell then over into what he could see of the lobby. He put his hand to his mouth and produced a few fake coughs that came out in a combination of a throat clear and take-a-shit moan.

"I can read to him," Ric said. His voice sounded strange, weak, not his.

"What you say?" The thundering voice from the lobby responded.

Now with confidence he lacked, Ric repeated, "I can read to him."

A chair squeaked. This time in combination with a scrape. A good-sized, woman came into view in a deputy's uniform. *HARPER* in bold letters above her right breast. Her size was nothing compared to her hair, teased, and taunted and stretched in every direction, the mass blocked out all the light from the lobby.

"What did you say, boy?" deputy Harper repeated. Her eyes squinted in his direction.

"I'm just sitting here," Ric started to say.

"You're sitting around is a temporary state. Lord, help you if you don't get that number to the Sheriff."

"I want to give him the number, but I don't have a phone charger and my parents—"

She held her hand up to stop his sentences. "I don't care," she turned back into the lobby.

"It doesn't matter. But I can read to your son if you want." Ric pointed to a spot on the floor just outside his cell. "He can sit out there, and I can sit here. That way he can see the pictures."

The woman looked away. "Do you have kids?"

"I'm only nineteen."

"What does that have to do with having kids? I didn't ask your age. I asked a simple question—"

"No." Ric said, "I do not have kids."

"How do you know he'd want to see the pictures?"

"Because I would want to," Ric said, then added, "Just forget it."

Ric took in a seven-count breath. He turned away from the lobby and spun his body down into a lotus position as he continued to breathe and count. His eye lids succumbed to the heaviness of his situation along with the boredom of another day. His lips started to rise on the ends.

Bam!

Ric's eyes opened wide. The woman was by his cell door, lips in a horizontal line. The book lay on the floor next to the cell door.

"You said you'd read to my boy," she said, kicking the copy of *The Fowl Twins* under the bars. "Make sure you do the voices too."

Ric grabbed the book while the boy sat on the floor, mimicking his pose. Jail bars separated the two. "Is this a new Artemis Fowl book?" Ric asked. "I read the whole series when I was in grade school."

"Really," the boy answered, wide-eyed. "I didn't know Artemis was that old." Mom's laugh sneaked in from the lobby and Ric had to smile.

"Yeah, well Eion Colfer happens to be one of my favorite authors," said Ric. A faint me too followed. "I didn't know he had a twin."

"I just found out this morning when we went to the library." The boy moved a little closer. "I haven't started yet, so you get to start at the beginning."

Ric nodded. The book had been checked out from the library in Pride Ridge. "You live in Pride Ridge?" He watched as the boy looked back at his mother. The clicking of keys gave way to the fact that she was focused elsewhere. The boy brought his attention back to Ric and shook his head side to side.

"Huh."

"I don't hear no reading," interrupted their conversation.

"Just starting now, miss," Ric replied. As he started to read, the boy slipped his legs behind him and lay on his stomach, his chin resting in his hands. Ric let out a small sigh. If only he had paid more attention to Artemis Fowl, he might already have an escape plan in mind.

L.M. Pampuro

MAXI

Maxi looked around her hotel room. Check-in had proved challenging without a reservation, yet management had found her a small room. The front desk clerk was apprehensive about the two dogs, but after a quick word regarding the dog's pedigree, Maxi and the clerk had reached an agreement. Now Bobby lay sideways across the king bed while Jerry snoozed on the bathroom's marble floor.

Both animals appeared more content than Maxi. She paced the room, lingering at the full-length windows to observe people entering and leaving the veranda. Their room overlooked the front entrance of the hotel. The constant people traffic on the other side of her vast window appeared to be another liability for showing up without reservations. If she could see people, people could see her.

As usual, her mind turned to Ric and his arrival back east. Maxi typed out another quick text to Ric. *Hey love. I am in your area and will meet you at the airport tomorrow. What time does your flight get in? Please send that and flight #'s. Miss you!* She ended with a purple heart emoji.

She also noted there wasn't a response to her last text, quickly adding, *And if I don't hear back from you soon, I will be on a plane to Fremont... or I will send Zack!* After a short debate she added a laughing smile emoji to the end. She clicked onto the text she sent Zack.

Another no-reply.

Maximum Panic

You know, if you texted me that someone was breaking into the house, I would show a bit of concern. Hello! I am no longer in VT and am awaiting Ric's arrival. The dogs are with me at the usual spot. A short laugh escaped as The Gideon was not their usual spot. Maxi enjoyed a walk around the downtown area in the evening. "Well, when he calls me I may tell him where we are or he'll just have to figure it out," she said, then added, *and by the way, Ric hasn't answered my texts in two days.*

The phone rang back as if on cue.

"What do you mean Ric hasn't answered your texts?" Zack's voice had a hard edge to it. Maxi wasn't speaking with her husband. This conversation will be with Zack Brady, Federal Bureau of Investigation agent. She had been here before.

"I texted him yesterday to say I was looking forward to his return. No reply. I texted today with the same only I indicated I was here."

"No reply," Zack finished her thought.

"Correct." While neither spoke, she could hear the clicking of Zack's fingers on his keyboard. The usually not affectionate Jerry distracted Maxi as he rubbed his side against her leg. On cue, her hand moved to stroke the dog just behind his ears.

"Are you okay?" Zack's voice had softened. Her husband now spoke.

"The guy in the backyard freaked me out, especially when he was sitting on the fence. Me and the dogs are okay now, but I'm worried—"

"I get it. There is a new assignment. I was coming home tomorrow. Should I go there instead or—"

"I can pick you up in Burlington?"

"Hey, we can get the tracker back while you are there." Zack's laughter filled the phone.

"I was, I am scared, Zack." Maxi's voice just above a whisper. "I'm really scared. No one has ever tried to climb our fence. And I think they shot a guy..."

"I'll have someone here check the area hospitals for gunshot wounds. Are you going to be okay tonight?" Although he couldn't see, Maxi nodded. "I will take the first direct flight tomorrow. I believe it lands around eleven-thirty. That I will confirm."

"I can pick you up in Burlington but know that I'm closer to Albany right now."

"Max, either way I need to go to the house and look around. If that is going to be too much for you—" The F.B.I. guy was back.

"I will be at whatever airport you fly into at eleven-thirty to get you. Commercial or transport?"

"Commercial. I will text details later." Zack hesitated, then added, "And I will call Ric. I am sure he is just in the groove."

"But he always," Maxi followed with an audible inhale and a deep whoosh of air. "I am sure he is okay too. I love you."

His voice came through the speaker in almost a whisper. "I love you, too, Maxi. This will all be okay. I promise and will explain when I get there."

She pressed the end button hard and threw the phone in the middle of the bed and watched it bounce across the mattress. Both Bobby and Jerry sat at high alert. Maxi dumped the dog's bag on the bed to extract their leashes. Bobby ran in small circles while Jerry brought his big brown eyes into the view.

"Just until we get on the path," Maxi said as she hooked the leash into Jerry's collar. His head hung low. She gave Jerry a quick pat with one hand as the other attached a leash to Bobby's collar. The lab pulled at the door. "Please behave until we get outside," Maxi said to both dogs.

L.M. Pampuro

ZACK

Zack stuffed his laptop into the small LL Bean pack that Ric had given him last Christmas, so he'd quit looking like a Fed when he travelled. He called Ric and when the kid didn't answer, Zack texted *911-MFO*, their code to call Zack as soon as possible because mom (Maxi) is freaking out. Zack had come up with this after Maxi drove to Ric's college and berated him for missing the weekly call.

Zack had laughed when Ric had produced the well thought out excuse that he was studying for a test in his trigonometry class and by the time he realized what time it was, it was too late to call her. Once Ric spoke, the neutral expression that stayed on Maxi's face confirmed that she wasn't buying what Ric was saying. Zack had told him next time at least pick a subject that he would need to study.

He took a quick inventory of his desktop - a mug full of pens, an empty blotter, giving each file drawer a quick tug, with none pulling open.

As he entered his office, Donald Atwood gave the one-minute sign then pointed at the chair in front of the desk. Zack made a show of checking his watch as he sat. In one hand Donald held the receiver to the desk phone near his ear while the other hand flipped the laptop screen around on his desk so Zack could read the contents.

Maxi's text appeared on her screen. Zack gave a quick nod, and again, Atwood held up an index finger. Zack's leg bounced as he waited, eyes focused between his boss and cellphone.

Zack jumped in his chair as Atwood slammed the phone down with so much force the handset cracked. "Gaddam bureaucrats!" he snickered. "I need to give you additional information on this case." Zack started to interrupt as Donald added, "I know you have a plane to catch so I will be brief."

The still that Maxi made took up half the screen. On the other half, two familiar faces stared back.

"Wait, that looks like my old boss Spencer Cabot. But he's—"

"In jail, yes, we know. I confirmed that fact just then." He gestured at the phone. "We think your friend here is a relative of Cabot's." He hit the space bar of the laptop to reveal a blown-up photograph of the suspect. "Unfortunately, we don't know who he is because whoever this is, he isn't in the system."

Zack leaned closer for a better look. "Could he be a she?" he asked as he pointed to the chin area. "That is a pretty clean shave."

Donald leaned into to look where Zack pointed. He picked up the receiver and dialed. Without a hello, he barked, "Check to see what female relatives Spencer Cabot has and put this through the scanner based on those criteria." Zack flinched as the receiver slammed down against the base.

"Donald, you need to relax. Think about how many phones do you go through a year." Zack pointed to the small crack in the base.

"Better smashing phones than people," Donald said. "I didn't get here by being nice. Okay so, I will forward this and any other information we have on file to the secured server. Should we use the usual password?"

"Yes, with the date, please." Zack made a quick note on his cellphone. "Are we good?"

"Yes, by all means. Give Maxi my best."

"Will do," Zack said. He moved the photographs onto the secure server and changed the access. Zack noted that views were now limited to him, Donald Atwood, and Kit Sellers. He backed out of the room, giving a quick wave as he disappeared to the sounds of keys tapping.

MAXI

Maxi left the building via the emergency back exit. Once she and the dogs cleared the parking lot to get across the massive lawn, she let both dogs off leash at the trail's head. "Now you two behave," she said as she gave each a quick pat on the head.

Jerry kept pace on one side, as Bobby hung back about ten feet behind. Maxi had seen this before – the dogs were now in protection mode. The packed down dirt path made the walk easy while the towering pine trees created a stunning canopy overhead. With each breath of pine, Maxi's tight shoulders sank a little further down her back.

As other walkers approached, Bobby's distance decreased. "Wow, what well-behaved pups you have," a woman who resembled her organic farmer neighbor in Vermont commented as she and her small child passed. "May he pet?"

Maxi let loose a small smile. "The Labrador, not the Shepherd, please." Maxi waved for Bobby to sit as the little one threw his arms around the dog's neck.

"Gentle, Arlo," the mother cooed. The boy broke his hold and smiled up to his mother. Maxi's heart ached as she thought about the early days with Ric. "Thank you for sharing."

"Our pleasure," Maxi said, adding, "Enjoy the moments," as she nodded to the child.

"You, also."

As the two walked in the opposite direction she heard a squeak of a "Thank you," float back.

Maxi let out an audible sigh. When Ric was little, they lived in a small beach house, the smell of the ocean brought calm. Then her ex, his biological father, took up with that whore, making Maxi the laughingstock of their small town. Yet if not for the whore, she and Zack wouldn't have reconnected, so Maxi would try to extend gratitude for that, and the whore shooting her ex's balls off.

Simple favors that happen.

Her laughter echoed off the tall cliffs on either side. Splashes from a natural spring soaked into the path. Maxi concentrated on walking as her sneakers slipped on portions of mud that accumulated just before the collected pool of water.

As they moved, small tidal pools of rust smelling water collected along the route. Orange sediment dried by the sun showed off the minerals in the water. A good-sized rim close to the edge showed the brightest hue. A few people carefully stretched across the rocks to dip cups into the liquid, the minerals said to contain the fountain of youth. Maxi gestured for both dogs to stay.

The trail went along a small trickle that ended at a significant stream; its waters gushed along a small picnic area. A few tables were covered with coolers, umbrellas, and towels. One table remained empty off to the side. Maxi sat on the bench and listened to giggles, the moving water, and occasional conversation.

Bobby's tail thumped at the sight of the water. "Go ahead," Maxi pointed in the direction of the stream. Jerry jumped up on the bench to sit close to her. Both watched as Bobby flew into the air, ending with a splash. The dog climbed up the bank, strutted over, and shook to share. Maxi laughed while Jerry just gave his partner the doggie stare down.

###

Back at the hotel, the message indicator blinked. Maxi retrieved the message, only to hear a bunch of static. She dialed the front desk for more information.

"Hi, I am in room 319 and I received a bunch of static for a message."

"Ah-yes, Ms. Malone, there was a gentleman here looking for you. I apologize his message didn't come through on the room voicemail. I had a line here at the desk when they arrived. Since you didn't answer my call the best I could do was connect them to your room via the house phone." The clerk's voice went distant. "Oops, I apologize. Is there anything else I can help you with?" Maxi could hear voices in the background getting louder. "We are very busy down here."

Maxi's hand rested on her stomach as she thanked the man for his time. She glanced at the clock on the nightstand. It was only five-thirty. She still had to grab something for dinner and take the dogs out again. They could just leave here and go stay closer to the airport. A long sssss of an exhale escaped. "Damn, if I didn't love my husband, I wouldn't have these problems."

Her mind traveled back to Aruba long ago. Outside the hospital, Zack and her sitting on a bench under a palm tree, her mom's cigarette smoke vacillating in the air around them. "Maxi, I think you need 24/7 protection," he laughed. Mom agreed, adding, "I am amazed at the situations you end up in."

Maxi's thoughts went back to the statement often. When Zack insisted on the fencing and the elaborate alarm setup at the Vermont house, he had reminder her that, "You don't piss off drug lords and go forward without a certain bit of paranoia." Yes, dodging drug lords with her son by her side had been stressful. She was told the wrong place at the wrong time, yet she couldn't help but wonder why her.

Her son by her side gave Maxi a sense of control, even if control didn't exist. If he was safe, she was okay. She shook her head to try to get the dark thoughts out.

Maxi wished that Ric was here with her now.

"I'll just send another text," she told the dogs as she snapped a photo of Bobby on the bed and Jerry's chin resting on the mattress behind her. *Guess where I am? Waiting on that plane from Niza.* She added a smiley face emoji at the end.

"When the kid is safe with me, everything else is okay too," she explained to the dogs.

RIC

Erik in the cell next to him hadn't returned. Ric paced the small area as he wondered why. The office had been unusually quiet. No Fox News, the little kid he read to wasn't around, and most of the time he couldn't hear the deputy on duty. Ric thought that maybe he was outside the building. The door scraping against the floor followed by a short blast of light gave away his location as he sauntered in and out of the lobby.

Inside perspiration seeped from every cranny of his body. The room got warmer as the sun rose. Even the cement blocks that surrounded his cell leaked sweat. He folded his legs under his behind and sat on the floor. Hands rested on his knees as his eyes closed.

As he began to doze off, a humming buzz in the background started to scream, yet no other sound existed. Ric awoke to the sounds of loud voices.

"Listen Hawk, if Susanna can't identify the boy, I am going to have to let him go." The Sheriff's substantial shadow took up the entire space that separated the jail cells from the lobby. "I know the drill you moron, yet nobody gets paid until we do. Drag that useless wife of yours into town."

The Sheriff emerged from the other room. Their eyes met and the Sheriff's smile sent a shiver through Ric. "That's okay, Hawk. I'll bring the boy by your place. Say around three today?" Now the Sheriff pointed his meaty finger towards the jail cells. "Yeah, let's say then. Thank you, Hawk."

The Sheriff jingled the keys around to open the cell door. "Go get yourself cleaned up, boy. A lady is waiting." He gestured down the hall in the area of the bathroom. Once inside Ric washed his face and hands. He pulled back the shower curtain to reveal a one-person shower stall covered in black tiles. With a closer inspection, he saw that the tiles had mold growing across all surfaces.

Ric let the shower curtain close and took a step back to face the sink. The same light green towel, covered in black spots lay on the holder. He wet the corner with the least filth and swiped it over the melted bar soap before rubbing both arm pits. He used his shirt, not much cleaner, to wipe the soap off.

Back in the front office, he observed the Sheriff and deputy give each other back slaps followed by laughter. The Pride Ridge Camp truck pulled up and an older man who Ric didn't recognize got out. The stranger said a couple words to the Sheriff who shook his head in response.

Just as quickly, the truck disappeared. A blast of sunlight extinguished his hope of being rescued.

"Okay boy, this is how this is going to work," the Sheriff said. "You are going to ride with me out to Hawk's place. His wife is going to I.D. you as the person who stole the truck, then you are going to be given a choice of paying the fine or labor. I sincerely hope you remember those numbers in your phone as your friend chose labor, and he's..."

The Sheriff let the end of the sentence drift. Ric climbed into the backseat. His body now matched the stench. The truck bounced its way through the canyon sending Rick flying back and forth across the seat. There was a huge meadow that stretched over to a red barn. The red barn had a single stream of smoke stretching into the cloudless sky. Ric didn't dare look back in the direction that he knew he'd see the old airstream.

The Sheriff turned down the dirt road that divided the meadow. He jerked to a stop in front of the barn doors.

"This look familiar, son?"

"No sir," Ric responded. His eyes glued upon the Sheriff, knowing if he looked past, the old airstream would be back there. "Where are we?"

Ric noted the Sheriff's attempt at a grin. The side door slid open, and the Sheriff motioned with his hand for Ric to slide out. Once his feet hit the dirt, the Sheriff pushed on his shoulder blade, moving him closer to the barn. The heavy vinegar smell overwhelmed Ric. His hand moved to cover his nose and mouth.

As the Sheriff's hand pushed hard against his back, Ric moved through an open door into the barn. The smell intensified. The space had workbenches set up down the middle with vials and beakers scattered on top. The makeshift lab reminded Ric of the chemistry lab at his high school that the board forgot to renovate. Five people in white lab coats moved liquids from one beaker to another. All wore masks and goggles.

On the opposite side of the room his cellmate's body leaned against a pile of boxes next to a back door. Erik's mouth hung open. A large wet spot, possibly drool, pooled on his shirt. The folks at the adjacent table didn't seem to notice or didn't really care. All kept going about their task as if on autopilot.

"Why the fuck did you bring college boy here?" the voice resonated from behind. Ric turned to see the gun-swinging-owner of the truck he'd borrowed, and behind him stood the stringy-haired girl.

"Hawk, you old dog, good to see you!" The Sheriff enveloped the man in a bear hug. The Sheriff whispered something in Hawk's ear. "Should we take a walk outside?"

Hawk nodded then pushed the stringy-haired girl out the door. The Sheriff and Ric followed.

"Okay, now we all know why we are here. Suzanna, dear, come over here." Hawk gave Suzanna a push. She flinched as the Sheriff draped his arm around her shoulders and faced her body in the direction of Ric. "Now Suzanna, take a good look at this boy. Is he the one that took Hawk's truck."

Ric stared into Suzanna's empty eyes. He still couldn't remember the night they had met, yet the next day got him here. She swayed a bit in the Sheriff's arms before shaking her head no. "Suzanna, answer the question," Hawk pushed her in the back.

Suzanna turned to glare back then said, "This is not the boy. I already told you the one who took the truck is drooly over there–the new tester." Hawk pushed her in the back again. This time she folded her arms across her chest and held ground.

The Sheriff turned back to Hawk. "Okay, this one pays the fine and goes." He looked over in the direction of Ric's former cellmate. "And do something about that."

"Are you getting his fine for the Sena—" The Sheriff sent his fist into Hawk's stomach.

"What did you say, boy?"

Hawk coughed. "Nothing Sheriff. We'll take care of the situation." He gave Suzanna a quick glance. "Both situations."

The Sheriff nodded. His sweaty hand gripped Ric's shoulder and pushed him against the car. Ric heard Hawk yelling, "You only had one job. Now the Sheriff's pissed. Damn you, Suzanna!"

Ric looked back at the barn as he slid across the back seat. Suzanna's body lay crumpled on the ground near the barn entrance. He paid attention as Hawk pushed his old cellmate onto the lump where she lay. The Sheriff walked over to point at both his cellmate and the girl then his hand gestured to a space behind the barn.

"Fuck," Ric mumbled as he pressed his back against the seat. Outside the window, the Sheriff and Hawk shook hands.

L.M. Pampuro

MAXI

With the lights off in her room, Maxi peered out onto the barely lit parking lot through a crack in the curtains. She got lucky upon returning and her SUV sat right below her hotel window. Even in the near darkness, the vehicle screamed cop! "I don't know what I expect to see out here," she said to the dogs. "Maybe a big white pedophile cargo van with a sign on the side reading *I'm here to get you, Maxi, because of your government official husband!*"

Maxi secured the drapes by using the clips on a clothes hanger to block out all the light. She turned on the light by the bed creating a soft glow within the room. Earlier, with the dogs in tow, she drove downtown to get a quick bite at Scallions then walked the dogs on busy Broadway, the whole time watching behind her in the shop windows.

Downtown Saratoga was as crowded as always on a clear summer night. The crowd ranged from old-time horse-racing fans to groupies of the band scheduled at SPAC the next night. The venue's calendar graced every window along the street.

Young and old, rich, and not so rich mingled the streets together. Their clothing styles ranged from Chanel to concert t-shirts and faded jeans. Maxi took in all the faces around her, unfortunately none of the faces screamed deranged killer, or at least the suspect left that t-shirt at home.

She waited on Zack to call with his flight information. Earlier, after a long debate, she had finally convinced him to fly to Albany and then they could travel back to Vermont together, yet if Ric didn't answer her soon, she had other ideas.

Maxi searched for the driving distance between Saratoga and Pride Ridge. "Crap, twenty-eight hours. We'll need Zack for this one." She stared at her last two texts to her son, without reply. "I could check the airlines to make sure he got on his flight." Bobby lay across the rug in the bathroom, his tail and butt visible in the frame of door while Jerry's head rested on her leg.

Neither dog moved on the suggested road trip idea.

"Okay, so you two are not up for another adventure. Maybe I will just relocate here to Saratoga and check in on him daily, since he can't reply or call me weekly." She had hoped by staying at the Gideon there would be a sense of peace or at least safety, yet the space seemed to shrink as hotel room closed in around her. "If we left now..." Jerry let out a low howl. "I know, Zack at the airport first. I wish he would call with details."

As if on cue, her cellphone buzzed. "Hello, love," she said.

"Hello to you too," Zack answered. Maxi let out a little sigh. His breathy voice suggested that Zack, her husband, instead of Zack the government official, was on the phone. She would have to deal with Zack the FBI agent once he landed tomorrow. "How's 'toga?"

"We had an awesome dinner at Scallions then strolled downtown."

"We?" Zack asked.

"Yeah, me and the dogs." That got a muffled laugh.

"They let the dogs eat at Scallions?"

"Outside, on the patio. The folks around us were impressed when I went to use the ladies' room and neither dog moved."

"They are well-trained machines. Either way, you were brave to venture out," Zack said.

Maxi thought about the message and decided to share. "Yes and no. After we got back from walking in the park, I had a staticky message waiting that I couldn't understand. The front desk host said whoever left it had asked for me by name." *Come on Zack, put on your concerned husband hat. Say something to make this better you idiot! Tell me that this will be okay. That I am safe. Someone was here! Asking about me!* "We left by a side door and parked the car under our room window when we returned. I just peeked out and saw—"

"Maxi, stop," Zack interrupted, "I'm on the first commuter flight from D.C. to Albany. I can get a car—"

"And arrive here at the same time if you had flown - sleep would be better. I am okay here at the hotel tonight. My room is on the second floor, I got the dogs, and I pushed the desk against the door. I will be okay."

"Alright then. Pick me up in Albany. I land at six-forty and will take an iced green from Uncommon Grounds along with one of their everything bagel egg sandwiches."

"Anything else?" Maxi said. The thought of being with Zack always made her smile, even if his antics complicated her life endlessly.

"Just your undying love and devotion," he quipped. "And Maxi, please try to stay in your room and not do anything stupid between now and then."

She blew out an audible breath. "You have my love and devotion; I can't guarantee the rest."

After the call ended, Maxi moved Jerry from her leg to stand. She picked up the scattered balls and chewed up stuffed dinosaurs, along with both feeders then threw them all in a canvas bag. Next her toiletries and dirty clothes went into a Ziplock then the suitcase. The clock on the dresser read 10:15. "Okay boys, we will sleep a few hours and slip out wicked early."

Maxi did a quick search to find out that Uncommon Grounds on Broadway opened at 6. She would get there as they unlocked the doors then let the dogs run around a rest stop on the through way right before she picked up Zack at the airport. As Maxi worked out all the logistics, which included handing the dogs over to Zack and hopping a flight to Niza to find and lecture her son, a plan started to form.

She'd wait to discuss the latter with Zack in person as starting an argument via text or phone was useless. At least she had learned something about her husband's personality.

SHERIFF

The Sheriff peered around the corner to observe Ric, eyes closed, with his torso against the cement wall.

"Boy," he said in a low voice. When no movement appeared, he dialed a number he'd memorized long ago.

A chipper voice answered on the other end, "Senator's office."

Without identifying himself, the Sheriff said, "Hi Bitsy, is he in?"

"One moment please."

Seconds later, the Senator's booming voice filled the receiver with his standard greeting. "How the hell are ya, buddy?"

"Doing fine, my friend, doing fine." The Sheriff continued, "We do have a couple problems, solvable, but problems."

"Money problems," the Senator said. The Sheriff coughed at that response.

"Yes and no. I got one who did a little tasting of our last batch and that boy ain't doing too good now."

"Not my problem. That set-up was all you…"

"Yeah, well," the Sheriff continued, "we can't have folks disappearing and all."

"You got that right–get the money, whatever there is from the parents and let them deal with the kid's drug issues, you hear me?"

"I will make the call. The other problem is the one here now," the Sheriff said again, looking to see Ric in the same closed eye position. "Kid keeps saying the number is in his dead cellphone yet that doesn't feel right. I mean what kid doesn't know his mama's number?"

That remark got a laugh from the Senator. "Listen buddy, get the kid's info from the camp and make the call. Marjorie will be by at the end of the week, and we can clean this up. I got my own problems here."

"Yep – we watched you take that federal agent down..."

"Yep – grilling that Yankee sure was fun and I did put him in his place—"

"You sure did Senator—"

"But beware, that Yankee boy is smart. He was the one who caught on to Marjorie and that dumb ass boss of hers working as double agents and Brady is directly responsible for the death of my nephew. Through all this I thank God I had the ability to help my niece out."

"And now she owes you."

"Now you listen to me. Family never owes family. Marjorie is just using her talents to help the family if you know what I mean."

"Yeah, I know. I will have the delivery ready for her."

"You do that."

The Sheriff slammed down the phone and took a deep breath. He looked over at Ric again. "Boy!" his voice vibrated. "BOY!" he said louder.

Ric jumped; eyes opened wide. "Yes, sir," the boy gave the right response.

L.M. Pampuro

RIC

The Sheriff stood just outside his cell door. "Boy I find it hard to believe you don't know your mama's phone number, but you people rely on this," he held up Ric's cellphone, "too much. So here is what I am going to do, you can make one call, right now, and settle up your fine..."

"What fine? I thought the girl said it wasn't me."

The Sheriff let out a belly laugh. "Suzanna is unreliable, as they say. I gave you room and board for how many days?" Ric opened his mouth to answer yet was cut off as the Sheriff continued, "Call your mama. Fine is thirty thou, more if you want a ride back."

"Thirty thousand dollars? For what?"

The Sheriff didn't answer him. Instead, he handed his cellphone through the bars. "Make the call," he said and walked back to the outer office.

Ric flipped the phone over in his hands and pressed the power button. A smidgen of a battery indicated there was enough juice for a call or a text. The Sheriff must have plugged it in or something.

He scrolled through his contacts to Zack's private line and typed quickly–*Zack–I don't know where I am, but some crazy ass Sheriff has me in jail for at least 3 days w/o charges. Think Pride Ridge is—*

"Boy, I told you to call your mama, not text. Gimme that," The Sheriff reached out to grab the phone as Ric's finger slid across the send button. He hit the power button as the phone was snatched out of his hand. "Lemme," the Sheriff yelled.

He continued to reprimand Ric, "Boy, there was only so much juice left in the tank, and you didn't do as I said." He turned and smashed the phone against the cement. Ric held up his hands to block his face as parts flew.

After the initial shock, Ric glared at the place where his cellphone hit the wall. "Your memory best be getting better," the Sheriff said, "cause tomorrow you'll be working down at the barn for a while if you don't call your mama." He tipped his hat as he exited the cell.

Ric started to pick up the jagged pieces that were scattered around. Hope faded with each new addition. His eyes grew wet and breath ragged. "I didn't even look at the number," he sighed out.

The only phone number that came to mind was his mother's old work number. At one time the line connected back to her cellphone, but that was years ago, before she sold the company. That had to have changed.

"Sheriff, may I use the phone?"

The Sheriff spoke as he unlocked the door, "Remembered mama's number, huh?"

"No sir," Ric said, "but I remember my mother's old office and they will have her cellphone because she still does consulting for them once in a while."

The Sheriff hesitated and then opened the door. "What the hell, boy," he said.

Instead of an old office number, Ric dialed the landline in Vermont. One ring. Two rings. "Come on. Pick up!" When a computer-generated voice instructed him to leave a message, Ric said, "Hi Mom and Dad—I am in a bit of trouble out here and need," he placed his hand loosely over the receiver, "How much do I need?"

The Sheriff hesitated and then threw out "50,000, no wait, bail will be a 100 grand. That should get their attention."

Ric continued, "Yeah so, my bail is 100,000 dollars. I can't tell you the charges." He looked over at the Sheriff again, "Should I leave a number?"

"No–tell em you will call back tomorrow morning. If we get an answer, you don't have to go to work."

Ric gave a quick nod then repeated what the Sheriff had said, adding, "I would have called on your cell but mine has no juice. I hope we talk tomorrow, and I love you both."

The Sheriff grabbed the phone out of Ric's hand and slammed it down on the handset. "Boy, that last part better not be no set up. Boy your age telling your parents that you love them. That isn't right."

"But sir, I tell my parents that I love them all the time," Ric's voice cracked. "And right now, I miss them both lots." Ric turned to walk back into his cold cell.

MAXI

Uncommon Grounds already had a line at six in the morning, yet parking on Broadway proved easy. Maxi left the windows open on the sidewalk side for the dogs. "You both behave. I will be right back." Jerry sat just out of view in the passenger's seat while Bobby assumed the same position in the seat behind. Maxi glanced back to see both dogs' heads hanging out the window, watching her progress. She stood behind the last person in a line of people waiting for the coffee shop to unlock their doors.

Their tails thumped hard against the leather seats when she reappeared outside the shop carrying a tray with two cups and a white paper bag. She walked around to the driver's side of the car and hopped in. Bobby placed his paws on the rest between the seats.

"Listen boys," she said, "if either of you touch that sandwich, Zack will turn you into coats." Bobby rested his head on his paws and gave a little whine. "However," Maxi reached into the bag and pulled out two dog cookies. "One each, don't fight."

Maxi pulled up at the Arrival Terminal to a waiting Zack, pacing in the loading zone at Albany airport. He threw his bag in the back, then pulled her into a tight hug. "I've missed you," he said as he kissed her bare neck.

"I've missed you, too," Maxi whispered. A blaring horn interrupted their reunion. Maxi hopped back in the driver's seat. She drove through the arrival area then followed signs for departures. "But I am heading out west," she said as she put the car in park, "When will that boy learn."

"He didn't text you back?" Zack said.

"Wait are you two having another bro," her hands flew up in air quotes, "bonding time? Seriously Zack, have you talked to him? I will kill my son! How dare he answer you and not me!"

Zack held his hand up, a gesture that stopped Maxi's rant. "I have not heard from Ric," Zack said. "I texted him to get in touch with you because you were getting concerned. He should have—" Zack pulled his phone out of his front pocket. From her vantage point she could see a blank screen. "When is he supposed to fly back?"

"Tomorrow. He is coming back here tomorrow."

"Okay – let me make a few phone calls. I'm game but the drive will take us a couple of days and we will probably miss him in the air."

Maxi let out a huff. "So why don't I fly out today and then we can fly back together? Problem solved."

Zack sat sideways against the passenger's seat. "How about if I make a few calls on our way back to Vermont. If I can't get a hold of Ric or any information of his whereabouts, we can go to plan B." Maxi opened her mouth to speak as Zack's hand went up. "Listen love, I don't know what plan B is, yet if needed, together we will figure that out." They connected both hands and intertwined their fingers. Maxi held back tears as Zack continued to speak, "I need to see the fence and I have a couple guys meeting us there to check the tape. Donald knows about our current situation and has offered any help within his capabilities."

Maximum Panic

She glanced down at the two connected hands.
Somehow this made her life a little less scary.

ZACK

Zack opened his laptop as Maxi turned north on the throughway headed for the Lake Champlain bridge. The rolling landscape of the beautiful Adirondack mountains and equally impressive crystal waters peeking in between the trees couldn't take his gaze from the screen on his lap.

The coffee had cooled to where he liked to drink although the cheese on his egg sandwich had congealed with the yolk. With egg slug running down his left arm, he ate and drank while his right typed away.

While Zack had been in the air, Atwood had sent a follow up on the list, that suggested he should concentrate his efforts in Fremont. The esteemed Senator's name was highlighted in bright yellow. Zack chuckled at the thought of investigating the head of the senate committee that forced an internal inquiry of his old New Haven office. As Maxi drove, Zack kept reading, compartmentalizing thoughts of his current situation with his stepson's whereabouts. On the spreadsheet, the biggest donations seemed to be coming from some county containing only Podunk towns about an hour from Pride Ridge. Zack made notes to look up industry and influential folks, if any, in the area.

His thoughts ran between work and Ric. If Ric doesn't show up in Albany tomorrow, maybe there will be more than one mystery in the same area. Of course, he might be off doing what teenage boys do. He looked over at Maxi who gave him a quick smile. Zack knew that if his wife didn't see her son, she would go ballistic and drive out west with the dogs. Anything less would not satisfy her.

"Crap," Zack said.

"Problem?"

"No," Zack fiddled with the angle of his screen as he leaned over to give a quick peck on the cheek. The laptop screen hidden from Maxi's view. "My Wi-Fi is shitty through here and I need to reply to some of these."

"Should I pull off into a Dunkin lot? We are close enough to New England that there should be one at each off ramp."

"No, that's okay. I want to get to the house." Because of his job, Zack had little control over the cast of scam artists and drug lords that found their way to him and Maxi. This job seemed to have another direct connection. Ric going to Pride Ridge was his idea and the people who'd scared Maxi out of the house had done so to distract him from his present case – he was sure of that.

RIC

The hand across his mouth kept air from reaching into his lungs. Eyes bulged wide open, gasping for a breath, the Sheriff's deputy, the mean one that had brought him to jail, was so close Ric could smell the cheese from his open mouth breathing. In a low voice, the deputy whispered, "Lie here and keep your mouth shut, boy." To which Ric nodded enthusiastically.

"Do so much as sigh, and I will kill you and dump your body where the coyotes will have a feast."

The deputy's eye faded to black. The man nodded then peeled his skin away from Ric's mouth, then brought his fingers up to his own lips. Limbs and muscles tightened as the slightest movement might produce a squeak.

In the lobby, the Sheriff's voice boomed, "Yes, mam, he was like that when we found him. Got him to the hospital as soon as we could."

A female voice followed, "I don't understand. Erik never did drugs. He was a good kid. How did this happen?"

"There are some unscrupulous people out there, mam, and I am sorry they got to your son." The sound of muffled tears followed. "We do our best to make this town a good patriotic place to be, yet these drug people are out of control. If I had it my way..."

The woman sniffled again. "My ex-husband and I appreciate all you do out here. Erik is our only child."

"It is my pleasure to try and save our youth. We started a non-profit to get the extra funds the government says we don't have. It is called *Drug*

Operation Potential Enforcement." Ric covered his mouth to quell a nervous laugh at the acronym. "That was what saved your son. We get donations and then add extra patrols and such. This flyer explains the program."

Ric couldn't see what was happening. He heard paper ripping. "I'd like to contribute as you saved my son's life. Maybe this will help get those bastards who hurt my son behind bars sooner. I never should have allowed my ex to talk me into that camp."

"I'm sure it wasn't the camp that did this." The sound of feet shuffling along the laminate floor got more pronounced. "And thank you, mam. This generous donation from you all will help the cause. Let me write you out a receipt for your check."

"Please be quick – I must get back to the hospital. My ex and I switch off, per the divorce agreement." She mumbled something before adding, "I just wanted to stop by and thank you."

"You are welcome, mam." Ric heard the door to the station open and the voices became muffled. The bed gave way, relieved of the additional weight of the deputy's body.

"You did good, boy," the deputy noted. "Let's hope your mama calls back today and gets us your check. I hate to put you to work in the barn as your friend didn't respond very well." He followed his statement with a big belly laugh. "They never do."

ZACK

Zack walked the perimeter on the outside of the fence. As he glanced back to his house, he could see Maxi watching his every move out of the kitchen window. His wife's silhouette paced back and forth within the frame of the glass. He couldn't see below her shoulder yet true to her form one hand was gripping onto her cellphone and she probably was screaming into it for their son to answer.

From Zack's review, the team his boss had sent up yesterday had done a good job of scanning the footage from the security cameras. They reported that along the fencing most of the ferns stood straight up, and there wasn't any breakage along their stalks as if someone had walked through the area. The only exception being where Maxi had seen the men trying to climb over.

The fence stood tall to appear sturdy. With a quick glance along the top, nothing showed itself to be out of order. His team had also reported that nothing was found along the perimeter with the exception of the broken ferns. No shoe prints, clothing tags, or any other indication that a human had tried to breach the perimeter.

The video on his phone from the surveillance cameras showed otherwise. He could see the outlines of three figures dressed in black from the top of their hoodies down to their ankles. The camera didn't pick up footwear, yet based on his experience Zack knew that whatever was on their feet probably matched the rest. He compared the angle of the footage to where he stood, trying to picture the objective of the folks breaking in.

Zack gave two sharp whistles, Jerry appeared on the opposite side of the fence. The dog led over to the gate. As they walked side by side to retrace his steps, Shepherd's nose kept bouncing into Zack's hand.

"I can't see it boy," he said, "but maybe you can smell better than those pups they brought in yesterday." Jerry gave a quick tail wag yet kept his nose between the dirt and the fence. Back and forth together they walked several times before turning down the trail along the neighboring farm.

Their neighbor Skye, owner of the organic farm next door, hunched over in the field. He would be easily missed if not for his bright rainbow ty-dyed standing out amongst fields of greens.

"Hey, man," Zack greeted. He noted that Skye rose slowly, dropping whatever he had in his left hand. This was normal for both Skye and his wife Rain tensed up around Zack. He figured their farm probably grew other stuff than veggies, yet that didn't matter to Zack. This was Vermont after all. The couple kept a lookout on Maxi when he traveled and made a point to invite Maxi out and about regularly. Having lived up here for a little over a year, friends were hard to find, and Zack was grateful for the two hippies next door adopting his wife.

Skye gave a slow wave back. As Zack approached, he stood up straight. "You're back," Skye noted.

"Yep – for a little while. Still commuting way too far."

"So…" Skye looked between Zack, the dog, and his barn. He blew out a loud exhale. "What's up?"

"A few days ago, Maxi almost had a break in—"

"Into the fortress?" Skye's eyes widened.

"Yeah, into the fortress," Zack laughed. "I'm trying to figure out who, of course and was wondering if you and Rain had noticed any strangers hanging around."

Skye rested one arm across his stomach. The other hand's fingers stroked a well grown goatee. Minutes passed without a sound. "Lots of lost hikers lately," Skye finally said.

"Lost hikers?" Zack wanted Skye to keep going.

"Yeah, you know, people end up walking along the fields asking where the road is, although I still haven't figured out where they are coming from because the trail is on the other side of the stream so how do you get lost on this side, know what I mean?"

Zack nodded and again waited for the farmer to speak. "You know Rain was out here with me the past few days. Her short memory is better than mine because I tend the greenhouse plants—" Skye's hand raised to cover his mouth.

"No worries, dude." The word dude felt wrong in Zack's mouth. "I am interested in two days ago. Did you notice anyone?"

"Maxi and the dogs," Skye said. "I remember because Rain and I were doing the beet dance and Maxi said she'd see us at the market." His hand tapped against his mouth. "Wait we didn't see Maxi at the market. I'm going to call Rain." With that Skye took in a deep breath then shouted, "Raaaain!" He repeated the bellow two more times before a "Whaaaat!" came from the direction of the house.

After another brief call and response, Rain came bouncing across the field covered in mud down to her boots. "What is so important?"

Skye leaned over to kiss her cheek. "Zack here has a few questions about strangers passing on the trails. I told him about a few getting lost the other days."

"Creepy dudes in the hoodies and camo?" Rain said.

"Yep, the creepy dudes," Skye repeated. The two shook their heads, shoulders, and behinds.

"What made those dudes creepy," Zack interrupted. Now the couple mirrored each other's stance, fingers tapping lips. Zack scratched Jerry behind the ears as he waited.

Skye spoke first. "Tell him about your spidey sense, love."

"Okay. Well, I have this thing that when I am around not nice people, my stomach twitches—"

"Like a nauseous pit?" Zack asked. Rain nodded yes. "Maxi has that too. Her hand rests on her stomach when something isn't right. Definitely a woman thing, no offense," Zack directed at Skye. "Any way, please go on."

"Yeah, so, some people came through the path and said they were trying to find some dog they saw by the river,"

"Did they say it was their dog?"

Rain shook her head no. "Just that the dog had disappeared and now they were lost too. I pointed back to the road," Rain gave a quick head tilt in the direction of the barn, "they said they came from that way and were on the road over there."

Zack felt a chill run up the back of his neck. "What did you tell them?"

"I said that that was our neighbor's house and land that way and the road they wanted was beyond the barn." Rain blew out a loud exhale. "They thanked me and went away from the road. I thought it was weird that they didn't ask if I saw the dog."

"Okay, Rain," Zack said, "How many were there? And did you see them again?"

"Did I do something wrong?" Rain chewed on her index finger as she leaned the rest of her body against Skye.

"No, not at all," Zack said. "I just need a bit more information."

"There were three," Rain held up three fingers for emphasis, "all in those outdoor shorts and tops the city folks wear, like I said before, hoodies and camo carrying one of those fancy backpacks."

"And you didn't see them after?"

"Honestly, Zack, I hightailed it into the barn once they were out of sight. The dudes gave me the creeps." Rain's head gave a quick shake to release the image.

"Thank you both. You've helped me a lot."

Rain gave a small smile in return. "Is Maxi, okay?"

"Why do you ask?" The two gave each other a conspiratorial glance.

"Well, you're here," Skye pointed out.

"Huh," Zack said. "I didn't think my patterns were that obvious."

The awkward silence that followed broke with a howl from Jerry. Zack turned to watch a group of teenagers pass into the woods.

"So is Maxi, okay?" Rain broke the silence.

"Yes, Maxi is okay," Zack hesitated how much information to share before deciding a few more details might spark more memory. "Someone tried to climb over our back fence, and we are just trying to figure out who."

Rain and Skye nodded, then together said, "It wasn't us."

"I knew that" Zack said. "Thank you for your help and please let me know if you think of anything." Zack reached into his pocket to pull out two business cards. He handed one to each. "I know you have Maxi's number, yet if you do remember anything, would you please call me?" Both accepted the cards with a nod.

"Oh, hey, isn't the Ricster due back this week? Or is he going straight back to school?" Rain's smile widened.

"Not sure of the Ricster's," Zack let out a nervous laugh, "plans as yet. If he comes home, I will be sure to send him over."

"Cool," both nodded in unison. Zack gave a quick goodbye and took out his phone as he walked the trail back to the gate.

RIC

To give himself more time, Ric tried Maxi's old office number. He left a new message, "Hi–This is Ric Malone, Maxi's son. I am trying to get a hold of my mom, and this is the only number that I am getting voicemail. Would you please forward this message to call me at—" Ric repeated the number the Sheriff gave earlier.

He knew it didn't matter what number he gave because the mailbox wasn't monitored. If they hadn't smashed his cellphone, he'd be out of here. The deputy led him by the elbow back to his cell.

"Hi, ya all," was followed by "Now do what I told," from the Sheriff. Ric moved to the corner of his cell to sit and lean against the bars. From there he could hear the two deputies chatting for a minute and as soon as the door in the lobby closed, a familiar face peered around the corner.

"Will you read to me again?" the boy's voice just above a whisper as his hands wrapped around another book.

"Sure, but that's not what we started last time," Ric said.

"I know–I finished that one at home. This is the next book." A small hand reached through the bars holding the second book of the Foul Twins series. Ric let out a sigh.

"I was hoping to finish the other one."

"I understand." The kid pulled the book out of reach.

"Maybe you can tell me about it and then we can start this one? That way I will know where this book starts." The kid started with "well" and didn't take a breath until what seemed like forever, now Ric had a long meandering synopsis about the book he'd started to read along with a brief update about where the kid was in the current book. "Little dude, you need to come by more often, so I don't miss parts."

"My mom floats," he emphasized floats with air quotes, "around the county, so she's only here once in a while. We spend most of our time in Luna, where we live."

Ric took in this new information as he started to read the book. The twins were in a similar jam except they were being held underground in the land of the fairies. The twins also had magical powers and a friend whose special talent was smelly farts.

Ric had neither.

The small boy laid his head against the cell door. A few chapters in, Ric looked up to see the boy's mother had repositioned her chair to watch from the outer office. Ric gave her a small smile as he kept on reading. A quiet yawn gave away that the boy was fighting sleep.

"We can stop for a bit, if you want to," Ric volunteered, already reaching the book back through the bars. A loud yawn followed by a quiet thank you as a small pair of hands brought the book to rest on the boy's chest. The boy then wobbled into the outer to the outer office and climbed onto his mother's lap.

Ric returned to his bunk to stretch. Time was measured in meals and Sheriff's visits. Every tick tock in between was just a slow passing of time. His eyelids grew heavy, and his breath slowed to a deep rhythm. A soft voice broke through his attempt at rest.

"Hey boy," he heard a woman's voice. "Dammit, I am not going to wake my son to help you." The urgent tone slapped Ric's body to a vertical position. His eyes now open wide. In between the bars the boy's mother's hand stretched extending his phone now taped back together. "I am not sure this will work or when the other two will be back so make it fast," she instructed.

The phone sputtered. "I still need a charger," Rick said as the deputy held out her hand.

She grabbed the phone back. "Give me a minute."

As minutes passed, Ric found himself pacing the cell. This could be his only chance—

"I got you some juice, now make it quick."

He grabbed the phone out of her hand and unlocked the screen. There were multiple texts pending that he ignored scrolling down to locate Zack's number.

"The number here is 303-555-5555," the woman said. Ric plugged the phone number into a text and added, *I am in hell. Please help!*

"Where am I?" he asked to confirm his location.

"Amity, Fremont," the woman answered. Ric's thumbs tapped out the words. "Okay, Dak, the other deputy is back. Hit send and give me the phone." Without finishing his thought, Ric hit send and turned on the locator button. The woman snagged the phone out of his hand and walked back to the desk.

"Greetings, Elma," Dak's voice filled the air. "Anything exciting I need to know about?"

"No sir," Elma answered as she pocketed the taped together phone. "Pretty quiet here today, Dak." Ric could hear items being moved around along with the jiggle of keys. "Guess I will see you in a couple days?"

"Maybe, maybe not. I have a feeling that our prisoner will be gone yet we might need someone to answer the phones," a low laugh followed.

"Just let the folks in Luna know so I don't drive out here for nothing. Come on boy, let's go." The door screeched open followed by a big slam. A loud squeak came in from the lobby. Within minutes Fox News sounded along with several "yeps" and "amens" to the commentary.

From the cement floor, Ric rose into a plank position and held his body straight until the commentator said the word "democrat." With each mention of the word, he moved from a plank to his stomach. Soon enough, he was moving gracefully through the Army style push-ups that Zack had taught him after they'd first met.

With each rise, his core got harder, while each dissent brought stronger triceps and shoulders. In every breath, he prayed that he'd have the strength to outmaneuver the people in the outer office.

ZACK

The phone call from Atwood was disturbing yet nothing to compare to the text that followed. Ric was in Amity Fremont, in jail. The same Amity Fremont whose Sheriff appeared on his list of donors to investigate. The man's name had moved to the top of the list after Donald's team uncovered a connection to a boy Ric's age who recently almost overdosed.

"I'm not sure the two are connected, yet there was another big deposit to the Cayman account we are monitoring." Atwood was usually on target with these things. Zack went back to the text. *I'm in hell - fake charges. My roommate - disappeared phone not charged - Sheriff keeps threat...*

That was where it ended. No other information except the kid had turned on his locator, bless him. The location dot beeped somewhere in the center of Luna, about thirty miles from Amity.

He had a phone number yet calling would eliminate the surprise element. Now that his two investigations are intertwined, it is time to visit the Rockies. Maxi of course would want to come along, and he'd need the dogs, in case of tracking. The SUV made more sense than flying, though flying would get them there faster.

Zack mumbled logistics as he entered the backside of the house. In the winter, Rain and Skye's farm lay in full view yet this time of year green foliage took over. He walked through the house to find Maxi lying down on the sofa, arms stretched out holding a cellphone above her face.

"What are you doing, love?" Zack said as he lifted her legs onto his lap.

"I am putting a hex on my child."

Zack grimaced. "Why?"

Without a preamble Maxi started, "My spidey sense tells me something is up yet you always say I am overbearing and paranoid—"

"I never said that." Zack met her stare.

"Maybe not those words – anyway Ric hasn't answered any of my texts or voicemails, so I have no clue when he is arriving tomorrow..." Zack made a show of looking down at his phone long enough for Maxi to notice. "Hey, my son isn't calling me back. He could be missing. Is my son missing not enticing enough for you?"

"Our son. Max, I need to tell you something and you are going to be pissed," she opened her mouth to interrupt at the same moment Zack held up his index finger. "We, meaning all three of us, have a problem, yet I think I have a solution, too."

Maxi's hands flew across her cellphone screen. She turned away from him and at that point Zack knew she wasn't listening.

"Listen, Max, Ric could be in trouble. I'm working to find out—"

"Got it," Maxi interrupted his speech.

Zack stopped mid-sentence, "Got what?"

"In three hours, a flight leaves from Burlington with a layover in Chicago. I can be out there by nightfall."

"Did you not listen to anything I just said?" Zack waited for a beat while a crimson glow merged on Maxi's face. He tried to control his voice as he said, "First, by the time you get to the airport, land, get the rental, and magically appear without a plan, we could be half-way there with a plan in place that includes back-up."

Pools of tears formed under Maxi's eyes. Zack put an arm over her shoulder while his hand extended to connect his fingers to hers. The phone clunked on to the floor.

"I know you are upset," he said as Maxi's shoulders vibrated under his arm, "and I am beyond pissed, especially because the camp was recommended by a colleague." Zack's jaw dropped. "Shit!" He pushed out of the embrace to punch a series of numbers into his phone. "Donald, are you alone?" He jammed his finger to end the call and waited.

"Zack—" His hand raised to silence her.

"Pack the SUV," Each word enunciated with force, "We need enough clothes for about a week along with dog food, beds, maybe pack a cooler as the drive will be straight through." When she attempted to rise, he pulled her back down to brush his lips against hers. "This will be okay, Max," his voice strained to sound calm. "And we are going to be driving for a while so would you please pack sandwiches too."

Zack's voice fluctuates while speaking with his boss. "Look Donald, this is personal. My family is now involved."

Atwood spoke in a level tone. "I understand that you are upset. Maxi too, but we can't just throw away months of investigating for one person. If you go in there guns blazing," he paused to let the implications of such actions sink in. "Zack, the two cases seemed to have merged." Donald's voice now quieted. "Off the record, I want you to go get your boy because family should always come first." Then in a brasher tone he added, "And do your f'ing job!"

Behind him, the duffle bags hit the foyer with a thud. Zack did not look forward to the questions that would follow once the two of them were confined to the car.

RIC

A huge hand lifted Ric into the air before slamming down his body onto the concrete floor. His shoulder snapped at the same time that a high-pitched scream expelled from his throat.

The hand grabbed onto his bicep to pull his body against the wall. "You listen to me college boy," he could smell whiskey on the Sheriff's breath, "I ain't running no bed and breakfast here. You either get your mommy and daddy on the line to pay me or you go to work for me and my colleagues, like your old roommate." A maniacal laugh followed as his body hit hard against the mattress.

"Since I got a feeling that mommy or daddy ain't bailing precious out this time, especially because you haven't called them," the laughter got louder, "you'd better be ready to work in the morning," the Sheriff grinned, "or maybe we use you as a tester like we did your useless friend. Of course, his parents came through after his unfortunate run in with drugs. That was different though—he made the calls."

The cell door banged shut followed by the main door to the street. A roll of Ric's left shoulder sent ripples of pain down his arm and up through the crown of his head, yet he managed to keep kneading his shoulder.

The opposite bicep sported long red markings. With intention, he crunched the arm at the elbow to get the muscles moving around, twitching with each motion. The pain receded, yet the markings remained.

Upon standing, he moved his left shoulder to rest against the cool cement wall. His arm hung with an unnatural bend at the elbow. The attempt to turn the rest of his body in the opposite direction resulted in small, muffled cries that he couldn't sequester. Each whimper released as his upper body moved.

With pain brought down to a numbing, Ric rested his left side against the cool cement. Sweat produced dark lines that slid into his torso. The cold touch of the cement made a small effort at taming the throbbing pain. As his body heat warmed each wall section, he took short steps to find another cool space. He moved across the wall towards the bars of the empty adjacent cell. Once in the corner, his entire body slid down to pool at the floor.

The door to the office bounced against the outer wall with a BANG. This was followed by the squeaking movement of the Sheriff's chair. Within minutes the Sheriff's loud snores filled the room.

MAXI

Zack fell asleep after setting the GPS for the Fremont office. The 2,000 mile trek would take about thirty hours driving straight through the night and Maxi had insisted that they do so although she prayed that her phone would buzz any second with an apology and flight information for her son.

Before Zack, Maxi would have contacted the local authorities and boarded a plane. Now her life revolved around a plan. The plan didn't need to make sense to her or even be practical, like driving from Vermont to Fremont, yet Zack having a strategy made her a little less worried.

Before leaving the house, Zack told her a little bit about his current investigation. The possible involvement of the Fremont Senator and even the county Sheriff of Ric's last location made her stomach flop, yet after he came to her rescue from her scammer ex Maxi trusted Zack enough to marry him, so she needed to trust him now.

All of the weirdness of the past 48 hours could be attributed to the pressure that her husband placed upon himself to solve these crazy work cases, or maybe something completely different. She could only conclude that someone Zack pissed off in the past tracked him to their Vermont home. That much he shared. As Maxi drove along I-80, she considered this thought. *What if the fence people's issue with her family is different from the Fremont situation?*

Crap! That idea put her current situation in a new perspective.

Maximum Panic

Twiddle's *Orlando* quietly seeped out of the rear speakers, prompting a semi-aware sing a long at the "ba da bump ba" part. The music was interrupted only by her snoring dogs and sometimes mumbling husband. The new states and state lines were somewhat confusing yet Pennsylvania splitting into east and west made it a little less. Once crossed into the eastern Hershey state, Maxi pulled off the highway into the combination Welcome Center and rest stop.

Jerry sat up at attention and stuck his face out of the open window to watch Maxi enter and exit the building. There was an SUV and an old Honda CRV in the parking lot, occupants hidden by tinted windows.

Normally she would have gone on high alerts seeing the same car multiple times along their route. A similar CRV had stopped at a gas station back in New York state. A quick google search on her phone confirmed that the make and model along with the gray color is very popular. Maxi chalked it up the random meeting as coincidence for now.

The sun had just started to set as she approached Scranton. Her jaw stretched as a loud yawn interrupted the music. Her eye lids fought to close, the big cup of green tea in the console had zero effect on her. At the start, they decided to break the driving into eight-hour increments so both could get decent rest along the way. Zack would take the wheel for the overnight shift somewhere outside of Pittsburgh, the capitol of the new state of Pennsylvania, and according to the last highway sign, Pittsburgh was only three hours away.

L.M. Pampuro

Jerry moved to rest his chin on the center console, Maxi's hand rested on his head, absentmindedly stroking the dog behind his ears, with the occasional tap to the beat of the music. At first her thoughts wandered to where her son could be and what she was going to do when they found him. The two plans that kept her awake involved changing situations. She prayed that the present situation is on Ric, and he had just spaced out or lost his phone, well that would be a major mama meltdown on her son, but if someone else was involved and for some reason, Ric wasn't able to contact her—

She let out a loud, almost manic laugh as her mind to stray further away from Ric just being an irresponsible young man. If he is being held against his will, and somehow those bastards figured out a Zack connection–her whole body shook at the thought.

"I need to stay positive," Maxi spoke in a tight, controlled voice, "for this situation to work out. I will stay positive…" Maxi repeated this mantra to the next stop, a gas station in the middle of nowhere just off the highway.

MARJORIE

Marjorie Lofsmen sat on the 18th-century sofa in her uncle's formal living room. The Senator's Virginia residence, an old townhouse in the Glendale section of Mclean, didn't match his yearly pay, yet no one seemed to notice. Her uncle had summoned her from her latest hideout, the family hunting lodge that her great granddaddy built in the Fremont wilderness for a secret place for politicians to have their own safe boys club. At first, Marjorie was fine with the changes because hanging out with the locals got boring quickly and anywhere was better than jail.

Family money bought her freedom, and the ailing trust partly paid for her uncle's influence, or it did before their latest venture took over. Now most of her privilege came from their little endeavor, the one that her ex-boss Cabot almost blew.

Marjorie looked out of the parlor at the servants vacuuming the hallway, dusting off tables, and replacing fading flowers with fresh. Although curious about which southern property her aunt inhabited that week, she wouldn't dare inquire, instead she'd wait until the end of the meeting to pass on her best. It was well known in the Senator's social circles that Aunt Harper hated the politicians and hanger's on along with all the rest of the cold, phony people, and from what Marjorie had gathered over the years, that included her uncle.

All of which kept her aunt out of D.C. except for a couple of public appearances and the family portrait above the fireplace. Even there, Aunt Harper wore a smirk of contempt for those who were present or maybe just for her husband's indiscretions, also known as Aunt Harper's D.C. friends.

The three o'clock chime of the antique cuckoo clock coincided with her uncle's harried arrival. His voice bellowed from the hallway, "This is a three-finger day. I will be in my study." Marjorie heard loud whispers of "no, she is here in the parlor" and "yes, now."

"On second thought, send my drink to the parlor." The Senator's imposing shadow reached into the room before he settled his glare on his niece. He gave Marjorie the once over before offering a "Humpt" as a greeting.

"Nice to see you too, uncle," Marjorie responded. She held back the urge to bow and instead stifled a giggle at the thought.

"I trust your travels were uneventful?"

"Yes sir," she folded her hands on her lap and waited.

The woman who was vacuuming the hall earlier walked in and handed the Senator a glass of amber liquid. He drank down the contents in one gulp then held up two fingers. The woman nodded and disappeared around the corner.

"Where are you staying?"

The question surprised Marjorie as much as her uncle's raised eyebrow when she answered "Here."

"Oh no," he said, "you can't stay here. I mean you were arrested for conspiracy against the government and are supposed to be rotting in a jail cell. How would that make me look?"

"What do you mean, how would that make you look? You were the one who—" The Senator raised his hand to stop her from speaking. Marjorie mirrored the gesture "Seriously, why am I here uncle?"

"I got word that our enterprise is under investigation. We need to take a hiatus for a bit. How soon can you break it down and have this completed?"

"You dragged me to D.C. to tell me to stop the operation in Fremont, where I was?"

Again, the hand rose, "We can't take chances via phone or text. There is a lot of manure going down." He ran his hand over his face. "Too much horseshit if you know what I mean."

Marjorie nodded. "What part of the operation do we stop?"

"All of it. Do you remember a fella named Zack Brady?"

Marjorie sucked in her breath as she balled both fists tight. "Son of a bitch. That is the bastard that killed Ken in Aruba."

"The one and only. My committee just interviewed him and although he didn't say much, I don't trust him. He had that smirk that the Feds always have when they appear before our committees. No respect from that one. There is something going down and his division is involved so either directly or indirectly, Brady is on the case."

"You know he was also the agent who brought the last charges against me," Marjorie pointed out as the Senator affirmed her statement with a quick nod. "Yeah, that ass pain is no friend of mine. So, what is the deal? Can I kill him?"

"No, you cannot, and if you do, at least don't tell me about it," the Senator instructed. "One of our guys in internal investigations said there are unusual donor lists floating around out there. Feds are making a comparison of means versus donations and a few of our top people's generosity do not match their income levels. In addition, we have that other stream." The Senator let out a loud hacking cough. "Like I said, shut down the operation for now, especially any linked to our nonprofits."

"Got it. The Pride Ridge operation along with Evergreen. Anything else?"

"Yeah – do this in person. No paper or electronic trails, understand? We don't need any of our electronics getting subpoenaed, especially at this point. We have enough cash now to cover my re-election and to take care of a few generous friends."

"Got it."

"Marjorie, if anything goes down this time, know that I can't save you." Marjorie's eyes twitched under her uncle's gaze. She shifted in her seat as he continued to speak. "Because of the extracurriculars you added in..."

"Yet you benefited from those activities, too."

"And you benefitted from my influence with splitting up those states in the Rockies from five to eight now with two more pending." The Senator rubbed his hands together.

"And when we get those other splits – speaking of benefits in the capitol. I guess we have benefits all around, wouldn't you say?"

"I have not benefitted as much as the locals, and Marjorie, stop right there because I will not take the fall with you. Remember, I can be a mean son of a bitch– just ask your dad."

The Senator turned and left the room, yet she didn't move. Her dad had died when she was in college. Her mother refused to talk about what happened, just that she'd needed to come home for the services. Her uncle had found the body. Her dad had been partners with her uncle in an Evergreen law firm.

A cool sensation floated up her spine. Her mother, like her Aunt Harper, lived a quiet existence in a small community in the south. Her uncle insisted on taking care of them because "we are family," yet Marjorie always thought there were unspoken reasons why.

As she reached the door, outside a taxi idled, and the driver called her name.

ZACK

They switched drivers somewhere near Pittsburgh. After a quick meal and a dog walk, Maxi dozed off. The curving hills gave way to the flat straightaways of the Midwest. The names may have changed yet the landscape remained flat, straight, and hypnotizing.

Zach looked over an updated map to see that instead of four, he was eight state borders away from Fremont. He mumbled that "it will probably be sixteen states on the way back."

He turned the volume down to barely audible then rang up Admiral Atwood.

"Zack, I am concerned about your stepson being in our area of interest in addition to the funds being moved from Grand Cayman to Cuba. The latter makes sense only if someone is leaving the country—"

"And a member of the senate is unlikely to do that, especially this one. I get the impression that he thinks he is bullet proof."

Atwood made a choking sound that to Zack covered a laugh. "Don't they all," he said. "Zack, the folks above us in the organization have brought up concern about your emotional involvement. I had to explain the Aruba situation and how well you did under the circumstances—"

"Donald, I have vocalized my concerns about some of those direct contacts, especially after the recommendation for Ric's camp came down the food chain. Do you think that the idea of me being too emotional is just a way to get me out of the picture? Think about it." Without waiting for answer, he continued, "Either way, I am still heading to Fremont to get my son back." Zack looked over at Maxi, who now smiled in her sleep. He did wonder how much of the conversation she heard as sleep might be an act for his sake.

"Now Zack, don't get your panties in a wad," Donald said. "That's a new one from my oldest grandchild by the way. You are knee deep and will be up to your neck as soon as you hit the Fremont border. Let me worry about the bureaucracy. There are those who voiced that you should follow protocol and go to the Niza office before proceeding out to Pride Ridge. We have a team set up, yes, all have been vetted by me along with the director, before you ask, we even made sure that none voted for the Senator or the Sheriff."

"I didn't know that information was public," Zack noted.

"It's not," Donald continued, "we asked in the interviews."

"Donald what the hell did these folks think they were interviewing for?"

With a laugh, Donald explained, "A special task force to protect upcoming candidates. From the narrowed pool, we looked for skills that this type of investigation needed, and well, here you have the top five that qualified.

Zack glanced over at Maxi. The little scar in the center of her forehead began to get deeper. "Crap," Zack said.

"Crap?"

"No not you, Donald. Something else. Anyway, please continue. I am going to need to stop for the dogs soon." The last sentence used as a code for Maxi might be listening.

"No worries, Zack. As soon as you hit Niza, head for the office. We've arranged for you and Maxi to stay at a privately owned retiree's bed and breakfast. There are many questions in Pride Ridge, yet the bulk seem to center on a small town on the outskirts called ironically Amity. The D.E.A. boys have been watching the area for a while and for some reason they are still waiting to raid and arrest. Before you ask, I do not know why they are waiting. That might be another link in our investigation." Zack heard a bit of static. "Zack, as always, be careful who you trust and if you would do me one favor," Zack wrinkled his nose in the direction of the car speaker, "please try to keep Maxi in Niza away from all this chaos. Things are going to get hot and two emotionally driven folks will not help."

With eyes still closed, Maxi brought her middle finger into plain view. Zack covered a laugh with a loud cough. "Yeah, Donald, I can't make that promise but know that I will do my best to keep my family safe along with getting some answers to our questions."

"Okay then we will talk when you get to Niza unless I get more information prior. Safe travels and give Maxi my best."

"Will do sir." The silence in the car festered into deep sighs. Zack contemplated how he could serve two bosses, his favorite pretending to sleep by his side. He placed his hand on Maxi's thigh only to have it slapped away. "Maxi, I know you are awake."

His wife turned to glare in his direction. With arms tightening across her breasts, her lips constricted. "Okay so I guess I'll go first," Zack said. "How much did you hear so I know where to start?"

"Why don't you just start at the beginning and then I will ask my necessary questions. Just promise me no bullshit."

"Have I ever not been completely honest with you?"

Maxi tilted her head to one side in response.

"Okay so in the beginning, yes, I kept you out of details for safety's sake—"

"And then my favorite boat got blown up—"

"Are you ever going to forgive me on that one? I can see you are in a hurry to replace it."

"Replace the old *Sludge Puppy*? I traded away that thought for you," Maxi added a face wide all teeth grin to punctuate her statement.

Zack looked over with a slight furrowed brow. "Anyway, Donald had little information to add to what we already know. The biggest addition was the potential drug lab connection, but you heard that part."

Maxi nodded. "Are you leaving me at a guarded bed and breakfast? Because if you think you are let me tell you that I will rent or even steal a car to go get my son."

"Our son and I do know this," Zack said. "And no, I am not leaving you at the bed and breakfast. I am making you part in the investigation that includes Ric. And Maxi, you have to promise me that once Ric is back with us, you will agree to go home, preferably on a plane.”

"I agree." Maxi shifted in the seat to face Zack, hiding one hand behind her back.

"That was too easy for you," Zack said, "yet for now I will trust that you will keep your word, and if you want to drive for a few hours, the path is straight and boring for a while."

In the darkness of the next rest stop located in Cargill, one of the newer states, the dogs ran a little, both Maxi and Zack used the facilities, then under the hum of the semi-trucks, they switched drivers and proceeded on.

Once settled in the passenger seat, Zack glanced out the window and took note of the only car in the lot: a Honda CRV idling a few spaces over.

RIC

With too little sleep, Ric found himself in the back of the pungent SUV again. This time he sported a bright orange warm-up suit, under the jacket an equally bright yellow T-shirt. His interrupted dream seemed so real, or maybe just wishful thinking that Zack would show up and beat the crap out of the Sheriff, who appeared visibly absent from today's activities.

The good old boy deputy hadn't said much besides, "change your clothes and git in the van."

Ric had thought about asking where they were going, yet at this point it didn't matter. Life or death would take place at the end of this ride, and he had no control over either. His eye lids lay heavy as his head bounced against the seat. Breath rhythmic.

Ric's neck snapped hard against the seat at the same moment his good shoulder hit the side of the van. He opened his eyes to see that they had come to an abrupt stop.

Without a word, the back door opened. A puff of dirt rose as his feet hit the ground. As his eyes adjusted to the blinding sun, rows of green swayed in between the gullies of dry earth. Sweat damped beneath the jacket to affix the t-shirt to his frame. Voices getting louder refocused his attention.

The deputy and another man, smaller yet dressed similar, walked around the van.

"Well at least this one's not a runner, Dak," the man spoke too loud for his frame. "You know that I got no use for a runner."

The deputy glared at Ric as he spoke, "The last one had listening problems and found out that running or trying to ditch out just got him a job where moving isn't an option." Dak then brought his attention back to the other guy. "Now this here is Ric Jacobs, one of those East coast people." He spat on the ground. "He volunteered to help you out today maybe in exchange for a phone charger later."

"What the hell is a phone charger?" the man responded as if on cue.

This got a laugh from them. Ric thought about telling both that his phone was smashed and the charger useless, but he didn't see the point, so he remained silent.

"What do I need to know about Mr. Jacobs? Can he do farmwork, or is he useless like the last one you brought me?"

"I think Mr. Jacobs will do a fine job helping you out here, Clem. And if he tries to leave, shoot him in the ass so he still has some use."

The Clem person nodded although Ric noted no visible gun. "You'll be back to fetch him when?"

"Sometime between one and four unless you need me to come back sooner. Boss man said to give the boy a taste today and then we will see where he goes next."

"Can I ask the same question I asked last time?"

"Non-violent, possibly stole a truck, been with use for about four days. What else do you need to know?" Dak focused his sneer on Clem.

"Not a thing. Let's go." Clem gestured his chin in the direction that he wanted Ric to follow. Both men turned to watch the puffs of dirt fade. "Anything I need to know about you?" Clem asked as they walked.

Ric hesitated a beat before answering, "My left shoulder is useless, but I will try to do whatever job you give me."

Ric felt Clem's eyes moved up and down, as if assessing him for a quick sale. The man walked a little further, stopping in front of a stack of metal and rubber. "Bum shoulder, huh? I need you to straighten these out and then move the pieces into the gully in between the dirt mounds in the field." Ric nodded in return. "If you finish that, we can talk about your next task."

Ric bent over to move a metal pipe. His shoulder snapped sending a shooting pain down his bicep. He repositioned his legs to give leverage to his opposite hand. With a single pull, the piece of metal refused to budge. Ric walked around the pile to see a small cabin close by with Clem sitting on a rocking chair on the porch.

"Could this be more of a stereotype," Ric mumbled as he proceeded back to the out of view side of the pile. He started to climb up one side, careful to test each piece of metal before putting his full weight in place. At the top, the structure weakened, and his feet slipped into the rubbery center.

Ric ignored the shooting pain in his shoulder as he used his other hand to begin to drag pieces off the top onto the ground. Anything was better than rotting in that cell. The structure started to tilt to one side as Ric climbed back to the ground.

The thick rubber hoses scattered around the bottom of the pile, connected into the metal frames. Ric guessed he was putting together some sort of irrigation system, although he could be wrong. Instead of working from the end of each hose to the start of the next, Ric dragged each connected part out to fit the next segment. After he had seven parts attached, he could barely move the structure. He detached one segment then dragged what was ready out across the dirt gully to the opposite end furthest point, away from Clem and the cabin.

Doing a quick calculation, he figured to cover each gully across the entire field, each row would take four segments, but he needed to complete three rows. In the center small green plants with a few leaves sprouted about a foot high.

Ric tried his best to drag the equipment in between the rows of plants without disturbing any of the greens.

The pattern continued across three rows as the segments attached and went back to the original pile. The task would have taken far less time if the Sheriff hadn't maimed his shoulder last night.

After dragging the last batch of hose into the field, Ric saw Clem waiting by the pile of rubber and metal, which now stood about half the size of the original. Ric followed Clem's gaze back across the sections he had completed. Segments ran along three of the rows with the open ends waiting for their next connection. Ric panted while waiting for Clem to turn his attention back to him.

"Wait here," Clem instructed. He walked back to the cabin and returned with a sweaty bottle of water. Ric nodded thanks then proceeded to chug three quarters of the contents. He spilled the last quarter over his head. "You are not averse to work," Clem noted.

"Yeah, I use to set up party tents for the rich folks around where I used to live."

"Party tents?"

"Yeah – I grew up on the Connecticut shoreline and that was my summer job. Before that I short ordered cooked and before that," Clem held up his hand and Ric stopped talking.

"You always had a summer job?"

"Yes sir. I had a job from when I was about twelve on. My mom said that working builds character."

"Huh." Clem looked back to the fields. "Did your mom work?"

"She had to – my dad left us when I started middle school and then died near the end of eighth grade."

"How'd your papa die?"

"His mistress shot him." Clem's mouth and eyes open wide. "I kid you not. You can google it."

"Huh." Clem regathered his thoughts. "How'd ya end up at that camp?"

"My college roommate was telling me about how he did work on the national park trails, and I thought it would be fun. And keep me from having to dig in shit all day at the organic farm next to our house." The last part got a laugh from Clem. "I did have a job lined up for when I get back to help with my tuition but..." Ric let that thought sink in.

"So, after hauling crap on those trails for a month you had another job lined up at home?"

"No sir, at school. My school makes all freshman work in the cafeteria if you are getting some sort of aid. I did that last year so this year I was going to work in catering and do some other odd jobs for cash."

Clem nodded then asked, "Who pays your tuition?"

"My mother pays some and so do I. It's not a fifty-fifty split but I try to pay my share."

Clem stared out at the rows that Ric finished and then back at the smaller pile of parts. Without a word, he walked about halfway down the first row, cut across the second, then came back over to Ric.

"Nice job," Clem said. "How's the shoulder?"

"Throbbing but good."

Clem gave Ric a nod. "Can you do a few more rows?" Before he could answer, Clem pointed at the pile and walked away.

MAXI

The bumps on the horizon started small, as the *Welcome to Fremont* sign greeted. A foggy hill appeared in the far distance. She had made this trek before, decades ago driving from what was Oklahoma City back to what was once Boulder with an old friend. The town names along with the borders have changed. What was once five states, Montana, Colorado, Wyoming, Utah, and New Mexico, there are eight with another two pending congressional approval.

Currently she could see that the flat Midwest was in her rear-view mirror and the majestic Rockies would soon be in full view. The optical illusion of bumps on the horizon gave hope that was at least another four hours away.

The average speed stayed in the eighties, only slowing when her phone warned of a speed trap ahead.

One of the dogs interrupted her thoughts with a high-pitched whine from the backseat. A few miles later, Maxi pulled into a replica of an old western town, complete with a covered wagon and a trading post selling tacky t-shirts. All the varieties are on display tacked up across a split fence leading into the shop. Maxi pulled into a parking spot close to the building and nudged Zack.

"Hey, I am stopping to let the dogs out," she said as she exited the car. Zack gave a wave and continued to sleep. "Okay boys," Maxi pointed to a small grassy area as both jumped from the back seat. The dogs ran around yet stayed within the boundaries of the grassy triangle.

As each squatted to leave a pile, Maxi approached with a bag. She deposited both in a nearby receptacle.

The two dogs jumped and played with each other for a few more minutes, then trotted to the car, waiting to go inside. Once the dogs got settled Maxi headed to the building. Inside, an older woman sat behind a desk surrounded by brochures and maps. She gave a quick wave in Maxi's direction. Maxi noted several eighteen wheelers idling in the back in addition to a few cars. The woman's presence gave Maxi a sense of safety.

"Where ya heading," she asked as Maxi approached the desk.

"Pride Ridge area. About how far am I?" Maxi gave her best tired smile.

"Ah Pride Ridge. Well, you are about five hours away. Look for signs for the tunnel after you hit Niza. From there you got another hour in the prettiest country your eyes have seen."

"Is there a way to avoid going through Niza?" Maxi focused her attention on the state map hanging on the wall as the woman spoke.

"You can," she pointed at an alternate route, "but you'll add a couple hours onto your trip. Are you going there for a getaway?"

"Business," Maxi answered as she concentrated on the map. She brought her attention back to the woman while producing a forced smile. "I just don't like cities," was followed with a shrug.

"Me neither yet driving through Niza is the best route. What kinda of business did you say you are in?"

"I didn't," Maxi said, then added, "dog training, since you asked." The answer seemed to satisfy the woman.

"You will lose your GPS several times along the way. Take this and here's a couple guides to the area." Along with a paper map, Maxi had a few visitor booklets for Fremont and specifically Pride Ridge area.

Maxi gave herself an imaginary head slap, a reminder to give as little information as possible to strangers. "Thank you so much," Maxi said, then asked, "Is there any other places you would recommend for trail training? I'm not completely sold on Pride Ridge because I hear the area is very developed."

The woman reached out to take back the Fremont state guide. Maxi paid attention as the woman dog-eared several pages. "If you want to avoid Niza, there are several entrances to Rocky Mountain National Park that take you around the city." She pointed to the map in the middle of the book. "I marked several areas for you to consider. Are you camping?"

Maxi laughed. "Oh no," she said, "We are looking at Airbnb cabins. I have a reservation in the Pride Ridge area, but I can cancel. The closer I get I am wondering if my destination is off."

"Can't help you there, yet I gave you options. Safe travels." The woman turned back to her book as Maxi gave a quick thanks. Outside, Zack leaned against the SUV as the dogs ran over to greet her.

"Do you need to make friends everywhere?" Zack said when she returned to the car. He followed with, "Want me to drive?"

"I'm okay," she said. Zack gave a chin nod in the direction of the building and disappeared inside.

A few minutes later he returned and asked again, "You sure you don't want any sleep? Once we get to Niza…"

Maxi stretched her hands up to the sky and then folded her fingers to the ground. Her head was as heavy as her deep breaths. "Okay, maybe I can use a few hours of sleep." She flipped Zack the keys. As he walked around the vehicle, she took out her phone and set the alarm for two hours later. She needed to be the driver as they approached Niza.

Zack

Maxi gave up the keys much too easily. Zack had expected some sort of argument and the fact that it didn't happen bothered him. Listening to her soft snores in the passenger seat brought him solace. Her kid was in the crossfire of this predicament and priority dictated that Ric's safety comes before the mission.

Family first.

One hand rested on the steering wheel while the other leaned against Maxi's side. Zack counted each inhalation and exhalation until he was satisfied that she slept.

He positioned his earpiece and hit the autodial. Donald answered on the first ring.

"Where are you?" he barked without a greeting.

"Just got into Fremont. Should be in Niza in four hours. I was thinking—"

Atwood made a loud exhale. "Zack, we talked about this. The plan states you are to meet the team and go into Pride Ridge as a unit. We have good intel that

Marjorie Lofsmen paid her uncle a visit and is on her way to Fremont as we speak."

"Explain again to me how Spencer Cabot is doing life in prison while she runs around free?"

"Who she knows - politics, Zack. It's that simple."

Zack considered this point along with the team from Niza, most of the members he had never met. "Donald, before I go to the Niza office, I would like to review each team member's profile again. I can't do that now because Maxi is asleep, and I am driving."

"Zack, you already reviewed and gave an okay for each member. Tell me son, what are you looking for?"

"Has the hacker seen any more activity from the Cayman account?" Zack looked over at Maxi, whose eyes watched each of his moves. Zack disconnected the earpiece and turned up the volume, finger moved in front of his lips.

"Not since the last deposit. Zack, tell me why do you hesitate on stopping in Niza?"

Maxi thrusted her chin out as Zack started to speak, "I understand the levels of what we need to accomplish yet I believe that if I have Maxi go in first and spring Ric, the rest will get easier."

"You know Maxi can't pay a fine or make a donation to that bogus charity, right? That would be—"

"A set up Donald. Yes, I am aware of the law. I do think that scoping out the situation first, especially with all the players involved, will bring better results. I just pray that whoever is running the show doesn't link me to Ric in the process. The longer he sits in jail—"

"The better the opportunity. I get it."

"Have you traced the locator on his phone?"

"That is the strange part, Zack. The locator has traveled to Luna, Niza, and Evergreen, in addition to Amity. The signal is pretty weak, yet I think that someone else has Ric's phone at this point."

"Can I get the last location?"

"Sure, Luna Sheriff's office and then a residential neighborhood. Do you want me to send?"

"Yes, please. We may be making an additional stop along the way."

"Just make sure you check in with the Niza office. And if you need to review the files again and let me know your plan, because I know you have an alternative plan. Just remember that we both have a lot invested in the outcome of this investigation."

"Not more than me," Zack muttered underneath his breath, adding, "I understand sir. I will be in touch within the next six hours," in a louder voice. He hit an end call before Atwood could respond. Zack had noted that Maxi's leg started twitching during the conversation. He brought his attention over to his wife and asked, "Thoughts?"

"Many," Maxi said. "I want to know what you know." She reached across the seat and punched Zack's bicep. "Everything!"

"Max I—"

"No more bullshit, Zack. Let me go take care of this. No one wants to mess with a crazy mama and right now this crazy mama is pissed off." Zack didn't reply, instead he reached over to take Maxi's hand in his.

"We will take care of this. I just need to stop and turn off the tracker on the car." Maxi gave his hand a squeeze.

"I already did that in Vermont—"

"Yeah, really cute throwing the tag in the back of that pickup. You do know that these government vehicles have multiple trackers?"

"Crap. I keep forgetting about that."

"Or blocking out the fact!" Zack gave an exaggerated eyeroll. "I think someone else has Ric's phone but it's up to you where we go, Niza to the office, Luna to the phone, or Amity where I got the text from? You decide."

RIC

Ric took a bottle of water along with a peanut butter and jelly sandwich from Clem then kept an eye on him as he walked down the driveway to meet the deputy out by the gate. The little remaining mound of pipes and rubber blocked most of his view, but Ric could see Clem's hands flying in the air with the occasional point in his direction.

The deputy stood with hands on his hips until what could only be surmised as Clem finishing his speech. This was mainly because his hands stopped moving as he waited for the other man to respond. The deputy said something as he took his hat off to scratch his head. He pointed back to the car. Clem shook his head no and pointed near where Ric sat.

Ric's stomach twitched as the two men got closer. "Boy, what the hell did you do?" deputy Dak barked upon arrival.

Ric sat perfectly still. "I, I," he started to say. "I did what Clem ask me to – put the hoses and metal frames down the rows and when I finished that we hooked up the rig to the water tower."

The deputy turned around to see the sprinkler system running in the fields. "Told ya," Clem stood with his arms folded across his chest, a slight smirk on his face. "Tell him what you told me," Clem said to Ric.

"About what? All we talked about were my summer jobs, you know, setting up tents for the rich folks and working in a restaurant."

"Wait – you had summer jobs?" Dak responded. "I thought you grew up rich."

Ric's laughter caught both men off guard. "My dad died when I was in middle school—"

"Tell him how," Clem said.

"His mistress shot him – but he and my mother were already separated. Anyway, my mom ran her own business for a while, when I was in school, but I always worked. The rule was if you wanted something, like school ski trips or extra sneakers, you worked for it. Everything except video games because my mom has major issues there. I was telling Clem that I had a job waiting for me back at school yet being stuck here I—"

Deputy Dak cut him off with a raise of the hand. Within the silence that followed, little puffs of dirt followed the deputy back to his car along with Ric's eyes, which he diverted when Dak leaned into the window of his car, sticking his enormous butt in their direction. Ric couldn't hear the conversation, even with the occasional shouting.

"Boy, you need to work off your stay with us here with Clem. I'll be back tomorrow to get ya." Neither spoke as he marched back to his car, gunned the engine, and left in a cloud of dust.

"Can we get a few more lines set up today," Clem broke the silence.

"Yeah, sure," Ric said. "Ah, Clem, what just happened here?"

"What happened is that I have your services for another day, if the deputy actually comes back tomorrow." He mumbled something incoherent then a bit louder said, "Leave space so tomorrow you can drag what you did today over to the other rows. If you are thinking of leaving, know that you are on my ranch which consists of crop fields and woods, and those woods have so many predators, you wouldn't make it through the night."

Ric gave a small nod as Clem continued, "You know I ain't going to pay you for your work, that is the deal between the Sheriff and I, yet I'll give you a place to bunk and something to eat. I have another stretch of field that runs just past that hill over there so after we finish the set up here, I got a few chores at the main barn. Any questions?"

Ric started to speak, "Where is the—"

"That question was rhetorical, college boy." Clem's laughter followed him inside the cabin as Ric moved to tackle the rest of the pile.

DEPUTY DAK

The shouting could be heard as soon as Dak parked in front of the office. He ran inside to find the Sheriff red faced while that young woman, Marjorie something said each word as if she was speaking to a baby.

"You." She pointed her finger into his boss' chest. "Will. Do. Exactly." Her voice getting louder, "What. I. Said." A growl came out of her mouth followed by, "And there isn't a Q and A." The deputy started to slip back out the door as both turned in his direction. "Make sure dim wad here follows directions too."

Her hand hit Dak's chest as Marjorie pushed past him out the door. He waited in silence as she climbed into a Mercedes convertible, gunned the engine, and bolted in the direction of the canyon. The Sheriff swore under his breath.

"How much did you hear?" the Sheriff directed at Dak.

"I couldn't make out the screaming on the street," he watched as his boss' eyes squinted shut. "Yet I have a feeling' that I am the dim wad she referred to."

His boss rubbed both eyes with the palms of both hands before looking around Dak. "Where's the kid? Please tell me you didn't—"

"No sir, yet the kid is a funny story." Dak proceeded to repeat what both Clem and Ric had said at the farm. His boss paced the length of the office as he listened.

"He really isn't a spoiled brat?" the Sheriff asked.

"Not according to him. Parents have a little money but nowhere near the last ones. Sheriff, I am confused to what do we do here. This is a new one."

"Maybe this is a gift," the Sheriff said. Dak waited for a further explanation as his boss' face brightened with each step. "The bitch gave orders to shut down the operation and clear out any stragglers."

"That come from the chief?"

This got an exaggerated eye roll. "Who else would make that decision," the Sheriff said his volume making Dak jump. "She left to shut down the farm, too, although I think she might have another idea there."

"Why is that?"

"She kept asking when the last time we went out to check on the place and how much had been shipped out. She also asked if we still had the pot fields in the valley. Lots of operational questions. Where is the kid?"

Dak said, "Left him with Clem. Apparently, the kid's a worker." Both men shrugged. "Do you need me to—"

"Maybe," the Sheriff said, "or maybe not. I don't like the way that bitch gives ultimatums. Her uncle bailed her out – she should be grateful she is even part of this operation." His boss wiped the sweat from his forehead. "Maybe Clem can help us out and the kid can just stay there and work, you know, disappear?"

Neither man spoke as both considered the options.

"I don't think that will work boss," Dak pointed out, "Somebody always comes looking eventually."

"Eventually comes long after we forget." The Sheriff responded. He twirled his gun in one hand. "We should get out to the barn and see what damage

Marjorie has done there. She's going in to shut down the operation?"

"Maybe Marjorie needs to disappear," Dak regretted the statement as soon as he suggested it.

The Sheriff's eye color shifted to black while his face stayed neutral. Dak had told the Sheriff plenty of times that he had no problem killing people. A dishonorable discharge from the Marines along with time spent in the Middle East proved that fact. The Senator pushed for his hire, so the Sheriff really had no choice. With the Senator's blessing he could just knock off his niece.

The family was strange.

"I think we should wait and see on that. The Senator might not like having family members killed."

"Understood." Dak gave a quick salute as he turned to leave. "The Senator doesn't mind when you knock off an obstacle," Dak said below his breath, "he actually gives you cushy jobs in the future."

RIC

He fought to open his eyes while a sandy layer blurred the surroundings. The bed contained a single pillow and blanket Ric kicked off as soon as his vision settled. The muscles in his body tightened then relaxed as he became more conscious.

He lifted his arms over his head, an attempt to stretch the sleep out of his body that was returned with a sharp pain along his left side. Immediately he brought both arms back to his side and slowly breathed to a count of ten until the pain subsided. Once the sharpness dulled, he pushed up to a sitting position to look around his surroundings.

Instead of steel bars, Ric found himself in a room that smelled like fresh wood and the inside of his dorm room. He lay on the bottom bunk of three sets of bunk beds, each butting up against one of the walls with the fourth wall containing a door in the center.

The sun peered through a single window to light up the space along with providing warmth to the room. "Maybe jail was just a nightmare," he said, testing his voice as he walked near the door. Here he noticed that a lingering odor moved with him. A quick sniff to his t-shirt confirmed the smell stayed on both him and his clothes.

He made an "eck" sound like the one his mother made when she'd enter his bedroom in Vermont. A short sigh released at the thought of the Vermont fortress, as boring as he found the area days ago, he'd much rather have been working on the organic farm than stuck wherever this is, and if that jail is real, this is far better than jail.

The handle on the door gave way to a good size room filled with the smell of bacon. Ric's stomach responded as he saw an unfamiliar person in an open kitchen, banging pots while singing and dancing to The Grateful Dead's Bertha. Ric waited for the crescendo before interrupting, "Hey now," he said loud enough to make the man jump and drop a pan on the floor. The clanging sound ricocheted in the room.

The guy said "Dude," as he spun around bringing one hand to his heart. "Don't do that."

"I'm sorry but Bertha ended and—"

"You know Bertha?" The dude's attention solely focused on Ric. "How?"

"My mom's an old deadhead. Caught Jerry over one hundred shows."

"Me too." The dude now jumped up and down. "Did she ever make it to The Rocks?" Ric tilted his head to one side as the guy added, "Red Rocks, best, most spiritual place to see a show."

Ric nodded. "Yes, though I don't know when. Maybe you can ask her?"

The guy gave a quick smile then reached his hand over the counter to shake Ric's. "You can call me Vittles as I come in to cook for Clem twice a day. Nice to see he finally has some help."

"Nice to meet you Vittles," Ric shook hands. "We set up the watering system yesterday. Though I am not quite sure where I am."

Vittles shook his head then shrugged. "Me neither," he said with a laugh. "I do know that breakfast is almost ready. Bathroom is that way," he motioned in the area of a door on the other side of the kitchen, "So get yourself ready because once you eat, you go back to work."

The bathroom had the standard toilet, sink and shower, along with a window that looked out on the surrounding valley. Any other time Ric would consider the view spectacular, yet now he needed a plan. He couldn't just stay here as free labor, and he couldn't go back to jail or whatever that place pretended to be.

On the side of the sink a basket held towels, soap, and a few unused toothbrushes. Ric pondered his situation as he splashed warm water on his face. By the time he finished brushing his teeth an idea began to formulate. He needed to wait and see what today's situation brought, yet if the opportunity came, he might borrow another truck.

Clem showed up as Ric put the last bite of a bacon, egg, and cheese sandwich into his mouth. He handed him two bottles of water along with a soft-sided cooler. "Come on boy," Clem said, "we are heading to the south field today."

"Bring me back some samples," Vittles shouted from the kitchen.

The two walked in silence out to a beat-up old Ford pick-up truck. Clem climbed into the driver's seat and turned the key. The engine roared to life as Clem shouted over the din, "She'll calm down once she warms up."

Ric gave a quick nod as the truck thrusted forward down a dirt road just beyond the last row of plants that he completed yesterday. Clem held the vehicle tight to the rising cliff on the driver's side. Although bumpy, the truck moved along the ruts like it knew every bump and hump along the way.

Around the third bend, another valley opened. In the distance a single line of smoke slithered into the sky from a small red barn. Ric's hand found his stomach as the structure, although in the distance, had an unsettling familiarity. "Can't be," Ric mumbled as he stretched in his seat to see if the trailer could be seen, too.

The truck lurched onto a well-worn trail to follow a line of trees further down into the valley. The smell of fresh pine and skunk weed filled the air. Ric thought the combination odd until the truck jolted off the trail into lines of dark green marijuana plants that extended at least the size of a football field.

"Whoa," Ric said at the same time Clem parked the truck next to a small metal building.

"Okay so this here is our other outside growing facility," Clem started to explain. "And I have a project for you." He gestured with one hand for Ric to get out of the truck and follow him into a row of plants. "I'll drop you off at the other end of this here field with a note pad and a pen. Don't lose either," Clem instructed as he reached into the front seat and handed Ric the two items.

"Not for every plant, but let's say every ten feet or so, I need you to pull the plant down and see if it looks like this." Clem reached up and pulled the top of a seven-foot stalk down and pointed at the flowers and seed cluster in the center. "If you see this, mark it down – before you ask, I don't care if you draw a map or what, just have a system that you could explain to me so my harvesters can find the plants."

Ric nodded.

"Now, I am going to start at that other end and do the same. We meet in the middle." Clem looked back at Ric. "Do not pocket or sample any of the plants, I mean it boy, and if you start to feel funny—"

That got Ric's attention as he repeated, "Feel funny?"

"You know, lightheaded, get out of the middle and sit on the edge for a minute or two. Understand?"

Again, Ric just nodded confirmation.

Clem pointed back to the truck. He drove Ric further into the field, closer to the barn. The barn where he last saw his cellmate alive and left him off in between the building and the field. Ammonia mixed in with the pungent of the plants combined to create a nauseous mix of stench. Ric pulled his t-shirt over his nose with one hand while the notepad rested in the other.

A door slamming in the distance brought his attention over to the barn. A familiar figure walked around the side of the building, stringy blonde hair moving as a solid in the slight breeze. She stopped to look at the field as Ric slipped inside the rows of plants. Although crops grew much shorter at this end of the field, Ric managed to duck in between the stalks to remain out of sight.

A puff of smoke left the girl's mouth every couple beats. After a few moments, he turned to start Clem's task. The penalty for not completing the work hadn't been revealed, yet Ric remembered the condition of his former cellmate. If all of this was connected, he needed to stay on the course until Zack could find him.

As he reached and noted the plant's conditions, he secretly hoped that his mother would be the one to confront the Sheriff, "Crazy mama would put that sleeziod in his place," he muttered.

ZACK

For the most part, Zack had always been a rule follower, which is why he pulled into a rest stop about an hour outside of Niza and told Maxi that he was too tired to drive the rest of the way. The stopping point was perfect timing. The sun just peeked about the foothills and all the area sparkled with a golden hue.

"Hey Max," Zack gently shook his wife's arm, "we need to stop. The dogs are getting antsy." Both dogs snored in the back until the SUV jerked into the parking space. Tails thumped against the backseat as Maxi stretched her arms over her head, a loud yawn filled the air.

"Where are we?" she said as she looked out at the bright sky and shadows of foothills.

"About an hour from the office. If you don't mind, I'd like to catch a bit of sleep, so I am fully conscious when I meet my team." He gestured at the steering wheel. "Driving is exhausting me."

Maxi nodded enthusiastically as she motioned to the bathroom. Zack watched her disappear into the building before pulling his phone out.

Again, Donald Atwood answered on the first ring. Without preamble he said "No."

"You don't even know what I am going to say." Zack's eyes stared at the door.

"Whatever it is no. Just follow the plan."

"Donald, this is my kid you are talking about. If anyone on this team is in cahoots with the Senator, I am screwed. Just listen to my thinking." Zack proceeded from here to sketch out a loose plan that involved Maxi going into the Sheriff's office while he observed the players. "I am also concerned if Marjorie is here, she would be able to I.D. all of us."

"How does Marjorie know Ric and Maxi?"

"She doesn't yet I had their photos on my desk and referred to Maxi as someone special many times. Donald, I need a team who I don't have to worry about inside back stabbings – like Aruba."

A short gasp came through the car speakers. Zack was fully aware that the additional personnel hired to take down that drug lord in Aruba had a connection back to Marjorie Lofsmen along with the drug lord himself. How those two missionaries got through the screening haunted Zack.

"I understand what you are saying Zack yet all but one on your team are veteran agents. I checked them out personally."

Zack considered this statement before saying, "Look Donald, Maxi is coming back to the car. Track the car and have the team members that you'd swear your life on meet me in Pride Ridge. The others, put on desk duty doing some kind of research, because Donald, this one is personal." The car door opened, and Maxi hopped into the driver's seat.

"Ready," she said, as Zack returned a nod.

L.M. Pampuro

MAXI

Maxi started up the car. All she cared about was finding her son. Whether she hugged him or killed him was still up in the air. She needed to find Ric to make certain he was okay. Late yesterday Zack confirmed that Ric did not make his scheduled flight, or any flight, back to Albany.

This, along with zero response to her texts and voicemails, had Maxi on edge, snipping at Zack often. Also, the fact she observed Zack's phone in his hand, and he hit the end button as she slipped into the driver's seat, told her something was up, and he wasn't sharing.

She automatically checked her phone to find zero messages. "Damn it," she muttered. After a quick glance at Zack's closed eyes, Maxi confirmed the directions to Pride Ridge she had inserted into her cellphone while chatting with the tourism lady inside the rest stop. The route through Niza to Pride Ridge appeared to be simple enough; just stay on the throughway and if Zack happens to notice her misdirection, oops.

Little beads of sweat dripped down her back as she gripped the steering wheel tighter than needed. The GPS from Zack's phone coming through the speakers interrupted the soft background music. The highway slowed to stretch through the downtown area with announcements for exit ramps coming louder and more frequently.

"Take the next exit and go left on the boulevard into the central business district area. Take the exit in three-quarters of a mile. Take this exit. Recalculating. Recalculating. Take the 16th Street exit. Get in the right-hand lane to take the 16th street exit. Take the immediate right-hand exit for 16th Street. Recalculating. Recalculating. Take the next exit..." Maxi pressed the off button on the car stereo. Faint voices could be heard coming from Zack's phone sitting in the cupholder. His directions kept recalculating so much, she waited to hear, "dumbass, take this exit" out of his speaker.

Her phone lay silent, yet she gave a quick glance to confirm the new route. Jerry sat up and alert to the surroundings, nudging his head out the window for a quick sniff. Bobby's halitosis breath filled the rest of the air combining with Zack's sleep exhales. Maxi had both back windows, along with hers, opened. They skittered closer to the mountains, passing signs for various tourist traps and the famous Rattlesnake Amphitheater.

Traffic ebbed and flowed along the way as lanes merged and unmerged for mystery construction projects until the throughway curved up in between two significant formations into the mountains. The speed limit slowed to accommodate the curves cut into the foothills. One side a vast incline up, the other a steep drop down.

Maxi concentrated on keeping with traffic while taking the occasional glance at her cellphone screen. The icon continued to move along the route, freezing up only for brief seconds as the SUV hooked around each mammoth rock formation.

Zack stirred several times. Maxi glanced over to find his eyes shut, yet his lips moved into a slight grin.

"If you are going to pretend to be asleep, you might as well get up and help me navigate," she said.

Zack realigned his shoulders to sit up in the passenger seat. "How far away are we from Pride Ridge?" he said.

Maxi opened her mouth to speak, then closed it again.

"Don't get mad—"

"Why is it every time you say that Zack, I end up furious?"

"Maxi, after all these years together I knew that you wouldn't listen to me, especially where Ric is concerned. I pretended to sleep—"

"So that we could bypass the Niza office and you could blame me for ignoring Donald," Maxi interrupted.

"We do make a great team." Zack reached over to pat her hand. Both let out a nervous laugh. "I do have a plan by the way."

"Zack, that goes without saying. Are you going to let me know why my rule following husband defied a direct order?"

"Don't you want to hear my plan first?"

"Zack, I want to hear both." Maxi pulled the car over into a small rest area. The view of the snow-covered peaks of the majestic Rockies looked like a fake backdrop against the safety rail. Maxi released an audible sigh. "You know under different circumstances that," she pointed at the view, "would be magical."

Both stared out the window. Jerry's whine from the backseat broke the silence. Zack leaned over to kiss Maxi on the cheek as his other hand opened the passenger side door. He stretched and noted another vehicle pulling in the lot with Virginia plates. Popping the backdoor open, both dogs jumped out to run around the car. Zack followed both to a small grassy area with a silhouette of a pooping dog on a sign that instructed you to clean up after your pet. His eyes shifted from the dogs back to the other cars.

Summer is tourist season in the Rockies, so it wasn't the out of state license plate that caught his attention, rental car companies had cars registered from all over the country at any given time. The Honda Civic's occupants did not exit to take in the view. The tinted windows showed the outline of two people pointing at something near the SUV.

Zack whistled for both dogs. He flung his arm around Maxi's shoulder as he opened the door for the dogs to jump back in and then escorted her to the passenger door. "Please just get in the car," he said, "I'll tell you why when we're back on the road."

Maxi did not say a word. Zack maneuvered the car out of the rest stop. One glance into the side mirror gave the answer to his question – the Honda Civic followed immediately.

DONALD ATWOOD

Donald Atwood kept their progress under surveillance as the tracker on Zack's government issued SUV bypassed both exits off the throughway for the bureau's downtown office. The dot on the map headed straight into the Rocky Mountains. The thought entered his mind to just call Zack to remind him of the plan, his mission, and the team that awaited in Niza, yet he knew this would be a waste of both of their times.

Zack Brady was infuriating stubborn when it came to running an operation his way, yet he usually obtained the needed results. This case felt different with his kid involved. Maybe finding his son, or at least the people responsible for the boy's disappearance could help Zack's focus. Either way, a text stating he changed the plan would have been appropriate.

He glanced over at the one family photograph on his desk. All fourteen of the most important people in his life. From his wife of forty years to their youngest great grandson. As his eyes volleyed between the moving dot and the photograph, Atwood started to visualize Zack's choices and new plan. He debated on sending part of the team over to Pride Ridge, instead opting to make a quick phone call to a trusted colleague.

Pete Malone answered on the first ring. "What did my sister do now?" Although in a different division, Maxi's brother and Zack kept in close contact and Pete had pulled Zack aside after the last hearings about his former boss. If anyone was in this loop, Pete knew the new plan.

Donald Atwood responded with an appropriate laugh. "I'm not sure except the vehicle they are driving missed both exits for the downtown Niza office. I was hoping you might clue me in."

An awkward silence followed with a grunt sound just as Pete started to speak, "I don't know. Last time I heard from Zack they were heading to Fremont with the dogs, and he didn't say much more. I asked if he needed a hand, but I am still in D.C. if that tells you, his answer.

"Thanks Pete. You know I trust Zack and that this one goes beyond your nephew's disappearance."

"Wait–I thought Ric was on his way back to New York. Last time I talked to Zack was after the hearings. I figured the Fremont trip was tied into that." Pete swore under his breath. "If this involves my family—"

"You need to be on the next flight out." Donald's fingers slamming into the keyboard reverbed across the room and into the phone speaker. "Commercial in four hours or military transport in two?"

"I will take the transport, thank you."

"Pete, I know you don't work for me, yet I will get you the highlights of the internal investigation."

"I have heard parts, Donald, not from Zack of course, yet there are many rumors swirling in regard to the Senator from Fremont and the possible involvement of his niece, again."

It was Donald's time to swear. "We were hoping to keep this all under wraps. If the Senator suspects that he is under investigation . . .," Donald let that thought hang in the air before adding, "I have a bit more information for you. You are on the right track, Pete.

What I am sending is classified to our department and not beyond. You can stop by my office to read a hard copy or on your phone. I ask that if you read what I am sending on your encrypted phone delete the message after. Zack already has this information so there is no need to hang on to it."

"I appreciate you getting me up to speed, sir."

"I appreciate you dropping everything to assist. Zack needs people he trusts and after Aruba—"

"—he doesn't trust many. I get it. Plus, this involves family—"

"Again—"

"And family takes care of family."

Donald let out a short laugh. "At least yours does. Pete, I don't need to tell you to be careful but be careful."

"I will sir and thank you for updating me on the situation. I will contact you after I meet up with Zack and my sister, and I hope my nephew too."

"Let's hope. Thank you again, Pete." Donald hung up the phone, his eyes drawn back to his family picture. He reached out to touch the frame before bringing his attention back to his cellphone. He typed *Trusted help on the way* and hit send. Now he'd wait for contact to be made.

RIC

The day passed as quickly as his queasiness. He worked faster than Clem predicted. The pungent smell of marijuana became the norm. Dust from the plants covered his clothes and body so thick that the beads of sweat that ran down his face made stripes in the pollen.

Ric stopped trying to wipe away the residue. The song Bertha that he heard earlier repeated in his brain, the few words he remembered escaping his lips. As much as he tried to remember another song, Bertha would not leave his head.

At some point Ric moved passed the middle of the field and just kept moving until Clem's truck appeared where the undertaking had started that morning. Inside the cab, a plastic bag sat stuffed with flowering buds next to the cooler that Vittles had handed to Clem that morning.

An audible vibration accompanied by a growling sound from his stomach had Ric reaching for the cooler. He removed one ice water along with a premade, wrapped sandwich. Clem had been smart enough not to leave the keys in the ignition.

The wooziness in both his stomach and head began to settle after a few drinks and bites of food. As he ate, Ric reviewed the rough map he had drawn for Clem. With the quiet of the field mixed with the satisfaction of food and a remaining slight buzz, he laid back in the bed of the truck to stare up at the blue-sky peeking through the high tree leaves and branches.

His brain wandered between Bertha and escape routes. If the barn on the other side was the same one near where this hell started, he could go there, steal a vehicle and drive to Niza. Yes, there was a Maserati parked in the driveway and those cars can fly above the crappy roads and over the peaks back to the city, wait – only if the car had enough gas. Gas would be the problem in this whole plan. Of course, being seen and ending up full of drugs could be an issue too.

In the next scene the tank was full of gas, but the car was an old Toyota Corolla held together by rust. His foot slammed straight through the gas pedal onto the ground below as the entire engine rested in the dirt. He tried for both car and gas, yet the next escape route got blocked by zombies on the way to him with syringes in hand.

As different thoughts entered and exited, breathing became more rhythmic, and the body relaxed. As his plans got stranger, new outside voices that were not in his head interrupted his weird solutions. These new sounds brought some awareness that others might be nearby. With limbs too heavy to move, Ric fought to bring about what little mindfulness he could by stretching his legs and arms, each stretch allowing a bit of fog to escape his brain at the same time the new voices rose in volume.

"You want me to burn my field? Are you nuts?" That sounded a lot like Clem. Ric started to bring his head high enough to look over the side of the truck. There was movement coming in his direction. A man and a woman walked side by side around the last row. Something or someone else's shadow followed behind.

Ric slid off the tailgate to reposition himself just out of view into the woods, crouching down alongside a pine tree. The truck rocked slightly.

"Where's your helper?" a female voice asked.

"Not sure. Maybe he's still in the middle of the field waiting for me. You know how these college boys can be." Clem answered. "Can't I send my crew out to harvest what's here then burn the rest? The stuff is legal in the state you know."

"Yes, I do know but your field isn't, same as the production going in in that barn on the other side—"

"I ain't got nothing to do with that," Clem's voice raised. "All I do is lend my barn to your people; you know that."

"Now calm down, Clem. Yes, we have a deal. How soon can you get this field clear? You can use some of that extra help you get from the Sheriff."

Ric wanted to look to see who this female was, yet the swish of greens along with footsteps had him making his body as small as possible.

"Why, does he have more people for me?"

"Not that I know of. I told our friend the Sheriff to stop his part this morning. My uncle is getting distrustful because of some internal shit going on. I think he's just paranoid, but who am I? Speaking of which," Ric heard the truck shift again, "If you see this guy and you kill him, you probably won't need to grow weed anymore."

"Yeah, I don't know this fella in the picture but if I see him, how about I just give you a call," Clem said.

"Your choice. His name is Zack Brady, and he is a thorn in both mine and my uncle's side." Hearing Zack's name got Ric's attention. He needed to warn his stepfather. "Yo, Dak, let's move!" Marjorie ordered.

Around the other side of the tree, much too close for Ric, the deputy's low drawl answered, "Just a minute, I need to take a leak." The smell of urine filled the air along with the jingle sound of one's belt being reclasped. Ric crawled his body up against the tree until he stood erect. The deputy's movements faded out of sight.

After a bit of idle chitchat, the silence returned. Ric stayed out of sight in the woods and followed the tree line to slip back into the fields. He arrived back at the truck in time to see Clem sitting on the tailgate eating the other sandwich.

"You already ate yours," he said by way of greeting. "Where were you?"

"Back in the field," Ric said. "I couldn't find my map after I ate." Clem held up the piece of paper. "Where did you find it?"

"Sitting beside the cooler," Clem's stare gave Ric the shivers. "How much did you hear? And don't you lie to me, boy!"

"Not a lot, or at least anything I understood. The other people were leaving as I was walking back."

The answer seemed to satisfy Clem. "Explain this map to me," he held it out to Ric, "and then get ready to work. We are picking up equipment and Vittles then coming back to pick as much of this as we can before sunset. It's just going to be the three of us, so we need to work fast."

A picture of Zack taken on a city street sat between them. "Who is that new guy?" Ric pointed to the photo.

"Let's hope that fella doesn't show up anywhere near us," Clem said as he crumpled the photo and shoved it in his pocket.

PETE

Pete Malone arrived at the Niza office to find Zack's team standing around drinking coffee and doing what looked like a lot of nothing. He observed the group for a few minutes before joining the babble in the break room. The chatter stopped with his entry and an awkward silence prevailed. Pete filled his water bottle with the filtration system. When he turned back to the group, he noted no one had moved.

"Meeting in the conference room in five," he said using his in-charge voice as his family called it, "and bring all materials related to the campaign funds investigation you are working on."

"With all due respect sir," a man about Pete's height stepped forward, "we do not know you and have no inclination to share materials that involve a top security clearance."

Pete brought his face into a practiced relaxed smile. "Pete Malone. I am one of the senior officers in charge of this investigation. If you check your emails, you will see my credentials and authorization. And you are—" Pete held his hand out to the spokesperson.

"People just call me Bombs, sir." Bombs gave Pete's hand a hard squeeze.

"Well, Bombs, please," Pete put emphasis on the please, "be in the conference room in four with materials. The same goes for the rest of you. I will answer questions then."

Pete walked out of the room before anyone could stop him. He did a quick sweep of the conference room for bugs before settling in the middle seat of the table with an empty wall behind him. On the table he placed his phone to the right of his laptop. A quick glance at his G-Shock watch gave less than a minute for the rest of the team to arrive.

One by one they filed in, each giving Pete a quick nod before choosing a seat on the opposite side of the table, leaving the seat directly across from Pete open. Pete had four tabs open on his laptop, all hidden from view. One featured photo and a short bios on each man in the room including each's specialty, the next, also hidden from view, contained highlights Pete had put together of the operation to date. The third screen was Pete's email, while the visible screen contained a detailed satellite map of Fremont that focused on the Niza, Amity, Pride Ridge triangle.

Pete waited for the last seat to be filled before he began. "We've lost three minutes waiting for the whole team to get settled. As trained agents you are aware that time is imperative during a highly secret operation."

"Should we synchronize our watches," the man opposite him interrupted to a few snickers. Pete noted the man sat back in his chair, arms crossed over his chest, a sneer frozen across his face.

"If that will get you here on time, do what you need to do. Now we've wasted five minutes." Some of the team shifted in the chairs while the two surrounding the man in the middle mirrored his pose. "As mentioned before, my name is Pete Malone, and I will be heading this portion of the investigation. Each of you was selected for this highly classified mission because of a special skill and your current security clearance status.

Each will have their part of the mission based on that skill and I expect that each person's role will be kept confidential." Pete paused to look each person in the eye before asking questions.

Three hands went up. "Yes, Bombs, although your actual name is Percy Welker."

"Yes, but Bombs is easier to remember. I have two questions; I want to know why we were not notified on the command change and where agent Brady is?"

Pete nodded as another man added, "I was wondering about Brady, too. We thought he was lead on the investigation."

Pete reached over the table to extend his hand to the second man. He stated his name again, "Pete Malone," as the man squeezed his hand tighter than necessary.

"Since you probably already know my actual name I am referred to Tracer," the squeezer replied with a smirk.

"Tech guy, so you are doing the deep dives?" Pete said. He noted this next to the man's bio as all that it said was tracer/tracker. Pete continued, "Yeah, I'm going to need to see your setup after this."

"My desk is your desk," Tracer replied, "although shouldn't we have some sort of authorization from back East before we start showing you our stuff?"

"Tracer, you are Parker Sinclair, correct?" Pete continued without waiting for a response, "You both bring up a good point, but first can I have the rest of you give a quick introduction and state your expertise, so I know if our records match your egos."

The latter got a snort out of one of his new colleagues. Pete flipped to the tab that contained a name, photo, and one-line bio. He then continued, "I will wait while each of you check your emails. You are looking for the confidential correspondence sent with urgency by Admiral Donald Atwood—"

"Alright, alright, we can see that you are legit," Bombs started to say. "Don't get your panties," Pete's glare stopped his comment. After a couple of the men let out loud coughs, Pete continued, "Well you know my name," he said, "and I am a demolition expert and sharpshooter along with the Bull here." He nodded to the man to his left who stretched his jaw before speaking.

"Hi," he started with, "I am called Bull and yes I am a sharpshooter and demolitions expert."

Pete gave Bull a quick head nod. "Bull?"

"As in Bull's eye. My legal name on your chart is Henry Morgan, sir."

"Welcome to the team, Bull."

The only woman in the room raised her hand. She sat with an empty chair between her and the next person, angled more in Pete's direction than the rest. "I am Special Agent E. Kit Sellers. You may address me as Kit. My specialty includes hacking and tracing."

"Nice to meet you," Pete said. "I'll need to see your setup after the meeting too."

"No offense sir," Kit started, "yet before I can share any materials with you, I need a direct order from D.C."

"Yeah, she doesn't even allow us in her space," Tracer added. "Triple locked." The three in the middle laughed a bit too loud.

Pete looked down at Sellers' bio. Donald had brought this one on board personally. "Since Admiral Atwood's email wasn't enough, I will get you the added authorization you request as soon as we are done here. Okay last person." He chin nodded at a quiet man who sat in what would have been the commander's chair. He lifted his gaze slowly to meet Pete's before he spoke.

"I am Director Archer Holey, the senior member of this team. As you may be aware, my expertise includes codes, money laundering, and I am a member of the internal investigation task force, along with agent Brady, who is visibly missing from this gathering."

Pete compared what Holey said to his bio to note he left out a significant portion of his training. When Pete glanced up, Holey gave a quick nod in the direction of his colleagues.

"Okay, so the mysterious Agent Brady was called away to another investigation—"

"Isn't that strange to do this far in?" Tracer interrupted.

"Yes and no," Pete continued. "Either way, I want to see where we are here and get started on our next moves. The two tech guys, let's start with you." Pete stood up.

"Excuse me, Agent Malone, please consider your word choice—"

"Oh man, here we go again," Bombs injected.

"Apologies Agent Sellers. I will be more aware. Now I will—"

"Wait," Kit said. "I thought this was a briefing on our next move. We don't waste time or resources in this office, Mr. Malone—"

"Captain Malone, please."

"We need to know our next step and to get moving forward."

Pete gave a small grin. "Agents, I need to see what the tech guys, er people, have first to confirm our next moves are valid. I will give you the official plan by o-nine hundred. Dismissed."

Pete followed Tracer into a dark corner where the only light emulated off a blank far wall from a prominent flat computer screen. A pile of printouts sat on the side of his desk and covered the top of the filing cabinet against the wall.

"What are those," Pete pointed at the largest pile.

"Forms, memos, mostly junk," Tracer waved his hand in the direction of the mess.

Pete stepped in the direction Tracer's hand pointed and began to flip through one of the piles. "Did you know some of these are stamped confidential?"

"No, they just printed that way." Tracer pointed at his screen. "Here is what I found yesterday."

Some of the information looked familiar, figures and timeline graphs stood out. He saw a list of names with several crossed out in black pen. Pete brought his phone out and held it as if reading a text. With a slight hand, he took a picture.

On Tracer's screen, a bunch of data appeared. Numbers distributed across columns with multiple headings. The graph was not familiar.

"Would you send this to me, please?" Pete pointed at the screen, "along with anything else you deem important." Tracer nodded. Pete shook his hand, now clammy, and gave a quick thanks. He circled back to the conference room. After another quick scan, he shut the door and dialed Donald Atwood.

RIC

Clem swore up a storm as he drove back to the camp, bringing the truck to an abrupt stop in front of the main building. "Grab waters and sandwiches from the fridge," he shouted, adding, "VITTLES," at a much higher volume inside the door.

Ric headed straight into the kitchen to start to pack up food and water. He could hear both arguing in the main hall as he moved to fill the boxes and load the back of the pickup.

"Are they nuts or you?" Vittles kept asking.

"Look we need to harvest as much as we can now," Clem shouted. "Or we can let the field burn."

"NO!" Vittles shouted back. He ran past Ric to grab something shiny out of one of the drawers, slamming it shut after. He took two of the three remaining boxes out to the truck then yelled at Ric to follow.

Clem added several boxes of garbage bags along with trimming shears and scissors. "You packing for a party?" he asked Ric.

"I wasn't sure how much," he stammered.

"Just git back in the truck." Clem opened the passenger door. This time Ric sat in the middle. Vittles, who appeared so calm this morning, vibrated in the passenger's seat, while Clem continued to sear.

"When we get there," Clem said, "we are dividing the field into thirds and moving as quick as we can. Ric where is that map you drew?"

Ric took the map out of the glove department and held it out. "Vittles, take a look at this. There are patches within each third that could be harvested. We are going to cut the buds and throw each filled bag in the back of my truck. We need as many bags as possible by each of the day."

"End of day?" Ric repeated.

"The bastards are burning the field," Vittles slammed his hand against the door. "Those bastards." He repeated.

Clem continued as if no one spoke. "I'll take the portion closest to the barn, working from the middle back in case anyone is watching. Vittles, you have the highest tolerance for the pollen, so you'll be in the middle. Boy, you will be at the end closest to the truck. Start in the middle and work your way out. Vittles will show you what to put in the bags."

Ric gave a quick nod.

"If either of you see or hear anyone, move in the opposite direction out of the field and try to get back to the truck. Instead of loading the bags into the bed, stack them up just off in the woods and we can drive around and pick em all up after." Clem chewed on his index finger as he spoke. "Any questions?"

No one spoke. Within minutes, the truck returned to where it had started, at the end of the field.

MAXI

Maxi pulled the car over into a strip mall parking lot just over the Pride Ridge border. The town, with its old west fronts, looked to her like a combination of a movie set and Disneyland, kind of fake yet with the illusion of safety.

One of the dogs gave an extended yawn and whined when the car stopped. "Okay boys, you need to sit tight," Maxi directed at her back seat passengers, "I will find you a place to run as soon as I can." She slapped Zack's arm with a little too much enthusiasm as she spoke.

Zack stretched his arms up pressing both hands against the ceiling. "Hey, we are not in Niza. What's the plan, Max?"

"You tell me. We just pulled into the Pride Ridge limits. I am thinking find my son and kick his ass for not returning any texts, but that might not be the right approach." A single tear leaked out of her eye. "He's in trouble, Zack. My spidey sense..."

She felt Zack's strong arms come around to squeeze her body. The strong appearance vanished as their destination became a reality. "He's going to be okay," Zack's breath heated against her ear. "We are going to find him."

Maxi broke the embrace, and Zack saw her eyes go dark. "And when we do, I am either going to beat the crap out of my son or the people responsible for his delay." Before he could speak, she warned, "No matter who that might be."

She went to grab the map that had fallen to the floor at the same moment that Zack bent over to do the same. Their heads bounced off each other. Zack focused on the open map, pointing to the location. "The camp is about fifteen minutes from here, but we need to go to this town, Amity, which is about thirty minutes outside Pride Ridge." He reached out to take both her hands in his. "Maxi, Ric texted me that some backwoods Sheriff was holding him on a false charge – the same Sheriff who is part of my money laundering investigation."

"What the—" She tried to pull back, yet Zack held tight.

"Yeah, I kind of figured you'd have that reaction and I deserve your wrath," she could feel his pulse quickening, "Listen Max, I don't think they know who Ric is—"

"—why is that?"

"Marjorie Lofsmen is involved in this mess too and is somewhere in this area." Zack gave her hands a squeeze. He added, "Feel free to punch her out when we meet again," Maxi just glared at her husband.

"A punch would be a day at the beach compared to what I will do to her if she has anything to do with Ric's disappearance."

"You scare me at times."

"Zack, you should be scared. Are you using our son as bait? Was the camp real?" Maxi's face had turned a dark shade of red. Droplets of sweat ran along her neck.

"I can't believe you'd even ask me that." Her husband shifted in his seat as his breath became audible. With hands balled into fists pressed into his thighs, he continued to speak, "Ric was at a legitimate camp to clean up the national park trails. Somehow, he got connected to this Sheriff, I am working on how, and I have been working on finding him, putting my job on hold and at risk. Finding Ric is my first priority," he stretched out his fingers before connecting back to Maxi's. "The fact that he stumbled into an investigation that has been going on for over a year is shit luck for all of us."

"Listen Zack, I'm frantic about Ric and my filter is off." Maxi reached to grab his hands. "I'm sor—"

"Please don't. Let's find the kid and the bad guys, charge the Senator, get Marjorie back in prison, and live happily ever after." He leaned over to kiss Maxi on the cheek.

Maxi returned the kiss with a quick salute in between a goofy grin with a few tears. "Let's do this," she said as she collected her emotions. "What's our plan?"

PETE

Pete's brief conversation with Donald Atwood gave him a little more information. The senior officer's genuine concern for Pete's family was always appreciated.

"Pete, I haven't heard from Zack in a while, yet he and your sister should be close to Pride Ridge. The plan is to give Maxi only as needed information at this point."

"Oh man, I feel for my brother Zack."

"What? You don't think Maxi will take this well?" Both men snickered. "The new information traced a small deposit of about thirty grand moved into a Cayman account—"

"Was this before or after the last kid overdosed?" He could hear papers shuffling in the background.

"The day after. Kit reported the deposit. She is also tracking Lofsmen's whereabouts for the team."

"Yeah, speaking of your agent Kit – she won't let me near her computer until you or another higher up confirm my involvement in this case," Pete added in a high voice, "because with internal investigations one could never be too safe."

"Did she really say that to you?"

"Yes, Donald, she did. Both Sellers and Holey have been stand offish and quoting from the rule book. I wanted to be out of here—"

Donald let out a laugh, "yes, the only reason I can see both grinding out the rules is to slow the process. I will try to ease their worries. Sellers was on the team who discovered the leak of confidential codes that set off parts of the Aruba investigation. I put her on this team so you or Zack would have an ally up front. I'll make a call."

"Please let's wait on this, sir, yet if could resend my authorization memo to her—"

"Done. Anything else, Pete?"

"No, I think I am good for now. I will be in touch." Pete added a few notes to his list of team members, most notably reasons to trust Kit Sellers, yet he had learned through the years except for a select few, to not give away his trust. The Niza office appeared well run, yet within these walls a traitor or at least someone working in the Senator's circle existed.

Pete moved Bombs and Tracer over to a suspect list, just because they both asked about Brady and in general pissed him off. Both men embraced that 'good old boy' personality that he found annoying. That trait always heightened his skepticism about their loyalty. All team members had been vetted by the main office, Atwood promised this much, yet a couple more hurdles would reveal who needed to be assigned benign duties and who would be an asset to the cause.

He looked up to see Kit Sellers standing in his doorway. "May I enter, sir?"

Pete waved her in, noting that she had shut the door behind her. Kit opted for a chair next to Pete, instead of the customary seat across. Pete's hand automatically rested against the handle of his sidearm.

Kit spoke softly, "Did you rescan this room upon return?" Pete nodded yes. "Good, good," her voice rose a little. "Look I was just following procedure asking for clearance—"

Pete held up his hand to stop Kit who continued. "I keep my office locked, both bolt and keypad, and have a micro-camera mounted on the door. Someone keeps trying to break in, I think to try to hack my computer." Kit Sellers swirled her head around the room. "There was another deposit made recently. I think whoever is in charge is starting to pull up stakes."

"Why do you say that?"

"Because my contact in the valley said that he was told to burn a marijuana field, and we are talking about close to a million dollars in weed."

"Marijuana is legal in Fremont," Pete stated.

"Yes, but this field, which is the size of a football field and has been in operation for decades, illegally and the grower failed to obtain a permit to grow when marijuana legalized."

"Where is this field located?"

"Right outside Amity Fremont. The Sheriff there—"

"Is on the list. I know."

"Yes, but the profits—"

"Help campaigns? Are we able to do a flyover or—"

"No to both. But here is the part that is setting off fireworks for me – we recently think there is a part two to this operation, a possible drug lab."

Pete sat up straight and turned his body towards Kit. "Why a drug lab?" he asked.

"The Cayman deposits spiked at the same time people started noticing an ammonia smell in the area. There is an old barn out there that the same person who owns the fields owns the barn. Not sure if the two are connected but if there is that much ammonia in the air that people are noticing—"

"There could be crack cocaine lab too." Pete finished his thought. "Shouldn't the D.E.A. have been brought in on this?"

"Yes, but they haven't been so far?" Kit looked over her shoulder before continuing, "we think that this is all connected to the internal investigation."

"Who is we and why do you think there is a connection?"

Again, Kit Sellers swirled her head around the room. "You sure you scanned for bugs?" Pete nodded then gestured to continue. "Mostly Bull and I. Holey brushed off our theory saying that it would be impossible to have a drug lab going that our office wasn't aware and to bring in the DEA would be waste of all of our time and an astronomical amount of paperwork that would only delay our investigation, and our work was more important."

"Does Holey know about the marijuana field?"

"Yes."

Both sat in silence as Pete took in this new information. "Have you sent this additional information to Donald, er, Admiral Atwood?"

"Not the marijuana slash drug lab part. I was told to keep focused on tracing the money, yet I think this is all connected."

"Why?"

"Because we are looking at campaign fraud and illegal donations but not really at the source of that money. Look at this chart," Kit pulled a tiny chart up on her phone. Pete strained to understand the graph.

"Please send that to me." Instead of downloading, Pete scanned the file to open in a secure server. Once opened, he said, "How long have you had this information?"

"If you look at the complete graphic," Kit ignored him as she typed a command to bring the complete document in view, "You will see that the spikes in both donations and Cayman deposits started in the last year, about the same time the ammonia smell started."

Pete swore under his breath as he hit the control print screen tabs to send copies to both Zack and Atwood in secure emails. "Did you bring this to Holey's attention?"

"A while ago. I have been working on this in my off hours because I was ordered to stop. I was going to go over the information with Agent Brady but since he is missing..."

"Who ordered you to stop? Someone on this team?" When the questions were met with silence, Pete continued, "I appreciate you trusting me with this. Please keep this confidential as I need to think about our next steps."

"Can I ask why you screenshotted the image instead of sending my file?"

"A screenshot would be safer than a file because of viruses," Pete said. His phone buzzed on the table, screen side facing down. "I need to take this," he said as he stood to indicate Kit should do the same.

As the two shook hands, Kit said, "Now I have trusted you with my life." Then in a louder voice as she opened the door, "thank you agent Malone, and yes, please come by my office so I may share my setup." She gave a knowing wink in Pete's direction as she exited.

Pete flipped his phone over to see on the screen that he had the two expected missed calls. He setup a conference call with both Zack and Atwood then started the conversation with, "you guys are not going to believe this one."

L.M. Pampuro

ZACK

Hollywood stole the old west look from Amity Fremont. Every building on the one main drag featured an old west front, right down to the similar signage for each business. "The historical society here must police the guise constantly," Zack said as he pointed to the only gas station visible that featured an area to tie up one's horse. "Must be hell to keep up appearances."

Maxi nodded in response. As the plan developed, his wife became quieter. At the town border, Zack noticed her leg started to bounce as she tightened and released her fingers. If energy could be seen, Maxi vibrated giving off tight pulses of blue light from her body.

Zack drove past the building with a *Sheriff* sign painted across the top gray panel, pulled a U-turn, and parked in an empty space a few doors back in the direction of Pride Ridge.

"Now?" Maxi said as she pushed herself up from the seat.

His hand reached over to rest on her thigh. "Let's give this a few minutes to see what we see." She sat back as if she understood the delay.

A white pick-up with the Pride Ridge logo on the side pulled in behind them. A thin young man with a wavy mess of hair jumped out holding a white mail bag. He disappeared into the building. Zack opened the door, leaned over to note the U.S. Postal Service sign in the window. Within minutes the same person came out with an empty bag. He caught Zack's eye and waved before jumping back in his truck to speed out of town.

While Zack took in the slow activity on the street, Maxi exclusively focused on the Sheriff's Office where shadows moved in the windows, yet no one went in or out. "Hey Zack," Maxi said, keeping her voice low. "Are you sure that is really the police station because it looks fake and there are no cop cars in front."

Zack rested his arms on top of the car to look in the direction of the office. "The town offices on their website list it as the police station," he said. "I do see your point, but we are used to the offices in New England and out here is different."

"Different but the same. Should I try to take one of the dogs in with me?"

"I was thinking about that. If you bring in Jerry, folks will get suspicious—"

"Because he looks like a cop."

Zack laughed. "Yes, because Jerry looks like a cop. Bobby might not set off alarms for his looks but if gets a scent—"

"He'll make a fuss."

"Exactly."

"I don't want to put Ric in any danger. Zack, do you really think he's here? And do you believe that I can do this?"

"I think," he opened the SUV door, took both her hands in his, and leaned in to touch their lips, "that you are the only one who can do this. Get as much information as you can, and I will do the rest. By the way, Pete is in Niza taking care of the other stuff. He should be here later today or tomorrow at the latest."

"Freakin' Pete," Maxi said as her face became wet. "I must be in real trouble if my brother was reassigned to your case."

"Let's just say," Zack wrapped her in a tight hug, "that family takes care of family. Donald thought we could use someone we trust completely. Pete is making sure the others fit that description."

Maxi let out an audible breath. "Let's do this." She marched in the direction of the Sheriff's office.

Both dogs jumped out. Zack quickly put their leashes on then waved one of Rick's t-shirts under Bobby's nose. The dog's tail started to thump. "You lead," Zack instructed. Jerry moved with Zack to stay in step. The shepherd focused on something straight ahead. This proved to be difficult with Bobby pulling his leash in several directions.

Although they didn't stray far from the Sheriff's office, the lab moved to the only restaurant on the street. He sat and thumped his tail. Zack noted that the place opened at five. He gave Bobby's leash a quick tug and the dog pulled him over to the post office, again sitting and thumping.

This time Zack pushed open the door to the post office and brought both dogs inside. From behind the counter an older woman said, "Sorry, the dogs have to wait outside," at the same time Bobby pulled to an empty chair. The dog sniffed and whined as he rested his nose on the seat. "What's that one doing?" the woman asked.

"Not sure," Zack replied as he gave the leash a tug. Bobby pulled back in response before moving to Zack's side. "He gets weird at times."

"They all do. How can I help you?"

Zack made a show of looking around the room. "Sorry, I wasn't paying attention to where I was walking."

The woman let out a small laugh and muttered, "Damn tourists" before bringing her voice back up to regular volume. "Well enjoy the town and next time, please leave the dogs outside. This here is a federal building, you know."

"Will do." Zack exited the same moment Maxi came out of the Sheriff's door. They met back by the SUV, out of sight lines for both buildings.

Zack said, "I got something to tell you!" in harmony with Maxi.

MAXI

Once Zack was out of sight, Maxi marched across the street and gave the door a shove like she owned the place. She stepped inside the lobby area to be greeted by a young boy reading at the desk with no adults in sight.

"My mom will be right back," he said. "She's using the bathroom. I can yell for her if you need someone fast."

"No, I just have a question or two," Maxi said. "What ya reading?"

"Artimis Foul," the boy answered. "I'm on the fourth book."

"Oh, I love those books. My son used to read Colfer all the time."

"Yeah, so did my friend here, but he left."

Maxi zeroed in on the word friend. "Was your friend here?" she asked, trying to keep her voice level.

"Yeah – but he left."

The boy's indifferent response bothered Maxi, yet she asked, "What was your friend's name?" and secretly hoped the mother had the shits.

"I don't remember," the kid shrugged. "He was really nice though. Taught me stretches and read to me here." In the background a toilet flushed. A hefty, female version of the boy appeared in the hallway, just behind the desk.

She stopped to observe the interaction for a breath, then said, "Sorry for the delay. Can I help you?"

"It's okay, mom. We were talking Foul. Her son read the books too." This got an eyebrow raise from the mother.

"Did he now," she said. "So, what brings you to the Amity Sheriff's office?" Her voice was pleasant, yet Maxi caught a slight edge.

She fingered Ric's picture inside her pocket yet did not pull it out. "We, my husband and I," she yanked her thumb at the door, "were just wondering how far we are to Niza. It's so beautiful out here we kept taking side roads and I think he got us lost." She said the last part in a softer tone, as if the woman were co-conspirators.

"You've got about an hour's ride," the officer said. Maxi noted the name Harper on her tag. "If you head that way," she pointed in the direction to leave town, "for about five miles you'll come to highway. Just hop on and that will take you straight to the city."

Maxi nodded and said a quick thank you as she leaned out the door. Ric had been here. She half walked half ran back to Zack.

L.M. Pampuro

RIC

Clem parked the truck just off the dirt road, about ten yards from where he parked earlier. As Ric and Vittles pulled gear from the back, he walked over to the field, turned in their direction, and stared for a minute. Once the truck bed was relieved of all the equipment, and the boys stood on the backside of the marijuana field, barely in sight, he drove the truck along the long portion of the field.

Vittles grabbed a box of trash bags, a pair of small hedge clippers along with a pair of scissors off the ground. He motioned to Ric to do the same. They met Clem as he jogged to meet them.

"Wouldn't it have been easier—"

Clem raised his hand to silence Vittles. In a low voice he instructed, "Here is what we are doing." He patted the pockets on his pants before focusing on Ric. "Where's that map you made today, boy?" Ric reached into his pocket to pull out the crumpled paper. Clem studied it for a minute. "Okay, Vittles, see here," he pointed at a cluster of markings near the center of the marijuana field, "I want you to start here and show the boy how this is done. Once he has the hang of it, move over to here," he indicated a clump of markings near where they stood.

"Start from the far side and work your way to this side. When the bags get heavy, they don't need to be filled, put them at the edge of the field. We'll git them later." Clem grabbed a hedge trimmer and a box of bags. "No tunes, Vittles."

"Got it, boss, stealth operation." Vittles saluted. Clem disappeared into the tall stalks. Vittles motioned Ric to follow him as they moved in the pine trees until the center field point. Both slipped into the row, the heavy stench of skunk weed filling the air.

Vittles inhaled deeply as they moved while Ric positioned the collar of his T-shirt over his nose. Once surrounded by plants, they stopped. A half-moon lingered just above the tops of the plants with a smattering of stars scattered across the darkened sky. A cacophony of forest sounds followed in their silence.

"That is beautiful," Ric sighed out and was promptly shushed as Vittles pushed him further in.

"Okay so here is what you do," Ric could barely hear Vittles speak. He pulled a plant down, much like Ric had done earlier. "This is a bud, and this is a flowering bud," Vittles tapped both with his scissors. "See the difference? You cut both of them where the bud meets the stem, no higher or lower cause it makes extra work for me in the dry house, get it?"

Ric gave a quick nod. "Do what Clem said and don't make the bags too heavy. I will catch you later."

The plants swallowed Vittles just as they had Clem earlier. Ric grabbed the plant Vittles had demonstrated. Bending the stalk came easy yet balancing the bent over stalk with one hand and cutting the bud off without losing it on the ground was Ric's challenge along with the light-headed feeling from inhaling the heady scent.

The more his mind relaxed, the sloppier the cuttings, yet he found the coordination to cut the flowering buds off the plant, then scoop up what he could gather from the ground into a trash bag. The illusion of moving at a good pace was shattered when Ric reached the end of his row.

In both directions at least a half dozen bags lined up in the space between the pine trees. Ric took the extra few steps to throw his bag into the truck bed, breathing deeply along the way, before walking back down the next row. He thought he moved a little quicker this time around, but when he returned, the number of bags had doubled.

As he worked, the thought occurred to him that if the deputy came back to get him, the marijuana stench was prevalent, and they might add drug charges on for fun. The other thing that bothered Ric was Zack's lack of response to his text. If his stepfather had received his message, why hadn't he sent in the troops by now?

He imagined his mother's reaction to this whole situation and let out a short laugh. If he made it through all this, it wasn't going to be pretty. She might never let him leave the fortress.

Now that would suck for him.

A faint chemical smell cut through the field's earthy scent as Clem's shouts took away the silence. "What the fuck are you doing?" he yelled. Ric could hear a woman's voice answer, "I told you we were going to burn the field." Clem shouted back, "After we harvested. Stop that you are ruining my crops!"

A hand reached through the plants to grab Ric by the shoulder, pull him further out of view, while a second hand cupped over his mouth. Ric swung his elbow into something solid. "What the freak—" was followed by a quiet, "Shush." He turned to see Vittles rubbing his side. "Dude, we need to get out of here. Take your bag and follow me."

"I said stop!" Clem's voice getting hoarser as anger turned to pleading.

Stalks hit Ric on all sides. Following Vittles turned out to be like running through bumper cars, some misses yet a bunch of hits. The bag started to tear, leaving a trail of plastic pieces and flowering buds. They plowed through the end with Vittles running straight into the same tree line that Ric had shadowed earlier that day.

When they stopped, both breathing hard leaning up against tree trunks, Ric said "Shouldn't we help Clem?"

Vittles responded in an equally wheezy voice, "Yes, but no. He said that if there was a commotion to take the bags and get the hell out of here."

Commotion was a good word. The stench of gasoline now dominated the air as bright lights from a pickup truck cut through the trees. The sssing sound of an automated sprayer slicing through the forest, drowning out everything else.

Ric saw that Vittles had grabbed a second bag of marijuana on his way out and wished that he had done the same. At least there were two in the truck's bed and here they managed to get couple more. For some reason that he couldn't explain, Ric liked both Clem and Vittles. The two had treated him okay under his situation.

BANG! "Fuck," said Vittles. "Follow me." He moved deeper into the trees. The arguing had stopped, along with the sprayer truck. Through the idles, voices rose. Both stooped down inside a field of tall ferns. From this position, they saw the truck turn back in the direction it came from. They waited a few minutes in the new silence before speaking.

"Was that a—" Vittles sat further back into the trees. He reached into his pocket, flicked a lighter, and took a long inhale off a stainless unbreakabowl. He offered the pipe to Ric who did the same, coughing out a reaction to the harsh weed.

"Gunshot," Ric said through inhales.

"Really? Fuck," Vittles responded, repeating this several more times. "We got to get out of here."

"What about Clem?"

"He'd do the same to us. Wild, wild west," Vittles shrugged and started to move in the opposite direction of the sounds. As he passed Ric, his foot slipped on some pine needles. Ric reached out to grab the back of his shirt and keep Vittles from falling against one of the visible tree roots.

"Do we get the truck? I put at least two bags in the bed?" Ric said in between heavy breaths. A boom brought on an orange glow that lit up both their faces as the bright ball of fire rose against the darkened night sky.

"Fuck," they both whispered at the same moment. Vittles followed up with, "We need to get the fuck out of here now."

"Where?" Ric huffed, "Back to the ranch?" A few long human shadows extended into their space. Both slipped behind an old tree trunk, Vittles signaling with a finger to his lips for silence.

Through the roar of the fire, they could catch every other word of an incomprehensible conversation. Bang! Bang! Bang! Now both inhaled and exhaled audibly. The two exchanged glances yet stood frozen against the trunk.

"Should we shoot into the woods too," came a clear voice. Another, maybe female answered, "No, we've made enough noise for now. I got to get back into town and tie up a few loose ends. Just take care of the lab and get the rest later." The truck's headlights did another full sweep lighting up the dark, after bringing just the glow and snap of the fire.

Vittles took a deep inhale, moved his head in the direction for Ric to follow him along the back of the field. They walked in silence, half drenched in an orange glow, breathing in the heady results of their labor. They followed Clem's tire tracks over to where he left the truck.

Vittles reached inside the passenger window. His hand came back with the quick flash of metal in the shape of a small gun. "Are you going to kill me?" Ric said pointing to the weapon.

"Only if I have to," Vittles answered. He relocated to the opposite side of the truck to haul one of the filled hefty bags from the back. "Grab another and follow me," Ric did as he was instructed. Sweat dripping off every part of his body.

Two bags proved awkward to carry, the plastic getting caught on any branch that stuck into the makeshift trail. Ric grunted every few feet from the weight of the load. He did his best to keep up with

Vittles and not trip over the stones and roots. The terrain remained on the flat side with various curves around trees.

A cayote howl in proximity was met with distant responses. The marijuana smell faded as the glow from the field dissipated into the shadowy cool of the night. Vittles stopped moving at an overlook. The curl of smoke from the heat of the ranch moving skyward in the distance.

The bags now torn apart, still about half full. Vittles lined up all four in an open space, held each briefly, then after the last, smirked.

"We did okay," he said. "I am guessing there is about fifteen pounds here, converted to ounces," Vittles held up a finger using the sky as a chalkboard, "would be about two forty yet broken up by the gram would be around six thousand." He looked over to Ric and repeated "Six thousand!"

"Okay," Ric said. When he fell silent Vittles did more math in the sky.

"We are talking about, shit, sixty, maybe seventy thou, depending on if I can get this to Niza or to my buddy in Pride Ridge." Vittles looked back at Ric, "How many bags did you say were in the truck bed?"

"I don't know, maybe four?"

"Holy shit! This is getting the fuck out of here and follow the old guys from The Dead money." Vittles started to dance around the bags. He opened his mouth to howl then froze. "Crap." He stared over at Ric as he rubbed the gun in his pocket.

"Vittles," Ric said. "Vittles," he repeated as he took out the gun and aim it in Ric's direction. The shot resonated through the valley as Ric crouched against the dirt. He rubbed his hands over his arms and legs, jumping up, mouth open, eyes wide. "What the fuck!"

Vittles walked around Ric to disappear just out of view. "Got it," he called from the shadows. Ric walked back to see blood leaking from a sizeable mountain lion. "All the predators are not human," Vittles said as he went back to the bags.

Ric breathed in deep to try to stop the shaking. He moved away and grabbed the two bags he carried earlier. Together they headed down the path to the ranch.

ZACK

Next stop was the camp where Ric was supposed to be staying. "Don't trust anyone," Zack kept repeating.

"I just want to get my bare hands on the people who have my son," Maxi lifted one hand to wipe her face, "and get my kid back," Maxi said, and she wasn't kidding. After they left Amity, she begged Zack to contact Donald for a warrant. He took his time to explain why they couldn't do that yet. "But the dog!" Maxie whined.

"Maxi, a retired drug sniffing dog's testimony wouldn't persuade a crooked or honest judge for that matter to issue a warrant. Come on now, we are talking about a dog, even if they both are smarter than most humans." He reached back to scratch Jerry under the chin. Bobby was out of reach, head leaning out the side window.

"How do you know the judge is crooked?"

"I don't—yet I can't take that chance until we look further into the donor list." That statement quieted his wife. Even when he added, "Pete will be here soon with back up," Maxi just nodded. This version of Maxi frayed his nerves because he knew from previous experiences that in that stillness his wife plotted and planned.

Zack just needed to get all the players to the same place, so his team could start picking up all the Senator's friends. He thought ahead about how the dogs could help with this task. Jerry and Bobby would remain glued to his wife's side, especially if something bad took place.

PETE

Pete Malone's arrival at Pride Ridge was anything but subtle. Holey insisted on taking the office's tech truck, a huge black motorhome that came equipped with its own Wi-Fi system, tracker, and full arsenal hidden in the underneath storage. The thing screamed FEDS!

Holey also insisted on Kit Sellers and Bull being part of the entourage. The only part that Pete agreed upon was leaving behind the other two agents to do additional searches for more money. Holey wanted the team to drive together so they could exchange added information during the hour and a half drive.

Holey seemed to want a lot of his decisions followed without question.

Pete took his rental car and followed the mobile unit instead of traveling with the team. The director offered to ride with him, yet Pete said he liked the silence to review and internalize everything discussed today. He made certain to drop back further behind the mobile unit, after the turn on to the main drag.

Pedestrians along the scenic wooden sidewalk turned to stare at what looked like a huge camper. An old-fashioned billboard at the main intersection pointed a huge arrow in the direction of the resort that doubled as a summer camp. The mobile unit turned while Pete drove straight ahead to park on a side street.

In the closest shop he bought two different versions of a logoed baseball hat, one light blue, one recessed gray, along with a green zip-up hoodie. He paid for his purchase with cash. Walking back to the center, he exchanged his black windbreaker for the hoodie, dropped the second baseball cap in the car, and wore the other.

Several times, Pete stopped to look in a store window, glancing back into the reflection behind him. Without any noticeable followers, he continued to stroll with the crowd on the main drag. His cellphone buzzed. The text read, *where are you?* Pete laughed to himself as he looked at his watch. It took this crack team a good twenty minutes to realize he wasn't following behind. *Where did Atwood get these people?*

He made a mental note then entered the Moosehead Coffee Company, one of the several trendy cafes that looked like all the others. He ordered a black coffee and found a seat against the wall. From this location he could see the small room, the entry and observe the street. Maxi walked by being pulled by a big black lab while a second dog, a German shepherd kept pace by her side.

The guy walking next to her broke pace to enter the café. Zack sat down next to Pete and said, "Wife shopping?"

"Where is yours?" Pete answered.

"Walking the dogs."

"With friends?"

"No," Zack said. "I watched some turn up the access road following the sign on main street. I figure that they are heading for the hotel not the camp. Interesting that there was some picture taking with cell phones from the tourists." Zack looked around the room, "I think we have one nearby, maybe across the street."

Zack got up and went to the counter as Pete looked over his coffee cup. Sure, enough two men stood across the street, one pointed in the direction of the café while the other nodded in the direction that Maxi went. Neither man followed in her direction though from experience, both Zack and Pete knew someone did.

Zack sat down with a matching cup. "I really wanted a tea," he said, adding, "This crap tastes like shit."

"So, order the tea," Pete tilted his head towards the window.

"I am trying to be inconspicuous." Both men laugh loud enough to draw the attention of those sitting close. "She can't not shop," Zack added to normalize their conversation and get out of observer's attention. "Should we move?"

"In a minute. Our friends across the street are watching."

Zack's phone buzzed. "She's back at the car with the dogs. Said there is a creepy guy hanging on the corner." He brought his attention back to Pete. "When does the sweep start?"

"As soon as we locate Marjorie. She is—" Pete stopped talking as one of the men from across the street entered the shop. They sipped their drinks and watched him order two coffees. When he turned to leave, Zack snapped a photo with his phone. He blew up and showed the photo to Pete.

"Look familiar?"

Pete shook his head no. "Brother there are far too many players in this game, especially in these parts. Our team is fragmented. Out of the four I got one is okay, maybe two, and out of the two, one is slightly paranoid about sharing. They keep asking for you."

"How lovely," Zack gave a smirk. "Why only two of the four?"

"One asked too many questions about you and the others followed this leader. The paranoid one gave up most of the updates that are going between me, you, and Donald, plus he's an Atwood pick."

"Those are usually good."

"The other, the head agent, is an okay guy, but a control freak—"

"Freak meet freak—"

"Whatever—at least I got you," Pete batted his eyes at Zack then added, "What is our next step?"

"I need to find the kid. According to Maxi, a kid in the Sheriff's office, son of a deputy named Harper, coincidence enough, had a friend who read Artemis Foul books and did stretches with him. Also, Bobby thumped and whined in front of a restaurant and inside the post office. Maxi wanted to get a warrant based on the kid and Bobby's reaction, and I had to explain that even a dog as intelligent as Bobby would not get a warrant from a judge, never mind the son of a deputy."

"Ah—Maxi. But at least we have confirmation that Ric is in the area. We now have a starting point to look. The friends we are staying with are the problem. Donald might not think so, yet so far none have been hospitable."

Zack stood to leave. "Listen I have to go have a chat with a creepy dude, maybe stir up the muck to get things moving." He took a long sip before adding, "Nervous people make mistakes. We were planning to check out the camp today, yet I don't think we will find anything there."

"Why do you say that?"

"Because of Bobby's thumping and wining. Anyway, the plan was to stay at the resort hotel, yet if your team is there—"

"You also might get ID'd if someone on the team sees you. There are several condos along the access road."

"I'll text you after we check in."

"Let me know how the camp goes."

"I will and I'll check the updates. I will try to do something within walking distance so we can meet up later. I am sure Maxi will be happy to see you."

"Not so sure but we will think that thought." Pete extended his hand for a quick shake. Zack went out the door, to the left, as did one of the men across the street. He watched the other lean up against the building, arms folded in front. After a few minutes, a man jaywalked over to the café.

L.M. Pampuro

RIC

The stench of marijuana coming off the bags made Ric a little dizzy. His body wobbled down the trail, tripping over the ruts along the way. Vittles moved at a quicker pace providing small flashes of color amongst the green foliage. The presence of the mountain lion had Ric looking back over his shoulder at each turn, and up into the trees overhead. This new habit slowed his pace even further.

The last bit of the cover came about fifty feet from the ranch house. Now with only the light of the moon, outlines of the structures created visible shadows. Vittles walked along the tree line as far as he could. Ric saw a quick nod of Vittles' head in the general direction of the building and followed him across the field.

With a jiggle of the handle, the back door opened into the kitchen. Vittles voice remained just above a whisper as he instructed Ric to keep the lights off. "Light pollution travels miles out here. We need to do this in as much darkness as possible." He then instructed Ric to grab a backpack and fill it with food and boxed water. "I don't care what you grab, just know that it needs to be quick and portable."

Ric went to the commercial refrigerator to be immediately blinded by the brightness of the inside light. He jumped as Vittles slammed the door shut, just missing Ric's hand. "What part of no light do you not understand?" Vittles hissed. He pushed Ric in the direction of the pantry and pointed before storming off in the direction of Clem's office.

Once he moved a couple cases of water, a warehouse store size box of Nature's Bakery bars, and a couple bags of Deep River chips to the main doorway, he followed Vittles voice and stood in the shadows just outside of Clem's office.

"Dude, listen to me, there are four bags here... yeah around sixty best I can figure but there are another four in the truck..." Vittles shadow paced out into the main room as he spoke. "I'm telling you that they burned him and the field, but I think we can get the stuff out of the truck..." His voice got a bit louder, "I don't know how but listen dude, I need you to come and pick me and the weed up along with another dude."

Ric stepped into the main frame of the doorway, yet Vittles didn't seem to notice. "No man, dude is cool. He knows Bertha and actually heard Jerry live in the womb. I swear to God dude. He worked in the fields and set up the irrigation system here. Clem trusted him so I do—" Vittles turned to the door and released a short "EEK!" Another voice could be heard shouting from the phone. "No, dude, it's okay. Just my little buddy. Hey man, I got to go. When should we expect you?"

Not hearing both parts of the conversation bothered Ric more than the little dude titles. The words, "at the pass near the lifts," caught his attention. As far as Ric could remember, the closest ski lifts were near Pride Ridge. He jumped at the sound of Vittles slamming the landline receiver into the base. "I love doing that," Vittles said. "Brings a release."

Vittles grabbed something off the desk and pushed past Ric. "We are traveling unconventional here – but at least we are traveling." The two walked past the outbuilding to the rundown barn hidden beyond the structure. Vittles fiddled with the key, jiggled, and reinserting several times. He slammed his hand into the door, and both watched as the lock slid down to open. "No wonder Clem was always cranky," Vittles said.

Inside the door, Vittles held out a small flashlight. The John Deere was slightly bigger than a riding lawn mower, covered in red rust, and attached to the back wall by spider webs.

Ric muttered, "You have got to be kidding me," Loud enough for Vittles to turn.

"I am not. This fine vehicle will top out at thirty miles per hour, take us through the trails, and move all our stuff too."

"This actually runs?" Ric walked back, "Doesn't Clem have a newer model? One we don't have to worry about disintegrating under our asses."

"Just give me a hand here," Vittles moved to the other side and placed one hand on the steering wheel and the other on the seat. Ric leaned over to mirror the image. After a few grunts and groans, the tractor slid out from its position.

"It looks worst in the light. Where is the other one?" Ric followed Vittles finger to a spot out in the middle of the adjacent field.

"I think it's out of gas," Vittles said, adding, "Clem said something about getting it later."

"Do you have the key for that one?"

Vittles shook his head no. "Clem always had that set on him. Look, this baby will start up with a little gas. We can hook up the trailer, throw all the shit in there and get the fuck out of here." Vittles went over to the back side of the other barn, returning a few minutes later with a gas can in each hand.

While Vittles tinkered with the old tractor, Ric moved all the boxes and bags to the wooden trailer in between the ranch house and the barn. As he loaded the last box of water, headlights bounced on the other side of the field. He ran to grab Vittles. "Push the trailer back around here," Vittles shouted.

The two grabbed the connector, hauling the beast to the side of the back of the old outbuilding. Vittles grabbed several moth-eaten blankets to throw across the back of the trailer, hiding the contents from sight. He then pulled Ric into the old building, closing the door just enough to peek out.

From their vantage point they saw the headlights stopped in front of the ranch house. The lights moved slightly as a prominent figure exited the car. After a quick try of the door handle, the man raised his foot in the air. The door banged wide open, and the figure disappeared.

Vittles leaned in the direction of the exit. Ric grabbed his arm and pointed. On the opposite side of the car a small red glow came into focus. "Someone else is there," Ric said.

From inside they heard, "Ain't nobody here," followed by the shadow exiting.

"You sure about that Dak?"

"Yes sir."

"I'll let the queen know. Let's hope they find more than Clem's remains in that other field. I guess we should tell her to have her guys burn this place too. No sense in leaving a trail."

"Sheriff, why burn this too. If the land is abandoned, we can eminent domain and start operations up here once it all settles." They heard some mumbling and then viewed the car bounced back down the access road.

Once back in the dark, Vittles broke the silence. "We will take the smaller tractor out to the big one. If I can get that one going, we will put the shit in the bucket. If not, we take this baby and the trailer. Let's move."

MAXI

Walking along the main drag in Pride Ridge brought back memories of her little shoreline town. Specialty shops featuring western wear, cowboy hats, and prairie skirts along with the same tacky souvenir shops that seem to appear in every tourist town. Maxi paused in front of a window filled with cowboy boots to glance back. Behind her stood the same buzz cut who tried to interject into her conversation at the last rest area. The man stood out because he wore dress shoes with shorts.

Maxi walked a little further, Jerry keeping pace while Bobby strolled ahead. Zack had taught her not to turn around when she thought that someone was following her. Another life skill she never thought that she'd need.

How the times had changed!

Now, instead of reading the menu at The Moose Meat Café, she watched buzzcut pause across the street. She decided to test out Zack's other lesson, reverse direction or take a turn to see if your senses are on target.

They parked the car back about four blocks. She gave the dog's leash a quick pull and both responded by reversing direction. The intelligence of her two companions surprised her. They walked back to the boot store, again looking over her shoulder in the reflection. Buzzcut, who she now renamed creepy dude, came into her peripheral vision.

She sent Zack a quick text then strolled at a slower pace back to the car, happy that they opted for the main drag instead of one of the remote lots. Out of street view, she sat on one of the scattered iron benches. Bobby hopped up next to her to lay his head upon the back. Jerry stood at attention on the sidewalk.

As Maxi bent over and scratched Jerry's throat, she whispered, "Doesn't it suck to always be the responsible one?" The shepherd gave a quick tail wag in response. Her eyes hidden behind dark sunglasses, Maxi gave a slow glance in both directions, noting that creepy guy stood a half block away.

Balancing her cellphone on her lap, she enlarged the screen to snap a quick photo, promptly forwarded to Zack. After she looked at the picture to see an average looking man with no identifiable qualities. Bobby let out a small whine that brought her attention back to the street.

Zack leaned against the doorway, a few feet away from creepy dude.

SHERIFF

Once back in range, the Sheriff dialed the Senator's private number, the one used by high end donors and his most trusted minions. The first attempt went straight to voicemail. He waited ten minutes then tried again. Without a preamble, the Senator answered, "Why are you calling me?"

"Did you send that woman to start fires, literal and figuratively?" The deputy bounced the rear tire off the curb as he parallel parked in front of the office. The Sheriff dismissed him out of the car with a glare. He started to ask if he should leave the keys or roll down the windows. His answer, a fully erect middle finger followed.

The Sheriff heard a loud sigh at the other end and started to repeat his question. The Senator interrupted before he finished. "What fire?"

"Your she devil," the Sheriff started with, "basically came in here and said to shut it all down and then proceeded to set a football field of revenue on fire."

"Huh. Any other complications?"

"Not sure, sir. I'm told there might be a body or two in between the stalks when the fire inspector comes through—"

"Do we know whom the remains belong?"

The Sheriff laughed. "Possibly. I cannot commit either way," he said, using one of the Senator's favorite lines.

The silence that followed through the Sheriff off as did a flushed Marjorie stomping into the office, phone in hand. The Sheriff looked around to see her Mercedes parked directly behind where he sat.

She emerged from the office, face scrunched in a scowl, phone in one hand, fist in the other. Their eyes met through the tinted glass and held.

"Sheriff," the Senator's voice interrupted his thoughts, "this is something that you and Marjorie need to work out. May I suggest that you two—"

"She's standing here outside the car giving me the bitch eye."

"Ah–good. Good. Then this is all settled."

Not for the first time, the Sheriff wondered what planet the Senator resided on. Then again, maybe this was all about the money and the rest was just an illusion. He jumped as Majorie's fist banged the window. "Family of freaks," he muttered as he opened the door, ready for whatever wrath spilled from her mouth.

In a calm voice that her body betrayed, Majorie said, "I took care of two of your problems today, did you finish the third?"

The Sheriff tried to mimic her vocalics, "I went out there and there was nobody there and it looked like nobody had been there for a while."

"What's that supposed to mean?"

"What that means," the Sheriff slowed his cadence, "is that the place was abandoned, no food, water, lights off, tractor left mid-field. It looked like they packed up and left in a hurry. What about the other property?"

"The other property no longer exists." Majorie said.

"Did you find Clem's truck?"

"No." Marjorie's face rested in a tight neutral.

"Did you look?"

"The field burned a little hotter than expected. We retreated to the barn."

"And how did the barn burn?" the Sheriff asked. He could feel sweat dripping from his neck into the collar of his uniform.

"It didn't. My guys took what was there over to our rental. There wasn't much–almost like someone cleaned the place out first." Majorie waited for a comment. When the silence stayed a beat too long, she spoke, "My contact at the Pride Ridge confirmed that the Feds arrived today in one of those mobile units."

"Idiots," the Sheriff said. "I suppose I should go up there and see how my office can help."

"In the meantime, I put a call in to my uncle to see what he can find out. Always pays to be on the safe side."

"Is that what side we are on?"

Marjorie said nothing, just walked away to her car. The Sheriff watched in the side mirror as she spoke into her cellphone, her free hand rubbed her jaw. After the Mercedes sped passed him, he moved into his office. Dak and Elma were exchanging pleasantries as he entered. He tipped his hat in her direction then disappeared into the toilet.

When he returned, the Sheriff found Dak staring at the television and Elma gone.

ZACK

Zack walked around the long block to arrive just behind the man creepy dude. His version of creepy dude followed close behind. Two against one isn't a fair confrontation, yet even a couple blocks off the busy part of downtown had too many folks wandering by to see a grown man fight.

Donald hadn't responded with an I.D. yet. Waiting for that information would have been the safer of Zack's two choices. That or meet with his team. Instead of either, he circled back around. From his observation point, Zack watched creepy two move in a circle checking in each direction.

An older woman approached the creepy dude. He pointed in several directions and shrugged. Zack heard a faint, "Good luck finding your friends" in between car engines breaking up the sound. Creepy two walked in the direction of Zack and creepy dude. He counted to ten, then followed.

"I don't know where he went. The guy is like smoke at times." Zack could hear their conversation clearly from his position around the corner. Creepy dude said, "Well let's grab her and maybe we can get him later." He sent Maxi a quick text to load up the car.

Creepy two nixed that suggestion. "Our part is to watch and report. Do you want a kidnapping charge because I don't."

"Yeah, but—" Creepy two's sentence got cut off by Zack's arm pressing on his windpipe. Creepy dude one raised his fist at the same moment Zack pointed his Sig Saurer at the man's face. Instead of forward motion with his fist, creepy dude turned to run. Instinctively, Zack stuck his foot out. Maxi seeing the man stumble, sent Jerry to greet upon the fall.

Zack quickly zip-tied his guy and placed him gently against the wall. Jerry let out low growls in front of the other.

"He really going to bite me?" the man stared at the dog's teeth.

"Depends on your next move," Zack said as he zipped tied his wrists behind his back. "Crab crawl back to your friend, please." Once the two were out of view, Zack bent down to frisk both. One had a small ghost gun in his back waistband while the other had a matching Sig Sauer to Zack's.

Maxi arrived with Bobby in tow, who wagged his tail as he growled in harmony with Jerry. She handed Zack a plastic bag out of his backpack. He placed both guns in the baggie then inside his backpack then took close–up photos of both faces.

"Gentlemen, you wouldn't by chance want to save me sometime and tell me who you are and why you've been following us since Vermont?"

"Wait, these two followed us cross country?" Maxi said, adding, "Don't you have better things to do, like jobs."

The two men let out a few snorts. "Loved when you put that tracker in the pickup. Couldn't stop laughing at that one, especially if you saw the owners and his buddies."

"Tracker. Pickup. Holy shit you have been with me since Vermont. Wait were you the ones—" Maxi's hand covered her mouth to stop her words. Neither man spoke.

She jumped at Zack's touch. "Please wait in the car and do me a favor, send the photos to Donald and ask for a trash pickup at this location. He'll understand what you are looking for." A moment later the SUV beeped open, and a door slammed.

Zack surveyed both men in the awkward silence.

After waiting an uncomfortable amount of time, Zack repeated, "Who are you and who do you work for?" This time when no answer followed, he brought his boot down to catch the side of his creepy two's thigh. The man winced with pain yet did not speak.

He turned his attention to Maxi's creepy dude at the same moment a plain black cargo van pulled up on the sidewalk. The passenger, a linebacker dressed head to toe in black, walked over to do a fancy handshake with Zack, as the driver, an attractive Black woman in a Sheriff's uniform came around the side.

"What the hell are you doing in Fremont," Zack said to his old friend Trooper Harper.

"Donald wanted to make sure you had back up to your back up. By the way, this here is my sister Elma, a floater for the county Sheriff's division."

"Nice to meet you, Elma. Ever do time at the Amity location." She exchanged a quick glance with her brother then nodded yes. "Well, it looks like we may have our first lead here."

"Oh, we do," said Trooper Harper. "What's up with these two?"

"Since they won't share their names, dipshit and dim wad followed Maxi from Vermont. I believe if we look at my property cams, they probably are the ones Maxi saw on the trails too." He looked over at the two men. "You can still come clean."

"Stalking over state lines? That's a big one. Federal offense, I believe." Trooper Harper sneered in their direction. "I guess we should feel grateful that I am with the Feds. What am I doing with these two?"

"I take it Niza is clear?" Zack got a quick nod yes. "Can we hold them there on stalking charges for now. As we get further in, we can add on the rest."

"The rest?" Creeper one spoke as creeper two shushed him.

"We will die," he whispered, sounding like a scared child.

"This was supposed to be an easy gig and so far—"

The other screamed, "Shut up!" over the end of the sentence.

"Separate cells?" Trooper Harper sported a wide grin.

"Separate cells." Zack said. He helped load the two in the back of the van, surprised that they hadn't drawn a crowd. "You feel like doing a gun trace for me?" Zack handed over the baggie holding the two firearms.

"You took the Sig off one of them? Possible complication."

"Yes. Can you keep the results between you and me? And if you don't have the time, let me know. I took photos of the serials and can run them via Donald."

"I'm going to do the same – keep the boss in the loop." Trooper Harper hesitated then added, "You know a Sig means—"

"Yep."

"Alright then. I will be in touch." They repeated the complicated handshake before parting.

RIC

In the back of the old barn sat two homemade wheelbarrows. Both had the standard three wheels and double handles for pushing. The sizeable half trailer differed from a traditional one as both the wheels and the steering were slightly off balance and pulled. Vittles moved the first with ease while Ric struggled to move the second one from its space.

"I think this one is stuck," he said as he pointed to the back tire wedged within the wall.

"Okay," Vittles said, "take this one and get the grub you took along with two containers of gas from the front." He went over to inspect the other wagon. "Yeah, this one's a bust." Vittles went around the back to pull out the two garbage bags from the field. He hauled both on top of the food, near the handles.

"Make sure the gas doesn't spill," Vittles started to say. He kept an eye on Ric as he lifted the handles. "Stop!"

"What?" Ric stood still.

"Don't move. I have an idea." Vittles took out the gas cans then nodded at the field. "Let's go. I'll carry these for now and we can switch in a few."

The tires proved wobbly, the rows of plants plus the ruts in the middle brought added challenges, yet he managed to move the trailer close to the tractor in the field. In the meantime, Vittles practically sprinted through the field, poured the gas into the tank, and passed Ric on the way back with a quick, "I think we'll need more than two."

On his second return, Vittles found Ric crouched in the field, breathing hard. "You pour this in there," he pointed to the open gas cap," and I'm going to try to start her up. Keep your fingers crossed because hauling that trailer through the old fire road will be a total bitch."

Vittles let out a few "shits" and "fucks" as he worked. Ric moved back near the trailer and waited. The strain of the engine trying yet not turning over followed by another round of "shits" and "fucks," made the process interesting.

After sitting to the side for what seemed like forever, Ric climbed up next to Vittles. The cover sat on the floor with all the wiring exposed. Vittles grabbed wires at random, held on for a spark, then went to the next set. The process looked strange to Ric.

"Did you look for the key?" Ric said.

Vittles returned the suggestion with a scowl. "Clem would never leave the keys here," he said. "This thing is worth around a quarter mil. Where the old guy got the cash, I will never know but used and sometimes new shit would just show up on loan," he held up two fingers and air quoted on loan, "and he'd tell me to use it."

"Huh."

"Yeah. Clem used to let me take this baby out to the other field too. There's a trail around the backside that leads to the other barn." Ric's eyes open wide. "No, we do not want to go there."

"No shit," Ric said. "That Sheriff dude took me there once. Pretty evil place. I said silent prayers that Clem wouldn't make me go back there."

"Yeah, for all of his faults, Clem was a good guy. Didn't like the chemical shit – just the natural weeds. It was too bad about his barn—"

"The other barn is Clem's?"

"Was Clem's. Until the Sheriff—" The roar of the engine turning over interrupted Vittles thought. "Yeah man. Okay, shove all that stuff in the bucket," he pointed to Ric. The food and weed took up only a third of the space.

"You want the trailer too," Ric said, "because if yes, I'm going to need a hand."

With the trailer and supplies loaded, Vittles steered the monster into the woods, running through a chain linked fence hidden by overgrowth. "This here old fire road...of Pride Ridge....trails are not used...okay....meet us...lift on the far side."

The bucket plowed along, spewing parts of bushes, gravel, and rocks along the way. The rumble of the engine bouncing off the mountainsides and valley, sounded like thunder up close. Together, they bounced along, hands clinging to the metal frame. Each turn brought a new level of anxiety, punctuated by the stench of nervous sweat.

The further they moved from the farm; the more Ric's concerns grew. In the distance, a rusted-out ski lift wheel sat amongst the overgrown brush. Vittles started to raise a victory fist at the same time the tractor sputtered and died.

"Man, so close to the promise land," Vittles said as he jumped from the cab. "Let's get the shit into the trailer." Ric climbed down, jumping the last few feet.

They had the trailer out and loaded it within a few moments. Vittles leaned up against the tractor and stared out over the ridge. "This hike will be a bitch, but worth it."

Ric studied the overfilled trailer. "Maybe we should lighten the load, drink a few waters?" Ric threw a bottle at Vittles who made a one-handed catch. He followed up with a couple granola bars from the box.

"Thank you," Vittles said, adding, "any ideas on hiding the tractor?" A quick snort followed.

"Do you think they know it's missing?"

Vittles stood and took hold of the handles. He moved through the tall grass, creating a path along the way. Ric followed the ruts across what might have been a ski trail to an actual gravel road.

"The good news is we are at the end of the old fire road," Vittles said. "The bad news is the road slopes up for and while, and" he gestured in the direction of the trailer. "Let me know when you've had it."

Ric took hold of the handles, leaned into his body weight, to push the trailer forward.

PETE

Pete allowed Holey about ten minutes to go on with teamwork and disappearing and how this affects the entire mission. He waited patiently while hearing about the D.C. prima donnas who come into his territory and decide what his team will be doing when they don't have a clue about how things are run in the west.

"You pussies think you know it all, well let me tell you—" At the word pussy, Pete stood to lean across the table. Holey ranted from a seated position, now Pete towered over the senior agent, who stopped mid-sentence to scowl at Pete. "Problem, sir," he spat.

Pete waited a beat before replying. Keeping a tight grin on his face, Pete said, "Listen, Holey, your team is to answer to both you and me regarding this case. I do not report to you. Admiral Donald Atwood is my superior. If you have a problem with my presence, call him."

Pete took in a deep breath, "Now, is there a reason we are set up in a conference room instead of using the monstrosity in the parking lot that you insisted on taking?"

Archer Holey continued his stare down, breath now audible. "We decided that the mobile unit will be used for research and testing," his voice strained, western accent getting stronger. "The unit is here because taxpayers paid for that thing, and we are going to use it instead of wasting it sitting in a lot in Niza. Does that reason work for you?"

Pete nodded affirmatively.

"I don't suppose you want to share where you were?"

Without hesitation, Pete said, "Getting a coffee. The tail you put on me will confirm. Now about that tail—"

"I never put a tail on you. I have no reason and do not like what you are insinuating."

"I'm not insinuating anything, sir," Pete's voice stayed neutral. "I am telling you that someone followed behind me from your Niza office, in an agency vehicle." When Holey didn't speak, Pete continued. "Any new details on the fire outside of Amity?"

"Just an unpermitted field of marijuana. No big loss."

"Did anything else burn besides the field?"

"Nope—there's a barn out there too. The Sheriff checked it out and said it was empty. Probably just a competitive grower. Happens all the time out here. Like I said, you are in the wild, wild west."

"And the Sheriff told you this?" Pete asked. "Did he mention any casualties?"

"Not that I know of," Holey said.

"Good," Pete said. "Where is the rest of the team and what are they doing?"

"Agent Sellers is in the monstrosity, as you like to call our mobile unit, tracking down a lead. Bull was heading out to Amity. Not sure how far he got. The two back in Niza are still deep diving into back-alley payments."

"Thank you for the update. I'm going to check in and make a few calls. Meet back here at oh-fourteen?" Holey nodded approval.

Pete checked into his assigned room, and did a quick room scan to find one bug. This made him smile. He then went on his secure phone and booked a one-bedroom home up on the hill.

He made some noises by opening and closing drawers, flushing the toilet, and opening the slider. After checking that both phones were muted, he started to speak.

"Yes, I am checked into the Pride Ridge hotel with the team from Niza. I followed their mobile unit while another agent followed me. We have three team members here along with two back at the ranch." He laughed, then added, "yeah, I couldn't help myself. Right now, agent Brady is missing. We were supposed to make contact today and he never showed up. Any advice?"

Pete waited for a beat as if listening to another party before saying, "Got it. Will be in touch." His hand reached around the ornate lamp on the desk to disconnect the bug. "I am not playing games," he said as he flushed the miniature microphone down the toilet.

L.M. Pampuro

MAXI

The instructions Zack gave were simple–go to the front desk and ask about Ric, say she was there to pick up her son, and get out as soon as possible. She wore her hair tucked into a baseball hat, non-descript t-shirt and black yoga pants, along with shaded glasses. When Maxi commented that she looked like a spy in one of those cheesy movies, Zack had said she was a spy, and this was real life.

Here she leaned against a rustic wooden counter waiting for some guy named Sully to get back from the bathroom. Maxi took in her surroundings, floor to ceiling glass that reflected green trees along the mountain range. A ski lift visible off to the left, the corporate sponsor banner hanging off to one side, shifting with each slight breeze.

Outside the main entrance, an older man gestured to a younger longhair in a bright blue tie-dye. Both walked in together, the older of the two moving to the back of the counter.

"Are you Sully?" Maxi said, hoping that she wasn't wasting precious time waiting.

"I am he," Sully said, adding, "How may I help thee?" He made a small giggle that those who think they are clever tend to use. The younger kid let out a snort behind her. He had moved out of her sightline to an old couch piled against the far wall.

"I am Maxi Jacobs. I am here to pick up my son Ric." She extended her hand to shake Sully's who let a tremble escape at her touch. Maxi froze a smile on her face, yet her eyes gave a slight squint.

"Ric Jacobs, you say," Sully busied himself as he pulled out a thick book with *Guests* stamped on the front. He turned several pages back, moved his finger up and down the next set, and flipped back to the second page. His index finger hit a spot in the middle. "Checked out yesterday. I think he was on the airport shuttle. Ed, did you take a," he made a show of looking at the name, "Ric Malone on the airport shuttle yesterday?"

Ed, the tie-dyed youngster answered from across the room, "I may have. The bus was pretty full, you know."

"Well, there you have it," Sully gave his best smile, "Your boy checked out and went to the airport. Sorry I—" Before he could finish, Maxi flipped the book around and snapped a photo of the page.

With a clenched jaw, she said, "Look, there is no proof my son was on that bus. Where is he?" She thrust a recent picture of Ric taken in the woods behind her house into his face.

"I don't know. Did you try calling on one of those cellphones you all tether to your children?"

Maxi raised her hand back and spun around to Ed. In two strides she had Ric's photo in front of his face. "Was my child on your shuttle yesterday?"

Ed reached out to take the photo out of her hand. He studied it for a moment. As he handed it back, he glanced passed Maxi to see Sully give a quick head shake. "I'm sorry mam," Ed said, "I can't say either way. Like I mentioned, the bus was really crowded, and I just wanted to get the kids to the airport with their stuff, you know?"

Maxi's eyes softened then at once hardened as she turned back to Sully. "Please show me his room." In the back of her head, she heard Zack say do not go off script, yet she had a hunch.

"Cleaning crew came by yesterday." Sully now matched her glare as he added, "You got a warrant?"

"Do I need one?" Maxi barked back. She turned away to give her eyes a quick rub, producing a few tears in the process. In a much calmer voice, she said, "Look, he's my only child and I haven't heard from him in days. I am scared. If I could just see his room—"

"Lady I'd like to help you—"

Maxi turned and marched out of the building. As she rounded the corner she plowed into Zack, who softened the blow by bracing her with his hands, so they hit in the middle.

"They lied—" Maxi's face bright red with tears moving downward.

"Did you go off script?" he said.

"I don't know, maybe? That jerk—"

"—is probably checking Ric's room as we speak. Go to the car and I will take Bobby with me for faster tracking."

Zack gave a quick kiss to her forehead before disappearing into the building. With Jerry by her side, Maxi started back in the direction of where they had parked, out of sight of the main building yet in an area with other vehicles.

When Jerry stopped to take a pee, Maxi turned back to the building. Ed sulked along the building. He started to run in her direction, his movements putting Jerry on alert. The dog started with a low growl that morphed into a single bark.

Ed froze about fifteen feet away, mid stride. "Look," he said with a glance back to the building, "please don't let your dog eat me."

Maxi clapped once and pointed to the ground. Jerry circled back to lay by her feet, still emitting a low rumble from his mouth. Ed came a few feet closer than stopped.

Again, he looked back to the building. "I wanted you to know that your son wasn't on the bus yesterday–that I know for sure."

"Why did you lie?"

"Because Sully is in on it and that dude is mean." Ed squatted where he stood and ran his fingers through his hair. "I got to go" he said as he sprung back to his feet.

"Is there anything else you can tell me? I just want my kid back, you know?"

Ed hesitated before he spoke. "Ask the Sheriff in Amity–you may get lucky. But be careful. There's some shit—" He jumped at the sound of an ATV moving down the main trail. "I got to go." Ed followed the noise before Maxi could ask any more questions.

After inputting the notes on their conversation into her phone, Maxi moved to the opposite side of the SUV to wait for Zack.

ZACK

The black lab moved along the main building, tail wagging nose down as he sniffed the gravel. The dog followed a zig zag trail only he could see beyond the mountainside entrance to a second building that set back off the main trail. Here he sat by the door, tail rhythmically hitting the stairs.

The door handle turned easily into Zack's hand. Bobby nosed his way inside and headed down the hallway in a fast trot. There was little light inside. The smell of mold filled the air. On both sides, several doors lay propped open. From his vantage point, each room contained dorm-like conditions; two twin beds, and an old wooden nightstand between.

Bobby's whimper caught his attention. The dog ran in and out of the room at the opposite end. A duplicate of the others except for phone charger laying across the nightstand. Zack entered to find Ric's oversized gym bag on top of the luggage rack just inside the small closet. Clothes spilled out onto the floor. Bobby lay down in the middle of the clothes.

The second closet appeared empty apart from empty Monster cans and chip bags on the floor. Zack took photos of both closets along with one room shot from the door. With a snap of his fingers the black lab rose to follow out the door, giving a short whimper on exit.

Zack went into the room across the hall. Similarly, cans of empty soda and chip bags scattered around the room. Unmade beds and empty closets confirmed the rooms had not been touched since the camp officially closed. He made the same quick inspection of each room on his way back to the side entrance. Two other rooms held personal items, clothes, suitcases, in the communal bathroom several toiletries' bags, including Ric's, hung on wooden pegs opposite the sinks.

Again, Zack took a quick photo.

Bobby's quick bark brought Zack's attention to the entrance door near Ric's room. Sully, the man from the front desk slammed the door against the wall and headed into Ric's room. "Son of a bitch," rebounded down the hallway along with several "shits." Zack scurried across to a room on the same side. He pulled the yellowing blinds to cover up the afternoon sun before leaning just out of view. Bobby lay at the base of one of the twins.

The shadow hovered against the opposite wall with one side in constant motion. "Someone was here asking about the kid," Sully said. Zack pressed the record button and turned his phone microphone into the hallway. "They had pictures of the boy." The shadow got more refined into a silhouette of someone leaning on a doorframe. Zack took a step backwards.

"Said she was his mother. Begged to see his room but I said no – not without a warrant." Zack's free hand clenched and unclenched. "What was I supposed to say. I got nobody to do the cleaning—" The door to the building squeaked open. The shadow now stretched down the hallway. "Ed confirmed he took the kid to the airport, so we should be okay." Zack heard the click of the door shutting along with "oh fuckinshit."

He waited for a minute then both he and Bobby went out the opposite way. One snap of the fingers and Bobby followed to the mountain side. He couldn't hear the conversation yet if one arm gestures were any indication, Sully was not having a good day. Far too engrossed with whoever he spoke to, Sully did not notice the man in the baseball cap and his dog strolling by.

Just past the main building, it was Zack's turn to make a call.

"I'm in a conference," Pete answered with their code for there are others in this room.

"Okay."

"I got my earpiece in."

"Pete, I got a lead on the nephew end that I need one of your guys to follow up on. I am going to send you some audio. Could you have an agent visit the manager of the camp, Sully something, play the audio, and get me his reaction?"

"No worries. Did you get a chance to review my last correspondence?"

Zack clicked on his encrypted messenger. Two files waited for his review. "I have been a bit busy. Would you like me to scan now or wait until I have the opportunity, one hour max, to digest the materials? There is one from the chief there too."

Pete let out a short laugh at their code name for Donald Atwood. "I have yet to scan that one also," Softening his voice, Pete added, "Just buy the dress. I am sure she'll look adorable."

"Why do I care about a dress? I take it your bossman over there is taking an interest in our call." A loud cough, followed by an *excuse me*, came through the speaker. "Doesn't matter. We went to Airbnb. Less traceable just up the mountain. Donald got us a house across from the C building."

"Look, it's not spoiling the kid if all of her friends are wearing the same dress. And we can afford it."

"Okay, see you in a few," Zack said.

PETE

"Love you too honey." Pete hit end and met Holey's stare. "You got daughters?" he said.

Holey dropped his shoulders, visibly relaxing. "Nope – no kids that I know of." He let a short laugh out.

"Well let me tell you…" Pete proceeded to rant about his imaginary daughter and her expensive middle school dance dress. The more he spoke about this mini crisis, the more his teammate slumped. After a good amount of time, Pete rose from his chair and stretched his hands up to the ceiling. "I'm going to head downstairs, grab a sandwich and look at the dress options my wife sent."

"Does your opinion matter?"

"Not in the least," Pete laughed at the thought. "Because I travel so much for work, the wife likes to keep me involved in some of the life events of the kids. Says it normalizes our life." Pete gave a quick shrug. "Could be worse."

Kit Sellers leaned against Pete's doorway as he stepped out of the elevator. He swiped his key and gestured for her to follow inside. Pete brought his finger to his lip, indicating quiet while he rescanned his room for bugs. This time the small device appeared wedged into the outside of the dorm fridge.

Pete took the device, reached into the refrigerator to gather, and pressed cheese around the microphone, then tossed the lump out the slider onto the weeds. He did one more scan that included the bathroom. When nothing showed, he smiled in Kit's direction. "We can talk now," he said, voice hushed as he turned on the television.

RIC

The ski patrol building had holes carved into the wood along with a family of birds living inside. The birds flew around the room, finally finding the door that Ric and Vittles had pried open. The single room, dust, and spider webs visible through the limited sunlight, had old skis and leftover gloves molding in the corner.

Vittles stumbled around, picking through the clothes, and slamming empty lockers, all the while stirring more haze into the air. "I can't find the damn thing," he muttered as he ripped open another locker.

"Can I help look?" Ric said, he backed into the sun as he spoke.

"My dude said he left a phone up here earlier. I'm supposed to call if we made it to this point."

Ric pondered the part about *if they made it* here for a second. "Maybe I should look in the other building?"

"Other building," Vittles pushed past Ric. Just up the hill attached to the rusting lift, an old shack where the lifties once watched skiers coming off the chair still stood. "Well, I'll be damned." Beyond the lifty shack, near the construction of a newer lift, a small, abandoned lodge added to the landscape. "I'll look in the shack. See if you can get into that lodge over there."

Ric gave a quick salute. He climbed up the straw covered hill, slipping a few times into the mud hidden underneath. Before he made it to the building, Vittles had yelled "not here" in his direction. The lower door had a newer padlock on the front along with plywood covering what must be a window.

Ric moved around the corner, keeping one hand on the building to steady his steps. He climbed up the creaky side stairs to meet the same fate at this door. As he rounded the corner, a newer pickup idled out front. *Pride Ridge* embossed on the side. The upper doors to the lodge lay prop open with cinder blocks holding both in place.

He froze as the memory of the last time he saw that truck surfaced.

First instincts said to steal the truck, pick up Vittles and get as far away from here as possible, yet Ric hesitated, chewing on his index finger, focused fixed on the idling truck. A hand on his shoulder made Ric jump as another covered his mouth before he screamed.

"Dude, you've got to relax," Vittles voice brought instant calm, "That there is our ride." In one motion Vittles bounced to the open doors, letting out a long "DUUUUDE" as he approached. In a tie-dyed blur, the two men bro hugged. "Dude" ringing out in harmony.

"I heard about the fire and thought you were dead," Ed said, as the two hopped up and down then did a serve around each other.

"I thought I was, dude, but then me and the little dude," Vittles waved Ric over, "did the ultimate escape, with two big baggies, ha ha ha." Vittles ended with a stoner laugh that made Ric wonder if he was sampling again.

Ed embraced Ric in a tight bear hug. "Oh man, you are alive!" He turned his attention back to Vittles and yelled, "He's alive!" Ed and Ric did the hippie bounce for a minute. When they stopped Ric caught sight of the tears in Ed's eyes. "Dubs at your service," Ed said with a bow.

"You two know each other," Vittles said.

"Remember I told you about the dude that Sully sent me to get?" Vittles nodded. Gesturing with both hands in Ric's direction, Ed said, "Wa–la!"

"No shit?" Vittles said, staring at Ric for an extra beat. "Let's get the baggies," he nodded, instructing Ric to "watch the truck."

Ed babbled as they walked away, "Man, I was worried about that dude, especially after the other one—"

"Yeah, man, that was a mess. Do you think—"

"Oh man, I got to tell him about his mom." Vittles turned up hill. "Hey dude," he waved both hands above his head getting Ric's attention, "Your mom is looking for you!"

"My mom?"

Ed held up his index finger, "Remind me when we get back." He turned, "That is important to remember."

The two vanished under the hill, voices becoming inaudible. Ric sat down on the wooden bench held back to the building with a heavy chain, wondering for the first time if safety was an illusion. As happy as he was to see Dubs again, all these connections gave him the willies. *Maybe this is just a small-town thing – like back home.* The golden overgrown stalks cut through groups of pines and maples, green vines climbing up both to create a barrier between path and woods.

The rustle of wind was the only sound. Nature's silence increased Ric's perspiration, sweat again dampening his armpits. His heartbeat increased, yet breath became rhythmic, and his eyes began to close. The sun, high up in a cloudless sky, beat down its warmth. The toll of the last twenty-four hours made an appearance as Ric slouched over the rail of the bench.

MAXI

Patience wore thin within the walls of the slope side house that Maxi and Zack rented from Airbnb. Donald had used fake names to make the reservation, getting Zack the code needed to enter. Pete showed up just after they arrived, immediately setting up his laptop and satellite encrypted Wi-Fi in the back, windowless bedroom.

The three huddled around the screen, waiting for Donald to show up for a briefing. Maxi paced in and out, first bringing back cups of tea for everyone. Her second trip included the prepackaged sandwiches she and Zack bought in town.

When no one touched the food or drink, she cleared it all out, only to return with three boxed waters. Zack now had his laptop hooked onto the system. A detailed map of the area took up his entire screen. Maxi pointed to one of the red circles.

"What are these?" she said.

"The red circles are areas that the D.E.A. are now investigating," Pete said. "This one," he pointed to an area just outside Amity, "is a marijuana field that recently burned. The senior agent from Niza, Archer Holey, keeps repeating that a rival marijuana gang is behind the fire."

"And you don't agree?" Zack interrupted.

"I think everything going on here is connected," Pete stated. "I'm not sure how yet, but as we know, there are no coincidences, at least from my experience."

"The kid at the camp yesterday had said to ask the Sheriff in Amity about Ric. Bobby already confirmed that he was there at some point." She glanced over in time to catch her brother give Zack an exaggerated eyeroll. "I know you two don't think that the dog's observations matter, yet if they didn't why do we bring them?" Maxi waited for an answer, foot tapping, arms crossed just under her breasts. She raised an eyebrow in the direction of both men. "Well, explain!"

Before Zack could respond, Pete said, "She's got a point. The Sheriff is on the list. Maybe it wouldn't hurt to rattle his cage."

"Yeah, let's rattle that piece of crap!" Maxi shouted.

"Maxi," Zack said, his voice softening, "I understand you are anxious, but please hear me out. Can we at least agree to wait until the morning to," lips curving up, "rattle the crap Sheriff's cage?" He waited a beat then continued, "See what Donald has and put a plan together—"

"A plan to what?" Maxi interjected.

"A plan to—" Zack didn't finish his sentence as Donald Atwood chose that moment to sign on.

"Okay boys," Donald squinted into his monitor, "and is that Maxi I see?" Maxi gave a quick wave. "Well okay. Why don't you boys start, Maxi I use boys as a gender-neutral term, and then I will add to what you already have as Kit Sellers is now sending reports directly to me and my team here forwards summaries back to Niza."

"Why is that, Donald?" Zack said.

Before he could answer, Pete said, "Zack did you scan the house for bugs when you arrived?"

"Yes," Zack said, voice tightening. "Why do you ask? That is protocol in this type of investigation."

"Chill brother," Pete said, "I found two bugs in my hotel room. The first was upon arrival. I had left the room to meet with Holey." Pete shook his head, "who was a bit pissed I took off earlier from the group to meet with Zack—"

"Did he know that's where you were?"

"No sir, but he did try to put a tail on me." All except Maxi laughed. "After the meeting, I went back to my room to meet with Kit Sellers. I, again, scanned the premises to find another bug, this one hidden a bit better. My original plan to stay here with Zack and Max might compromise what we are trying to do here, so I am thinking about making a show to stay there and taking out each bug as I get back to my room."

"You think there will be others?"

"Sir, if I have learned anything in this investigation is those guys are consistent. Sellers shared two important items," Pete said. "First, Marjorie Lofsmen is in the area and has offered a bounty on Zack."

"Holy shitter bugs!" Maxi exclaimed as she reached for her husband's hand.

Zack opened his mouth to speak, and Pete shooed him away, "I was going to tell you about that. The second and this one I see as an immediate concern, is, again according to Kit Sellers, the deputy, Dak something, just made a twenty-five thousand-dollar donation to the Senator's PACT account in the Caribbean. The key here—"

"How much does a deputy make a year?" Maxi said.

"That is the million-dollar question, sis!" Pete said, excitedly changing his voice to a higher pitch. "According to the state website, cause salaries are public information, between fifty-five and ninety a year, including overtime."

"That's not good news. I mean the deputy could treat donating to the Senator as some do donate to a church or non-profit. On the higher side of those numbers, twenty-five grand isn't a lot," Zack added.

"It is if your tax return shows you making only forty and we all know that political donations are not tax deductible, even in Fremont," Pete added. "Now would this be reasonable to start the pick-ups of people we know are involved in this mess?"

"Could be. Could be," Donald said. "I will add his name to the list I have. Right now, I see these lower-level guys taking the fall unless they turn evidence against our internal suspects." He let that thought sink in. "Zack what do you have?"

"Donald, I have two questions, first, any word on the two yahoos that were picked up in town today?"

Maxi sat erect. "Please tell me you got those two," she whispered.

Rustling of paper and clicking on the computer could be heard as they watched Donald flip through a stack of hard copies. When that produced nothing, he concentrated on his screen, the sound of keys filling the pause. "I don't see anything here. Please give me the details."

Zack went on to report on the two men who followed him and Maxi ending with the pickup in town.

"Did I miss anything, Max?" She responded with a head shake no.

"I see nothing about a pickup of either party. When did this happen?"

As he gave the additional information, Zack presented the photos he took earlier. Donald confirmed receipt and forwarded the pictures to Kit Sellers for more information. "I trust Kit Sellers with my life," he added.

"Then I guess my second question isn't relevant."

"Go on, Zack, ask what's on your mind."

"Donald, I did a quick search of all members of the team to try and see who might be on our side. All came up with bio's except—"

"Kit Sellers. I know Zack. She was once in witness protection and now works for us—"

"Donald, can you share her agency connection?"

"Zack, can I ask why? And don't say you have a feeling." Both men fell silent.

"I have a few questions, if I may?" Maxi interrupted.

Before the others could speak, Donald said, "Go ahead, Maxi," surprising both Pete and Zack.

"I want my son back," she started to say in a relatively calm voice. "Ric is my priority and although I see many connections to this other stuff," she made a sweeping gesture with one hand, "all I care about is my son. So, what I want to know is when can you start officially interviewing these people," her voice now raised, "so I can get my son back."

Zack reached to rest one hand on her shoulder, gently rubbing her neck. She tried to shrug him away.

"Maxi," Donald said, "I know this is hard for you. If you remember Aruba—"

"Aruba was hard for all of us, Donald."

"Yes, yes. I understand." He waited for a pause. "Maxi, go see the Sheriff tomorrow. Ask him any questions you have; yet may I please ask that you don't indicate that Zack is with you or that you have a connection?"

"She'll need back up, Donald," Zack said.

"I know that" Donald snipped back. "And you will be close by. Maxi is going to kick the snake's den and believe me boys, what slithers out will not be pretty." He turned his attention back to Maxi. "Now Maxi, once you find Ric, and you will find him, I need you to promise me the two of you will high tail it out of Fremont as soon as possible. Can you promise me that?"

Maxi gave a quick glance to her brother and Zack before nodding yes. Donald asked Maxi for privacy, and she obliged.

In the hallway she could hear bits of conversation, most of which she already knew. Her hand reached down to scratch Jerry's head. She waited for Zack to exit, proclaiming, "I just sold my soul to the devil," to which he replied, "Not even close."

L.M. Pampuro

SHERIFF

The Sheriff stood just outside on the main throughway in his town. He leaned up against his patrol car and watched the Mercedes crawl down the street to stop in front of him.

As a woman approached, he said, "I just got off the phone with the boss, who is not happy."

She stopped mid step. "We should discuss this inside."

"Not sure we have anything to discuss." The Sheriff took a long drag off the cigarette in his right hand, his eyes not leaving hers. "The boss said to get this mess under control, and he wants to know how I'm, not you," he pointed at her chest, "is going to clean up this mess and make up one hundred thou in revenue."

Marjorie kept her voice low and steady. "We still have the barn. That's where the—"

The Sheriff raised his hand to cut her off. "Are you as dumb as those fancy colleges you supposedly attended?" He didn't wait for an answer. "We have the D.E.A. crawling up our butts because an illegal pot field went up in smoke along with that other thing." He let that sink in before adding, "And according to my friend in Niza, the Feds are holed up at Pride Ridge, taking over the conference room and half the hotel."

"So, let's burn it down. We can have a pig roast with Feds." Marjorie burst into a laughing fit as the Sheriff's mouth hung open. Each time he started to speak, he considered what he was about to say and stopped. As he watched Marjorie sputter while wiping tears from laughter away from her face, his right hand dropped the cigarette butt to rub against his revolver, a gift from his father when he joined the force.

He pointed towards the office door, yet Marjorie waved him off. "I have some recon to do," she said as she stalked back to her car. The Sheriff watched her drive away then observed a plain SUV take the empty spot. The driver lowered the windows on all sides just enough for him to see a couple dog noses pop out.

Upon exiting, a large German Shepherd followed, off leash. The woman waved one hand as the dog sat and between her and the car. A second dog's nose could be seen hanging out the window. The Sheriff couldn't make out what the woman said to the other animal as she closed the door.

As their eyes met, her face went from a small smile to neutral. With a German Shepherd by her side, she stepped in his direction.

"That is one well behaved dog you got there," he said, noting the breed.

"Yes," Maxi gave her fingers a quick snap as Jerry sat at attention. "I am looking for the police chief or Sheriff of this area." Her tone gave zero emotion.

"That would be me mam," the Sheriff performed a well-practiced tilt of his hat. "What can I do for you?"

"We should talk inside your office," the woman said as she pushed past him to open the door. The dog followed.

"I'm sorry but the dog can't come in. And even as behaved as he is, the animal should be on a leash."

"This animal is a trained emotional support animal. By the American Disabilities Act, he can go anywhere with me, including government buildings." Maxi gestured with one hand, "Sheriff."

The Sheriff looked around to see if anyone heard the exchange. Apart from a family across the way, the main drag appeared empty. Unusual for midday. He followed her into the lobby area, pushed open the swinging door, and took a position on the other side of the counter. The dog circled the perimeter of the lobby, thumped his tail twice, and sat next to the counter with only the top of its head in view.

"How can I help you?" he said.

Maxi noted the attempt to take back the lead. "My son is missing," Maxi said. She waited for a response, yet the Sheriff only stared back.

After a few moments of silence, a shake of the head returned his focus to Maxi. She stood perfectly still and glared at him. "Let's see, we have a form for that," the Sheriff said as he shuffled through a few papers. He brought the yellow form to the counter before stumbling for a pen. "If you wouldn't mind—"

"I would mind, Sheriff. My son was supposed to be on a plane back east two days ago yet never made it on the plane. One of his last know locations was here, in this office." She could see the sweat forming on his forehead, near where his hat met skin.

"If I may ask, why would you think that?" The Sheriff's voice level. The woman picked up the form as the Sheriff stared her down. "I asked you a question," his voice now rising.

"I am thinking how to respond to your query, Sheriff as so you will not think that I am crazy." The Sheriff's shoulders came down a few inches. "This therapy dog," she pointed down, "was my son's dog and has the ability to track my son's scent, which is present, at least in the lobby out here."

"A lot of people come through this lobby. Do you have a picture? Maybe I can recall your boy." The woman handed him a photo taken on a hike right before Ric had left to come out west. The Sheriff's eyes open a little wider with recognition. He waited a minute before handing the photo back.

"I'm sorry mam, but your boy looks like all the rest who have stopped recently. I can't say I recall him." The dog let out a low growl. "Now if you'd like to fill out that report form, I can get him in the database, and we can see if one of my colleagues knows your boy."

He watched as the woman stuffed the form into the canvas bag on her shoulder along with the photo. She thanked the Sheriff for his time. "I guess I will try the next town over."

"We could just do the database," the Sheriff said.

"Thank you, no. My son was out here at a camp up the road. They suggested I try here. I think I'll go in another direction close to the camp."

The Sheriff gave a quick nod, adding, "Let me know how I can help. We are a small force, just me and my deputy, yet we cover a lot of ground."

The woman looked over with her eyes wide, mouth slightly open, in a hopeful expression. "Maybe your deputy has seen him?"

"Maybe. He'll be here tomorrow if you want to come back."

"Yes, yes, that would be great! Thank you, Sheriff. You just gave me hope."

The Sheriff watched her through the window. He slammed his fingers against the numbers on his desk phone as he extended the cord to lean against the window. The woman's SUV turned the corner, plate out of view.

He listened to the phone on the other end ring. When a voice answered, the Sheriff stated, "We got trouble."

MAXI

Maxi made a quick exit, forcing herself to walk back to the car. Jerry jumped in the back seat.

Maxi pulled out of the parking space and turned down the side street before he could make her plate. The Sheriff had Ric's name and little else.

"It took all my restraint not to punch that gas bag in the face." She pulled over and turned her focus to Zack, "That buffalo butt lied to my face. The eyes gave it away and the cow shit brains had sweat pouring from the rim of that dumb cowboy hat." She took in a deep breath, "He's a sleaze and guilty of all of the above. I just know it."

Zack petted Jerry. "You did great boy!" He smiled Maxi's way, "as did you, my love. Did you plant the bug?"

"Yes, right under the rim of the counter. Do you think he'd be that stupid?"

"I sure hope so. We got Pete's guy doing the monitoring so we shall see." Zack pulled out his phone. "I say let's take a ride by that pot field that just burned and grab a late lunch a couple town over. There is another ski town along the way, and we can circle back on the highway."

"Why do you want to see a burned-out marijuana field?"

"I think this is all connected, the dark money, the Senator and Sheriff, and I hate to even say this, but I think Ric's disappearance figures in somehow, but I haven't figured out the how."

L.M. Pampuro

Maxi nodded as she drove, trying to solve the puzzle.

ARCHER HOLEY

Archer Holey hated the inefficiencies of his current situation yet loved the additions to his bank account. Using civilians was a brilliant idea yet each presented its own challenge. At least the ones they used could be eliminated without much fuss. And in the end, everyone would win!

As the talk radio host debated with another D.C. punk about getting guns off the street, something that Holey knew would never happen, although he also thought they'd never legalize weed either. Too bad on that one as the Senator had to branch out into other things to raise added campaign funds.

Why Marjorie ordered the field burned, he'd never know. There was at least half a mil of harvest ready to go. His high school chum did a good job-some really good times.

The road curved around a group of pines and Pride Ridge Two's new lodge glowed in the distance. He let out a chuckle. Those damn environmentalists never had a chance of blocking that thing. A shiny new Leitner-Poma lift sat ready to roll once snow hits. What a brilliant deal that was bringing both jobs and resort expansions.

Now he just needed to cut a bit more dead weight Marjorie created. If the woman wasn't so good in bed, or his boss' niece, she would probably be worm food by now too.

Another situation that he should have known better but didn't care. Holey followed the service road that ran parallel to the mountain, parking next to the old bunkhouse. In the winter all the workers they brought up from some island would be housed here. Last week's college boys slash trail cleaners are now long gone. Rooms should be emptied of their existence and waiting on the others.

Inside the lobby, Sully sat behind the desk, the light from the computer screen reflecting in the dark of the room. Holey had hired Sully as a favor to his then wife. "He'd be a good one for what you need," she had said.

And for the most part that had been true. Sully was a good guy, just a few doughnuts short of a dozen, in his opinion, not that his thoughts mattered. Sully called the Sheriff, and the Sheriff called him. "If you can burn down a weed field, you can do this too," he was told.

That damn weed field. His boots still smelled like gasoline.

He screwed the silencer onto his Glock 17, placing the gun in the waistband by his back before rising out of the car. "Hey Sully," he greeted his friend since high school at the door.

"Archie Holey well this is a surprise."

"Yeah, I got headquarters set up down the way and thought I'd stop in. Marjorie tells me you had visitors."

Sully scratched the left side of his head with his right hand. "Yep," he said. Holey waited for more, yet the other man remained quiet.

"I thought I'd take a look around. Do you mind?" Sully gave a shrug.

Holey walked out in the direction of the old ski lift, then moved back around to circle the old bunkhouse.

He walked through the hallway to the other exit, followed the side of the building, and appeared again in the entrance door, Sully now leaning out the opposite side of the building, trying for a glimpse.

With a clean motion, Archer Holey brought the gun around. Two puff sounds discharged into the air. He watched Sully's body go rigid and fall against the frame.

L.M. Pampuro

RIC

"Yo, Ric," Vittles shook him awake. "We got to go, now." Dubs sat in the driver's seat of the running pickup; garbage bags loaded in the back. "Good job guarding the truck," he added with a laugh.

Ric stood and stretched, the stench from his pits bringing tears to his eyes. "Where are we going?" he said as he climbed in between Dubs and Vittles on the front bench seat. A mist of marijuana lingered in the air with Chalk Dust Torture by Phish filling in the silence.

"I told you I'd take care of you," Dubs said, adding, "Bonus you hooked up with Vittles here." The two-fist bumped across Ric's view. "We need to get to our distribution center just outside of Niza to get rid of this stuff—"

"Before anyone comes to look for it," Vittles said.

"Or you." Dubs sounded serious. "I can't bring you back to Sully because he'll turn you in to that dangle bag in Amity. Sully turned out to be not so nice." Dubs said this as if a new revelation had just formed.

"And we can't take you with us on the drop, because our guy is tweaked when we come in, never mind a new face." The truck bounced in and out of the ruts that melting snow created on the service road. Dubs held tight to the wheel, occasionally letting out a "Wee" or a "Whoa" along the way.

"But no worries, dude," Vittles said, "because I got this. There is this old ranch that my buddy Clem runs—"

"Vittles," Ric placed one hand on his shoulder, "that's where we came from. Remember we took the tractor and carried the bags from the field."

"Oh yeah, dude," Vittles turned his attention back to Dubs, "there are about four more bags in the bed of Clem's truck down by the field that burned.

"No shit," Dubs said. "That would bring our haul to—"

"A lot of tour money. But we can't go there because they burned Clem too and his ghost will haunt us."

"And the people who shot Clem," Ric said. The three sat in silence as "Black Peter" by The Grateful Dead mixing with static played through the speakers.

"What if," Vittles started to speak, "wait no." He reached into the glove compartment, pulled out a packed pipe, and with a flick of a lighter, took a long inhale. After a pause, he slowly released the smoke into the air. "Wait, Dubs man, are they working on the old mid lodge up by the ridge?"

Dubs shook his head side to side, as Ric jumped in, "As part of the National Parks program I was working on," all three gave an eyeroll, "that old lodge had supplies in for us, when we were clearing trails. We closed it up the second to the last day."

"Dude!" Dubs high-fived Ric. "We can hang there. Brilliant."

"Hey Dubs, can't we just go to your place?" Vittles asked.

Dubs foot hit the brakes, sending all three forward against the dash. "What the hell?" Vittles screamed.

"My place! You want to go to my place?" Dubs' voice shook the truck. "Dude, we have garbage bags of stolen weed in the back—"

"Not exactly stolen. We saved these from the fire," Vittles joked.

"Yeah, that would be a good explanation to my landlord and roommates. Plus, this one's mother– imagine the trouble we'd all be in." Dubs sat back and let that thought linger. Ric blocked his hand from shifting back into gear.

"What about my mother?" Ric cut through the stoner ramble. "You said his mother, what about her? Are my mom and stepdad here?"

Dubs rubbed both eyes with the front of his wrists. He snuck a glance at Vittles who just shrugged. "Weed would be a two-way split," Vittles mumbled.

"Come on man, did you see my mother or stepfather?"

Dubs put the truck in drive to continue on the unkempt road. He held his index finger up to indicate he needed a minute as he went, finally speaking after a few miles. "Your mom came looking for you at the camp. She had a police dog with her, I didn't see a dude."

"Police dog," Ric said as he tapped his hands on his legs, "Oh, you mean Jerry. He's retired F.B.I."

For the second time Dubs slammed on the brakes. "Retired F.B.I.?"

"Yeah, my stepdad got him somehow and mom renamed him Jerry Garcia. Our other dog, a black lab, is Bobby Weir."

"You named an ex-F.B.I. dog after Garcia?" Vittles said with awe.

"No, my mom did. Remember, my mom, the deadhead?" He turned back to Dubs, "Did you talk to her?"

Dubs nodded. "I told her to go see the Sheriff."

"You did what?"

"Look dude, that was the last place I saw you before today. We are happy to get you back to your family, but business first."

Ric swallowed hard and rested his head in one hand. Vittles leaned over, in a quiet voice, he said, "Look man, we have waited for this our whole lives—"

"I don't care about the weed or the money or any of this. The Sheriff wouldn't help me charge my phone and I finally get an S.O.S. text through to my stepdad, my mom is here, and..." The truck veered around an old water tower and an abandoned lodge appeared.

Dubs slowed next to overgrown weeds that surrounded the loading area. "I thought you said that you campers cleared this?"

"No, I said this is where we stashed our gear and food. Now about my mother..."

Both men jumped out of the truck at the same time. One pulled open the garage door while the other grabbed one of the garbage bags. Ric sat and waited.

"Hey, can you give us a hand with this stuff," Vittles voice came from the truck bed. Ric slid across the seat to move just outside the back of the truck. Vittles handed off a case of water and the box of granola bars they took from Clem's. "Dubs will tell you where this goes."

L.M. Pampuro

By the time Ric dragged a bag inside the garage, long folding tables scattered with sandwich bags and three beam scales were set-up in the middle. Dubs already had the garbage bag open at one end, buds spilling out. Vittles followed with the second garbage bag.

"There's a lot of weed here, dude," Vittles said.

"I got a deal for you," Dubs looked up at Ric, "Help us divide up the first bag and when I bring the breakup to my Niza contact, I will drop you off wherever."

Ric hesitated yet agreed.

MAXI

They drove out of Amity along an old road with a severe drop off on the passengers' side. Zack maneuvered around the deep potholes and ruts, while keeping all four tires on the surface. "This will be easier on the way back," he said a few times, doing a head nod at the rocky slopes jetting upward on the opposite side.

Their path followed the faint spell of marijuana that rose from a field that had burned, its only indication of existence being a large black rectangle in the middle of a lush valley.

"Arson," Zack said more to himself, yet when Maxi asked him to explain, he continued, pointing at the shape. "See how none of the trees along the side or the space in between the field has burned marks?" Maxi sat up taller to look out. "That is a sign of a controlled burn. Whoever set the field on fire wanted the crop gone but didn't want a wildfire to start."

"What does this mean for us?"

"Someone wanted that field gone. Donald said that there were two bodies in the charred middle." Maxi tensed as Zack reached for her hand. "From the DNA samples, neither were Ric."

"That should have been the lead, buddy."

"You are right, and I am sorry." He gave her hand slight squeeze, then continued, "I'm curious what is in that barn. The D.E.A. folks reported it to be empty, yet the building was spared for a reason."

"How do you know that?"

"Because, darling, there is always a reason." Zack pulled off into an area marked *Scenic Overlook* just as an old pickup towing an older airstream pulled passed heading in the opposite direction. He gave the driver a short chin nod as he went by. "I want to get closer."

"Why and how?" Maxi thought she was used to Zack's mind leaving the scene. In these focused moments, she, and everything else around them disappeared, yet at times like this, her hands rubbed against her stomach as it churned acid.

In between the SUV and the barn rested some scrubs and dirt, yet very little cover. "I could just walk up. I don't see any cars. Or you can drive me, though if someone were to show up, I could get away on foot easier than in the car..." Maxi waited as Zack mumbled through different options, most of which she couldn't visualize.

Without a word, Zack went back into the driver's seat and brought the SUV around the bend. The road is divided to continue around the ridge or move in the direction of the barn. One stayed paved while the other turned to gravel.

He chose the gravel, which he followed around the side of the barn, into the woods along the well-done field. Zack stopped behind an old pickup truck, just out of sight. "Hang here for a minute," he said.

Two large garbage bags sat untouched in the bed along with a good-sized picnic cooler. Inside the cooler Zack found about a dozen sandwiches and some water. He felt one of the wet water bottles, cool to his touch in approximate to the melted ice.

Maximum Panic

He went around to the cab. Keys hung in the ignition, cellphone resting in the middle of the bench seat. With his cellphone, Zack took photos of the cab of the truck and the bed. He left the cab open, then walked back over to Maxi. "I need Bobby for a minute."

The lab ran around the truck three times before hopping into the cab with a single push. The dog sniffed around the entire area then sat in the middle, tail thumping while releasing short whines. "Just as I thought," Zack said as he patted the dog on the head.

With a wave of Zack's hand, the dog leaped out to run back to Maxi. Zack opened the cooler in the back and took out two sandwiches. Both flew like frisbees into the woods. In the first bag, he placed the other phone, before concentrating again on the garbage bags. One whiff of the contents gave way that they were harvested before the field burned. "But why are they here?"

In the second sandwich bag Zack placed a few samples from each garbage bag. He knotted both ends back to their original form. Turning back to his vehicle, Maxi appeared at his side. "Car," she said, as he followed her finger past the barn, puffs of dirt kicked up behind a Sheriff's car and a convertible.

"Move the car further down this path," Zack pointed passed the pickup to the dirt road beyond. "I am going around the side to try to hear who is there. If you see me in trouble, call Pete and get the hell out of here—actually text Pete my location and go to the other end of this field." His arms went around Maxi's still body, as he kissed her on the head. "I'll be right back, promise."

Maxi watched as Zack followed the tree line that led to the barn before climbing into the driver's seat, the SUV still running. Once in drive, she let the engine boost its own momentum while she finessed around the pickup in between the trees. At the opposite end, just into the pines, she parked and texted Pete.

Location. Found weed and truck. Zack sneaking around the barn. Two cars Sheriff plus.

Both dogs got out to pee at the same spot. Bobby ran further into the woods, while Jerry prodded Maxi to follow by sticking his nose against the back of her legs.

"Okay boys," Maxi said, "I hear you and we will go after Zack gets back." Both dogs lay on the ground, releasing quiet whimpers.

ZACK

Zack gave Maxi a quick kiss and let his eyes rest on hers for a beat too long. A slight headache developed, his mind waxing between his devotion to the job and his love for his family.

Here he put Maxi in the middle of another mess, possibly one that he had created. And it sucked. "I will meet you just beyond the field," Zack said. "Stay on the dirt and keep the dogs quiet, please."

Maxi gave him a quick thumbs up, adding, "I love you and after we find Ric—"

"You are going to kick someone's ass. I know, you have been planning." Zack leaned in for one more kiss, this one longer than the last. When their lips broke, he slipped out of sight before he might note any reaction from Maxi.

The overgrown bushes and tree line offered some cover. The barn had a large, garage style door along with a smaller one on the same side where he stood. From his view, the smaller door had the only visible window that looked out on the field.

Zack followed a rough path of bent ferns noting that someone had trampled through here recently. The idea of human or animal popped into his mind as slow movements from tree trunk to tree trunk kept him out of sight.

On the right side of the tree, he could hear the SUV fading. Maxi's distance helped him focus on discovering who was in the parking lot.

The packed down plants muffled bits of sound coming from his shoes. Without any noise worry, he could move a bit quicker. He arrived between the woods and the field, the details of the barn coming further into view. Although his initial assessment had been a traditional rustic structure, he could now see that the building was outfitted to give that impression from a distance.

Each corner of the roof held a security camera similar to what he had on top of the Vermont house. One camera pointed out across the field, another at the back door, and two focused on each side. Zack used the camera application on his cellphone to zoom in. A small red light beeped underneath each, an indication that the system was active.

Sticking to the narrow passage in between the tree trunks and green vines, Zack swore quietly noting that like on the backside, the pattern of security devices followed along this side of the building. A quick text query to Atwood, including a couple photos of the system, superseded his questions about the field investigation.

The towering trunks gave way to dirt and scrub, the front of the building still out of view. Zack still needed about thirty more feet of cover to get to the barn. His options were thin, at best.

A car door slamming followed by second slam froze his body in place. Voices rose just as fast. "Okay so we are here. What's the plan?" (male).

"We're going to level this sucker like we did the field?" (female).

"Wait – what? You said that you wanted to spare this part of the operation." (male). Followed by a cackle that sent jolts of recognition crawling up Zack's spine.

"Just follow me," (female). "Let me turn off the alarm and I will show you what I mean inside."

"Stay out here and watch the place. Somethings not right," the male voice directed to another who responded, "You got it, boss."

Zack zoomed his lens onto the cameras. The red dot blinked four times then stopped. He backtracked to the field side to see the others did the same. "My lucky day," he mumbled. With a deep inhale, Zack moved across the space between him and the barn, creating as little dust as possible.

What should have been a rough exterior turned out to be a metal wall, painted to look old and feeble. One hand stayed on the side of the barn as he headed for the front, glancing at the sleeping cameras. Occasional low laughter suggested another human in proximity.

In a crouching position, Zack leaned up against the wall and slipped his cellphone perpendicular around the corner. He blindly snapped a few photos. A Sheriff's vehicle came into focus along with a hefty man leaning up against the wall, full concentration on his phone.

Using one finger he focused the camera to see a law insignia on the man's shirt and a Glock within reach, on his side. Zack positioned the top of his head around the corner to confirm what was in the picture. The law man now leaned against his left shoulder, blocking the door, yet giving Zack the opportunity to snap a few photos of the car next to the Sheriff's.

As he zoomed in on the license plate, voices rose. "Are you sure this is what the boss meant?" (male).

"Look, I know what the boss wants," (frustrated female). "We can keep this going quietly. He already took care of the Feds—"

"What about—" (male).

"Kill him and you'll never have to work again. Come on let's get out of here." (female).

Zack moved his phone around the bend to click one more photo before counting to ten and running back to the tree line. Four cameras clicked on to capture a still of his backside. A loud click took his attention upward as two cameras barely visible in the trees snapped a clear frontal view.

PETE

"Fucks," a few "damn it," and all telling "son of a bitches" filled the hall as Pete made his way to the conference room for the morning briefing with the director and his merry men. Zack's nickname for the team stuck in Pete's thoughts. He gave a short laugh at the sight upon his entrance.

The other team members, apart from Kit Sellers, were already seated. One of the two empty chairs offered a view of the entire room. Once seated, Pete noted the Holey's computer screen reflected in the window.

"Bonus," he murmured as he sips his bottled tea.

"Pardon?" Holey turned to focus his glare on Pete.

"I said Good morning," Pete clarified, adding "where are we?"

"We," starts Holey, "are in fucking Fremont in the middle of a huge god damn mess. In case you are not aware, a football field of marijuana burned up a few days ago. The grower's body and a member of a crime syndicate were both found dead in the middle."

As Archer Holey took a long, dramatic inhale, Pete interrupted with, "How does this fit into our investigation?"

Holey turned to give the side eye in Pete's direction. "You tell me. If we had that answer, then we would be all set. That, Mr. D.C. is the problem." Holey's computer flashed. Pete's attention shifted to a photo of a man walking into a forest.

With a slight gesture, Pete leveled his phone to appear to be reviewing something. He snapped off two photos of the reflection. "Not to aggravate the situation further," Pete asked. His statement got a few laughs, "but if we don't have a connection why are we wasting our time on this? Shouldn't we be focused on our investigation?"

Holey's shoulders rose to his ears before sinking down to rest about an inch lower. A wheezing noise came from his nose. Archer Holey bought time, reaching for a napkin from a pile in the center of the table and wiping his brow. "Well, I will be damned. DC boy here makes a good point." His chubby finger shook as he pointed. "Now you listen, Bull, contact what's his name at the DEA and find out if there is any connection to what we are doing here." His eyes moved down to his screen as one hand nonchalantly clicked on the second photo. For a second time Pete took a photo of the screen reflection just before Holey slammed his computer shut.

"What did I miss this morning?" Kit asked in between puffs. "I heard the swearing and turned right around. I mean really, do we all need to be referred to as son of a bitches on a daily basis? Can't Holey remember anyone's name?"

Pete let loose a short laugh in between a strong exhale. The idea of taking a run along one of the packed down ski trails had been Kit's. And just like she had predicted, none of the others would follow. "Bunch of lazy asses," were her exact words. "Just using the word run turns them all off."

The wide path sloped uphill at a forty-five-degree angle. The Fremont blue spruce and Wasatch maple created shade along the way while Rocky Mountain Jupiter filled in to provide a divide from the other trails. Their rhythmic breathing came with a cadence different from the other inhabitants of the area.

Out of caution, they waited almost an hour into their run to slow and speak, each having their own story to share. Pete took a long swig from his bottled water before starting. "My room is still continuously bugged. I found another two this morning when I got back from the gym. Instead of removing at this point I am going to use a jammer—"

"Those don't always work," Kit jumped in. "So, nothing has changed and Holey still doesn't trust you?"

Pete continued his train of thought. "I think for the Holey's team end of our investigation I can use that plus limit my in-room communications."

"What about a computer reader? If someone is taking the time to bug your room, they may have installed something that can read the shitty Wi-Fi in the hotel. I know it's a pain, yet if you stick to the encrypted network—" Pete agreed. "Okay so now getting to why we ran up here, I think Archer Holey, our illustrious director, and Flash are part of the problem."

"I agree yet why do you think that?"

"Because Holey is downplaying the pot field situation, and he told the DEA counterpart in this area that it was his investigation and to back off."

"His investigation? He told everyone at the meeting that he was waiting on those DEA bastards before he did anything, and he thinks we should stay on the pot field until he hears. But that is just the start of our problems. I took this shot of his screen reflection this morning. Even without enhancing the photo, I know that's my brother-in-law."

"Ah, the famous Zack Brady." Kit pointed at the figure.

"One in the same. You've met him?"

"Once, in Donald's office when I was added to the investigation."

"Then may we assume that it was the Senator that sent this to Holley, yet now that I'm thinking about it, it could be his crazy ass niece, who put a bounty on Zack. Kill him and be set financially for life."

Kit scratched the side of her head. "Set for life, huh?"

"I would hate to have to kill you," Pete said. His face held no expression. "My family comes first, always. Which is why I am here in the first place."

Kit Sellers shifted her weight leaning to each side and raising one hand overhead to stretch. "I thought you were here because Donald Atwood needed to bring in someone that he and Brady trusted. Am I wrong?"

Pete considered the conversation about Atwood trusting this woman with his life, "I don't know. I get the call, and I show up." He gave a quick shrug.

Kit looked off into the distance. She stated, "That being said, we need to start taking players out of this game to get to the prize."

"And in your world the prize is?" Pete chin nodded in the direction of the trail. Side by side they started to descend the path back to the hotel.

"I think of the top as the prize, so the Senator needs to be indited or killed," she laughed.

"I agree with you on the first part, not on the second, but I need to get my nephew home safe too."

Kit's pace slowed. "As you say, family first. Where are we on that end?"

"We know he was in the Sheriff's office yet from there the trail is cold. I have someone observing movements in Amity."

"Anything interesting there?"

Pete thought about the photos on his phone that showed Marjorie and members of the Sheriff's office at the meth lab next to the field. Pete opened his mouth to speak as Kit interrupted his thoughts.

"I am a very family orientated person myself, so since you have family involved, concentrate there. I am one or two accounts away from connecting Holey to this whole mess."

Pete grabbed a hold of Kit's bicep. "The whole mess?"

"Okay maybe not your family mess, but I can show deposits into both Holey's and the Sheriff's offshore bank accounts going back three years." Kit let out another high-pitched laugh. "The dumbasses used the same bank!"

"And you are waiting to tell me this now? Have you shared this with Atwood?"

"Not yet," Kit held up her index finger to stop Pete from interrupting. "Mainly because in Donald's world we need to get to the top."

"Can you link the Senator in there too?"

"That's where I am getting bogged down. I can see a few shell corporations, yet none make a direct link at this point beyond the mystery campaign donations."

"What about our other teammates? Anyone else in your crosshairs?"

"Not connected on this level. I think most are just following boss' orders if you know what I mean. Bull has been stopping by my room quite a bit to chat about non important items." Kit lets out a sigh. "I get the impression he is disappointed that I am there so now I make sure that if I am not in my room, Bull is in my sight."

"Good plan, I haven't heard anything from Niza." Pete reached into his jacket pocket to pull out his phone. The screen opened to one of the photos of Marjorie and the Sheriff at the barn.

Kit stared at Pete's screen. Choosing her words with care, she said, "Circumstantial yet it connects both parties, one who is supposed to be in jail on espionage charges, together at a known drug lab. Let me guess, Brady took the photo?"

Pete confirmed this with a quick nod.

Kit said, "Could you send—"

Instead of texting, Pete uploaded the photo to the common file where Kit, Donald Atwood, he and Zack had access. "In the common file. Now—"

A snap of a branch followed by leaves rustling silenced their conversation. Both froze to concentrate on the direction of the noises.

SHERIFF

Sheriff sat back in his squeaky chair, thankful for the moment of an empty room. His phone lay lit within reach while his other hand balanced half of a roast beef sandwich. His phone beeped continuously, each interruption bringing slower chews. He read Archer Holey on his screen, flipped the phone over, and brought his second hand to rest on the back of his neck.

Mayonnaise and tomato juice dripped down his arm to pool into a wet spot on the thigh area of his pants. The Sheriff took breaths as deep as the bites he tore off the packed roll. A flash of light emulated the desktop with each buzz of his phone.

He wiped both hands along his pant leg, reached his sidearm, and placed it on the desk, hidden underneath the paper wrapping from his sandwich, grateful that the cells were empty. No witnesses.

Bam! The door from the street entrance slammed against the back wall. Archer Holey strutted inside. As the door closed slowly behind him, the Sheriff got a glimpse of Dak across the street.

"You don't answer your fucking phone?" Holey's voice rose. The Sheriff examined as his old buddy moved to the opposite side of his desk, Glock in hand.

"There's a reason you have that thing out?" The Sheriff pointed at the gun. "And why are you here, Arch?"

"I am here," Holey leaned over the desk to enter the Sheriff's space, "because you and the goober out there are fucking up our operation!"

The Sheriff sat back in his chair and nodded his head. He waited a beat then spoke, "How is this on my end?" his voice stayed calm. "Me and my men are following orders from D.C. brought to us direct from the princess." The princess comment got a forced chuckle from both. "What makes you think that you can barge into my office, gun waving, and threaten me?"

With a jerk of his body, the Sheriff stood to send the chair flying back behind him. One hand rested under the deli paper - fingers wrapped around the metal handle of his pistol. The other helped him balance against the desk. "I asked you a question, boy," the Sheriff sneered.

Without moving a muscle, Archer brought his firearm even with his chest. Ignoring the gun, the Sheriff continued to meet his old pal's glare.

"Why are you emailing me photos of Zack Brady? If you remember correctly, he was to be your problem, not mine."

"The photos came from the security camera over by the field. I got someone—"

"You mean that goober across the street talking shit with my guy?" Both brought their attention to the window. Dak and another man stood in active conversation. "Flash is my demo guy. He likes to blow shit up if you know what I mean." Archer gave an exaggerated wink.

"So, what do you want from me? You got your demo guy, and I assume a directive from the boss?" Archer looked away from the Sheriff's glare. "You ain't got no directive? Boy let me tell you something, I have been working for the Senator for a long time and if he doesn't say to do something, I don't get my panties in a wad."

"You don't panic, huh?" Archer brought his sidearm back into the holster. "Then tell me why there is chaos."

"I got a better question for you, Arch, where is my guy Sully and why was that field burned?"

"Your guy Sully was a liability, as us law enforcement people like to say, and I got nothing to do with that field. Talk to the boss on that one." Archer glanced passed the Sheriff at the empty cells. "Shouldn't you be out looking for Brady or anywhere but here?"

"Brady is both our problems, huh."

"And actually why I am here, not to get into a pissing match with you. Show me on a map where those photos were taken along with any pertinent places close by. My guys," Holey said, "are going to get rid of that turd once and for all."

The Sheriff didn't say a word as he pulled out a map of Amity and the surrounding area. With a red Sharpie he circled the area near the drug lab along with Clem's place and pushed the map in Holey's direction.

"What the fuck is this?"

Using the Sharpie's tip, the Sheriff pointed to the drug lab, "Barn," he said as he moved the marker to Clem's place, "abandoned marijuana growing facility," he said, then drew a big X in-between the two points. "Forrest." He threw the marker on the desk. "Any other questions?"

Archer folded up the map. "I'll be in touch," he said as he exited.

The Sheriff sat back down and re-holstered his gun. Dak came through the door, waving at someone as he entered. "Those Fed guys are a bunch of putzes," he declared. "I just spent the last half hour listening to that fella tell me how they are going to get Brady and take over the operation out here. Geez, talk about elk crap."

"You and I need to make a visit to the barn and then Clem's place. Bring some explosives so we can git into both safes."

"What are you planning boss?"

"Dak, your job requires you to be seen and not ask stupid questions. We need to do this shit now, along with a sweep of Clem's property."

"Are you thinking about heading out now?" Dak scratched his head as he focused out the window. "Do we need to have Alma come in to watch the office?"

The Sheriff let out a loud sigh. "I would prefer that no one notices our absence."   He pointed at the door. Dak gave a short salute before exiting. Once he was gone, the Sheriff went into the safe and retrieved another gun, one that had scratches where a serial number should have been etched in. He checked the chamber before placing the metal in his pant, barrel against his butt crack.

MAXI

Maxi parked the SUV on the opposite side of the field, just off out of sight into the pines. Both dogs sat up straight; Jerry staring in the direction they had just traveled. Steady pants coming from his mouth.

Bobby took his position on the front seat, expelling a similar breathing pattern as he focused on the narrow dirt path that led further away from the barn.

Max had cracked her driver's side window open, straining to breathe fresh air and hear her husband coming back to them. Both her son and Zack were pissing her off – each for different reasons. Her husband needed to stop dismissing her gut feelings. They'd have a long talk about this after they find Ric.

That Sheriff had something to do with Ric's disappearance. The dogs both confirmed it and if the same tail thump happened next to someone carrying drugs in an airport, they'd be busted. "Ha–I need to remember that one next time they argue with me."

She fiddled with the buttons on the dash wondering how she might have prevented this whole mess. Keeping Ric closer to home would have been one option. *And teaching him how to charge his freakin' phone!* Maxi let out a short snort at her last thought. "Yeah. Right. Like me pointing out that the phone can't work without a charged battery would have made a difference here." *But it would have, as long as he kept his tracker on.*

She chewed her index nail, focusing back on the rear-view mirror.

"Where the fuck is he?" she whispered to the dogs. The distinct sound of a gunshot brough her foot down hard on the gas. Bobby lurched forward off the passenger's seat onto the floor onto the floor mat. "Sorry baby," Maxi said as she concentrated on missing the pine trees as she sped along the narrow trail.

"I hate when he does this," she mumbled. Her hands turned white on the steering wheel. "You know the drill," she repeated out loud. "I'm pissed off at you, Zack Brady!"

She could hear Zack's voice answering. "You hear guns, you run in the opposite direction." A hole leftover from winter run hit the passenger tire, sending the SUV bouncing to the right. "I will find you..."

"We are on our own," Maxi stated. Both dogs now in the passenger's seat stared back at her. "We will be okay. Zack will be back soon." Both dogs let out whimpers at the sound of Zack's name.

Maxi pulled over to the side and listened. "No footsteps or gunshots," she informed the dogs. Bobby's yelp turned her attention from the trail's end to a small compound.

From what she could see, a dilapidated barn and possible garage, both leaned to the side and appeared to be collapsible with a touch. Just beyond the two structures, another one-story building sat with both a commercial kitchen vent on one side and a massive chimney on the other.

"Well, what do you make of this?" Maxi asked the dogs.

The entire area appeared deserted of life. Maxi eased the SUV into drive to move cautiously down the bank, stopping about fifteen feet from the entrance to the building. She blew out a breath and looked over at the dogs.

"I know, this is your job, but you two are retired..." Jerry slipped his head under her hand and looked up to meet her eyes. "I know," Maxi said as she scratched under the dos's chin. "but…"

Bobby gave a quick whine and started to bang his head against the door. "This is a bad idea," she told both dogs as she opened the driver's side door. As she slid her butt off the seat, both dogs pushed her body aside to jump outside. Together, they took off in a run towards the building.

"Guys, no," Maxi called after yet by the time she reached the door, Bobby's whines had increased in volume and Jerry scratched at the door handle. Maxi tried the handle which opened with ease. "Damn it," she muttered while both dogs ran around the room, sniffing and barking along their path.

"Please, shush," Maxi begged as she called out "Hello" into the empty room. She followed the dogs to an open room with a bunk bed. Bobby jumped up on the lower mattress, sat up straight, and thumped his tail to make pounding beats.

Maxi walked across the room, bent over, and smelled the mattress. "Oh my god," she said as she hit her head on the top bunk stepping back. "He was here." Bobby gave a quick bark to confirm.

All three's breathing became audible. "We need to get out of here," Maxi turned towards the door at the same moment her hand flew to her stomach. "Now!" she yelled at the dogs.

No sooner than she maneuvered the SUV away from the building, puffs of dirt came from the road leading in. Her heart sunk as another SUV embossed in gold with SHERIFF across the side pulled up at her driver's side.

"This is private property," he said. "You are trespassing on private property."

"I understand sir," Maxi answered. Without thinking she started to babble, "I don't know if you remember me, but I was in your office. My son is missing," she said. The Sheriff shifted his gaze away from hers.

"Okay," he answered in that slow drawl that annoyed her.

"I went to the camp as you had suggested and the guy behind the counter," she stopped to consider making up a name before the Sheriff interrupted her.

"Sully?"

"Yeah, I think that was his name. Anyway, he told me about this farm where some of the kids did chores during the camp to help out some elderly farmer."

"And Sully sent you here?"

Maxi let out a small laugh. "I'm not sure. See we followed the road that went by your office but then I thought I took a wrong turn. Doesn't matter though, no one is here, or at least no one answered the door." Maxi gave her best *I am going to cry any minute so please be nice to me* face and waited.

She gave a quick glance in the rearview mirror at the car behind the Sheriff to make sure no one was sneaking up on the other side. Bringing her attention back to the man sitting level with her, she observed that he hadn't moved either.

"So, you didn't go in the building?" Maxi shook her head no and the Sheriff continued, "as I mentioned this here is private property. I'm not sure what you are used to back east, but in Fremont a person could get shot for noising around someone's ranch."

Maxi let out an audible gasp. "I, I mean, I..." She waited until the Sheriff's hand rose up to stop babbling.

"Because you are unfamiliar with our customs, I will not arrest you for being here—"

"—Thank you, sir—"

"But I am going to tell you to go back into town or wherever you are staying and let me do my job. Understand?" Maxi gave a quick nod. "Now if you follow this drive in about a mile or two you will come to the main road, where you turned to get here—"

"Oh yes—"

"Head back to wherever you are staying, and I will be in touch when I have some information."

"Okay, thank you sir." The Sheriff gave a quick tip of his cowboy hat and pulled forward. "Good luck with that without my contact info," she muttered.

The second car drove by slowly, yet with the tinted windows, Maxi could see nothing inside. She slid into drive and eased on the gas, moving the pace of someone trying to avoid the ruts in the dirt road. She guided the SUV around a slight bend and stopped to park on the side of the road, noiselessly praying that the SUV was out of the Sheriff's sight line.

Resting Zack's high-powered camera on her forearm, Maxi focused on the second vehicle's plate, taking three or four photos before returning to the dogs. "No, I cannot let you two out right now," she instructed.

Jerry had his nose out the window and was quietly whining. "What's up, boy?" Maxi said as she brushed under his chin. Jerry moved his nose around to push Maxi's hand onto the steering wheel. "Okay, I'm leaving…"

In a matter of minutes, the drive turned more into a road with less potholes and smooth pavement. Around a second bend, the compound that she had just left came in full view along with both the Sheriff and the other car heading back in her direction. Maxi stepped on the gas at the same moment a loud BOOM along with a shaking ground sent her off the road.

Looking back, flames soared above the compound. "Oh shit," she said, hitting the gas. Another loud noise fell on top of the SUV roof. "What the fuck was that?" she yelled over the loud barking.

Maxi hit the brakes hard, and a body slid off her roof onto the hood. Zack jumped off, pulled the door open, and shouted "GO" as he slid into the passenger seat that both dogs vacated.

Maxi brought her gaze back and forth between him and the road. A hard left onto the paved road brought Zack's body against hers. The phone on the dash rang, Pete's name on the I.D.

ZACK

One hand rested across his stomach, fingers massaging the side that hit the roof of the SUV. For a minute Zack said nothing, he just stared at his wife as she drove, hands ridged, clinging to the steering wheel as if she could control their circumstances. He raised his free hand up to caress her right arm, only to be met with a slap against the offending limb and his side.

"Oww!" Zack jumped in the opposite direction. "That hurts you know."

Maxi had streams running out of both eyes and scrunched her lips as she spoke. "This is crap. You are crap. Donald's crap and probably my brother too. I have had it—"

She slammed her foot on the brake pad, both dogs hit the back seat while Zack's seatbelt torn into his shoulder. "Maxi—"

"Don't Maxi me. I want my son back. NOW!" She slammed her palm against the wheel. "Zack, I am so sick of this procedure shit, and we need to complete A before B can happen. That kid at the camp said the Sheriff knows. The dogs confirmed that Ric has been both at that god forsaken jail and in the building that just blew up."

"Wait, what?"

"You heard me. Both dogs ran into a room with bunk beds and around the kitchen there, barking, tails wagging. He's close, Zack. And I want him back, safe with me." Her shoulders shook violently as Maxi let out a scream that shook the car.

Heavy breathing followed.

Bobby fit his paws on the seat divider and whipped his head around to lick Maxi's face. His tail wacked into Zack's side. Her hand brushed against Zack's arm to reach under and pet the dog's throat with a quick scratch.

Zack opened his mouth to speak and was immediately interrupted.

"What's our plan hotshot?" He laughed at Maxi's nickname for him.

"I have a—"

She interrupted, "Cause I think we should get a map and see where the closest structures are to that camp." She turned to face her body towards his. Zack took note that her palm was turning black and blue. "Those assholes torch that field that we were near and now blew up this building. I think that if we narrow the structures off that trail I was on, we could find Ric."

"I think—"

"And we should probably go back and get Pete, but not that Kit Sellers person."

"Why not Kit. She's working directly with Donald."

"She's not family and family first." Maxi held out hand for a quick fist pump.

"Uh, Max," Zack said, holding her hand back from moving the gear shift. "Do you think that I could drive?" Her eyes bore into him. "I mean I just think that in case someone chases us."

RIC

The bag of weed seemed to keep refilling itself as the table wasn't clearing fast enough for Ric. Never mind that Dubs and Vittles kept taking breaks to sample the harvest. Stoner giggles floated in and out of the garage, depending on which way the breeze blew.

An old cassette player played the same two bootleg tapes, scratchy versions of both shows, people screaming or talking over the music in the same spots. "I would be happy to never hear *Uncle John's Band* again for the rest of my life," Ric mumbled as Jerry's voice strained in the background.

Now covered in oil from the plants, his hands, shirt, and forearms stunk so badly that Ric was surprised he didn't have the stoner giggles too. He imagined hearing Dub's truck fading off into the distance at the same moment Vittles turned off the tape.

"Thank god," Ric exclaimed. "I love The Dead but how many times can someone listen to that same first set."

"It's a classic from Red Rocks," Vittles explained. "Wait, how did you know that was from a first set?"

"My mom's a deadhead, remember? I probably was rocked to sleep with that tape." Ric stood up and stretched his arms over his head, feeling his muscles release from fingers to toes. "Where'd Dubs go?"

"Get us dinner. We can't live on granola bars alone. I mean we ain't on tour and broke."

"That's half true," Ric said. The table lay covered in various forms of weed. A stack of sandwich bags filled with an ounce of uncleaned weed each covered a third with a few extras having slipped off the table to scatter on the ground. Ric worked from the middle part of the surface reaching to the bag on the opposite side from the baggies to drag stems onto the scale and then fold the leaves into a bag.

"You know, Vittles, I was thinking that your contact is probably going to want to dry this shit out. I mean you really can only bake with the fresh stuff."

Vittles let out a short laugh then explained, "okay, so Dubs bud owns a bakery near Niza that makes, like, cookies and shit. This makes it easier for his crew, kinda like how butter sticks are measured out, you know?"

"For real?" Ric thought about each baggie turning into a batch of cookies.

"I don't know!" Vittles fell over laughing. "Dubs said to break up the haul so that's what we are doing. I have no idea why, but Dubs knows because he has been doing this a while." Vittles looked around the room then focused back on Ric. "Can you keep a secret?"

Ric gave a quick nod.

"Me and the Dubber have been doing this for a while. See the field behind the ranch—"

"Where I did the irrigation system?"

"Yeah, there. So, me and Dubs have been poaching a plant or two before each harvest and investing," Vittles did a quick air quote around the word investing, "in our future touring. You know, like staying in hotels instead of sleeping in the car and having tickets to the shows–that was a nice change."

"You'd go without tickets?"

"Yeah, summer tour was easy. We'd sometimes hop the fence or at some places you could hang near the fence and see the screens." Vittles got that faraway look again. "But Fall and Winter tours were harder. Had to rely on a brother popping the door or a kind folk handing off a miracle."

Ric's hands kept moving as the two spoke. From the garbage bag to the scale, into a baggie the green leaves folded in. What seemed like a never-ending pile of marijuana moved across the table.

Without music, Vittles paced the garage swaying and hopping to his own beat. At times, he stuck his head around the corner at the open end. Ric tried to make out his mumblings yet only the occasional "fuckin'" was audible.

"Dude, you are making me paranoid. Stop that," Ric said.

Vittles froze at the door, his hand upright in a stop position. Both listened intently as a combustible engine sound came closer. "That's not Dub's truck," Vittles said as he pulled the garage door shut. Ric sucked in a breath as car doors slammed nearby.

SHERIFF

The Sheriff paid attention as Clem's place erupted into a fireball that reached up into the sky. "What a waste," he said, giving a glance over to Archer and Flash, both pointing and giggling at the flames like little boys with a stolen lighter.

Archer now approached where he stood, holding out a bottled Coors. "Here's to another fine mess that's disappeared," he said.

The Sheriff looked back and forth between the beer and the smirk his old buddy Archer wore. "I don't drink on the job," he said as he pushed the bottle away. "We need to call this one in, although with Dak gone, I'm not sure who'll respond."

The comment got a hardy laugh. "Yeah, nice touch using the Senator's gun on that idiot deputy. I guess that took care of two problems. The less people in our circle at this point the better. Now if we can just find Brady, no worries there as my guy is working on that." Archer bounced on his toes as he spoke. The movement had the Sheriff back up a step. "I got a guy that can hit a mouse with a shotgun, and Bull is also an expert tracker. Plus, you know," his elbow connected softly into the Sheriff's girth, "our gal there is doing a bang-up job passing on Brady's whereabouts. How did that brother-in-law get promoted being so dumb?"

The Sheriff ignored the last part of Archer's rant. He studied Pete Malone's bio, and the man was far from dumb. Malone appeared little too straight and narrow for him, but then again, that didn't mean the man should be underestimated. He brought his attention back to the smoldering building. "Brady is close."

"Oh, does the Sheriff have psychic powers too?" Holey teased.

"No, I do not have psychic powers, I just know Brady's type and he'll want to see this through." He looked passed Archer to Bombs. "What's his deal?"

Archer followed the Sheriff's gaze. "He's a good kid, just a little off his rocker. Got here mighty quick from downtown Niza. Bombs got his nickname cuz he loves to blow shit up."

"You don't say," the Sheriff said. "How did you two meet?"

"Was part of my unit in Afghanistan a while back. His body came back but most of his wits stayed over there, if you know what I mean."

The Sheriff let out a slow breath. Dak had been over there too. He wondered about the connection yet decided to instead ask, "How much does he know?"

"Less than you or me. Thinks we blew up the place to kill off the drug dealers. Told him that other fella was working with the lab people making crack. Kid's sister died of an OD." Archer brought his attention back to the Sheriff. "You just got to know what buttons to push."

The Sheriff gave a small nod and got into his car. He hadn't meant to let it slip that the gun came from another murder scene, or that the Senator had given it to the Sheriff to "do something with." He just wanted his old buddy Archer to stop bragging about his "family" connection and how he and the Senator were tight. Laughter filled the cruiser with that thought. The

Senator was only tight with people he could use, with even family being an illusion.

The smoke could now be seen coming up over the ridge that separated the property from the road. If he called it in, he'd have to go back, and that wasn't going to happen. Not with dufus and dumbass on the scene. Up ahead he found a spot on the side of the road that had both the old barn and burnt field both in view. *What a mess this all turned into.*

The smoke now took up a significant amount of sky. He took a photo with his phone and texted it to a familiar number. Within seconds his phone rang.

"What the hell is that?" the Senator's voice blared through the car speakers.

"That my friend is what's left of Clem's place thanks to those psychos you sent here."

"Now Sheriff, I had nothin' to do with those people coming over into your area. That was all the feds investigating things that shouldn't be. Where's Marjorie?"

"Damn if I know. Dak and your guy Clem are incinerated, and I need an out, like now. They are getting closer."

"Now listen, you don't worry about a thing. Those guys go on my orders, you know that. Just sit tight and we can go back to our business soon. Kay?"

He agreed knowing that there was no reasoning with the Senator. "Boy, you get paid to do shit my way or..." was one of the baby–kissing elected officials favorite lines.

Not for the first time, the Sheriff wondered which babies held the Senator's DNA. With a fluid motion, he disconnected by hitting the stop record button on his phone. After labelling the file with the date and the word Senator, he uploaded it to a cloud file named CMA. "You betcha," the Sheriff said as he made a U-turn to head back to his office.

ZACK

Zack hit the answer button instructing Maxi to just drive. Pete's voice came through clearly on the speakers. "We got him," Pete said, "thanks to that bug Maxi planted. We got the Sheriff and Archer Holey discussing the situation on tape, and I hate to tell you this brother—"

"That the tape was obtained illegally?"

"Ah, no. But we now have semi-proof of collaboration, and that, my friend, is going to help us in our next moves. So no, not submittable in court."

"So, what could you tell me that I haven't already heard," Zack replied, giving Maxi's shaking arm a squeeze.

"Well, I suppose this is probably nothing new for you, but Bull and Bombs, a.k.a. one Henry Morgan and Percy Welker, are both in town with one job—"

"Let me guess—"

"To kill you, buddy. Atwood said to get you out of there and we will round up Holey's team and the Sheriff. We have the folks from D.C. on route providing a welcoming party for the Sheriff at his office."

"I'll be damned." Zack said. "I was going to say to blow up a ranch over near that marijuana field that was torched. But I guess I'd be wrong?"

"Yeah – you'd be wrong. I hope that him or his deputy will want to save their asses, and we can start charging a few levels higher."

"The deputy might not be much use."

"Why is that?" Pete's voice got a little statically.

"For one thing, the Sheriff and the deputy went into the building prior to the explosion—"

"And only our friendly Sheriff came out?"

"You got it brother." The jolt of Maxi's foot against the brakes sent Zack's head inches from the windshield. His back slammed into the passenger's seat. One look over at his shaking bride told him to cut the call short.

"Hey, uh, Pete, I gotta go."

"Everything okay?"

Maxi cut into the conversation with a solid "No."

Zack noted that her breathing had become more audible. "Listen brother, keep me in the loop—"

"Wait! What about Ric?" Maxi interrupted. Zack rested his hand on her shoulder as they waited for Pete's response.

"No word as yet but we have a few leads. Keep the faith, sis. We will find him." Maxi gave an audible choke as she tried to fight back her tears.

"Listen, bro, I really gotta go, we will be in touch—" Zack pressed call end as Pete still spoke. "I got a plan," he reassured her with a quick squeeze of her hand. "I will give you more details as we get the heck away from here. Now would you please climb over the console—"

"I'm not in the mood, Zack," she said as she moved her body away.

"Yeah, always going in the direction away from me," Zack said. "I want to be driving in case any of our friends show up. I am going to run around the car while you get settled." He reached back to give both dogs quick pets as Maxi slid closer to him. "Good work guys!"

His head came within inches of the dash as Maxi stomped the brake pad. She heaved the door open, and Zack could hear the crunch of her boots as she stomped her way around the vehicle. The door on his side tore open. The blank stare that met him was all Zack needed to know.

He moved around his wife's stiff body to the driver's side. By the time he got to the open door, Maxi was already seated, back fixed against the seat. Zack took her closest hand from her lap to give a quick squeeze, then turned the wheel back in the direction of town.

RIC

As Vittles clung to the garage door handle, his body weight could not keep the door closed. Ric retreated to the far wall of the garage; body hidden in the shadows, yet he could see just above the table where people stood in the doorway.

A loud thud was followed by deep laughter. Vittles stood to full height next to two men.

"Ah, Sandy my boy," the man took Vittles into a bear hug. "I am so glad to find you. I can never tell if the other one is lying." That statement got a nervous laugh, Ric assumed from the other man.

"Ah, what do you mean the other one," Vittles air quoted the last few words. "I thought Dubs was on his way to meet you."

"Yes, Edward was on his way before the dumbass got pulled over by the D.E.A. Seems his boss over at that camp was shot." The man brought his full attention to Vittles, "I tried to save him, Sandy, but you know how these things go." He pointed at the contents on the table. "Is that the rest of Clem's weed?"

"There were a couple bags in his truck, over by the field—"

"The field that the D.E.A. torched?" The man moved to slam his fist onto the folding table and said something in a language that Ric didn't recognize. "You only took what's here and in that other truck?" He walked around the table, his back now to Ric's hiding spot.

"We couldn't get to the truck to get the rest—"

"Who's we?"

Without missing a beat, Vittles continued, "Me and some kid from the fancy camp—"

"Where's the kid now?" Another voice came from behind Vittles.

"Don't know. He took off when Dubs, I mean Edward got to the ranch. Said he needed to get to an airport. We offered a ride, but." Vittles gave a little shrug.

"So, you really don't know where this kid is?" Back to the wiry guy a few feet away.

"For all I know he's sitting in the floor behind you," Vittles said. Ric's muscles tensed as laughter filled the space.

"Okay, Sandy, I believe you. Your friend, Edward has decided to take a leave so now me and Archie here will take the rest of your harvest with us."

"Unless you have a problem with that," Archer called from the doorway.

"Nope. I will even help you load this up." Ric could see shuffling and clumps of pot leaves hitting the floor. Vittles swung the almost full bag over his shoulder. "Where do you want this?" Vittles asked, his steps getting faint.

The fainter the footsteps, the less Ric could make out of the conversation. He stayed in the shadows and waited.

"Yeah, thanks anyway but I think I'll just wait here for Dubs, I mean Edward to come back," he heard Vittles say followed by a muffle of words. A car engine kicked over and with a stomp on the gas pedal, the sound faded.

Ric counted to one hundred before calling out "Vittles?" After a few minutes of silence, he crawled out from his space. At the garage door, a silhouette of Vittles' puffy hair leaned on the other side of a rock about twenty feet away.

"Damn it, Vittles, this shit ain't funny," Ric said as he approached the body. Vittles stared back; eyes wide open. His body still. "Oh fuck."

Headlights flashed up over the hill to light up most of the area. Ric dove back into the darkness of the trees wedged between two ski runs. The now familiar voice of Arch bellowed in the direction of the spot where Vittles lay.

The man mumbled as he approached, "Why the fuck do I need to toss a corpse? It's your turn, Archie," he whined, followed by, "wait 'til I tell the boss about this one. Ha!" The man lifted Vittles up like he was carrying a case of beer. "Over the cliff or in the explosion?" he yelled.

The wiry man strolled within yards of Ric, carrying a cardboard box on his shoulder. "If we are blowing up the evidence here, mind as well through the kid in. Not sure what the fuck they were doing out here, but the air reeks of the good stuff." He disappeared inside the shed. "What about the other one? Do you think that's Brady's kid?"

Ric moved further out of view, praying he didn't hit a branch, hole, or snake as he moved.

"Not sure, but that would be par for this one, huh? We can only hope that the Tracer gets to him at the airport. Convenient we have a ready team in Niza." Both men laughed. "Even if they collect a paycheck from the Feds too. I hope he finds Brady too. That bastard has been a hemorrhoid to me for too long."

"Yeah, to all of us," Archer said. "We should finish this up and get out of here." Ric heard shuffling as he backed up further to watch the man dump Vittles into the garage.

As both trudged back into the headlights, Ric heard "This one will only take out the garage and maybe ten feet around. Our investors wanted to put a new lift over here anyway. We'll just save 'em a few bucks." The car door slammed, and Ric climbed up the hill heading to the tower, branches ripping into his clothes and skin.

PETE

Pete was out the door as Zack pulled up to the condo, gun in one hand, backpack in the other. Kit Sellers followed close behind.

Both slid into the backseat.

"What's the plan?" Pete asked. He caught Zack's eye in the rearview mirror as he continued, "Donald's guys are heading to the Sheriff's office and the main lodge as we speak."

"When did he confirm that?" Zack asked, holding his gaze.

"About fifteen minutes ago," Kit chimed in. Zack didn't comment. From the hatch, Jerry let out a low growl.

"Jerry, shush," Maxi said. She lowered her voice to add, "Did you get that confirmation?" Zack responded with a slight jerk of his head.

With Zack's eyes still on his, Pete started to speak, yet when he caught an ever so slight movement of Zack's head, he stopped, instead opting for, "Did you bring your laptop?" directed at Kit.

"I did not. It's back at the hotel. I thought we could just use secure lines, no?" she answered.

"What's in the laptop bag?" Zack asked.

"My lunch," Kit answered as she pulled out a KIND bar.

"Ooo, I'll take one of those," Maxi's hand brushed against her brother's as she reached for the bar.

Kit hesitated before placing the bar into Maxi's hand at the same time Pete moved his backpack to the console between the seats, forcing Kit's onto the floor.

"Okay Zack, where we are heading?"

"Max and I mapped out the area and our best move is to pick up a few of the team guys in Amity and then head over to the old barn. That seems to be the center of their activity," Zack pointed to a printout sprawled across the main console.

"The old barn, huh," Kit repeated. Pete noted that she held a secure phone in one hand.

"You are sure that Atwood said the team was starting at the Sheriff's office?" Pete said.

"That's what the text said. I can forward it to you if you want," Kit offered.

Zack interrupted from the front. "Not necessary. Max, would you switch on the GPS please so I can figure out where we are going." Pete heard the glove compartment open, with a slight click that followed.

A jolt followed as Zack made a U-turn on the access road. "Whatcha doing there, buddy?" Pete asked, keeping one eye on Kit as he spoke.

"Maxi has to use the bathroom and I don't want to stop later," Zack answered. Pete waited for his sister to comment and when no wise crack came, he rested one hand on his gun with the other on the door handle.

Maxi hopped out before the vehicle had stopped. "Be right back," she called back as she raced up the stairs. The SUV vibrated in silence.

"Are we actually waiting for her?" Kit asked. "I mean aren't we on a timetable here?" Kit's focus swayed between the car and the door to the condo.

"Yes," Zack replied.

"So, we are heading to the barn." Pete asked as his phone buzzed in his hand. The text from Donald Atwood was short and clear. *Team still on route from Niza. Heading to the last explosion. Watch yourselves and leave Maxi home.* The last line made Pete laugh.

"Something interesting there, boss?" Kit interrupted Pete's thoughts.

"Nope. Just another plea for cash from my daughter." He caught Zack's grin. "Now she wants a tiara to go with the dress. And not just any tiara, one the size of a Texas ranch."

"Huh?" Two vertical lines appeared between Kit's eyebrows.

"Texas ranch," Zack said, "You know, like big and tacky." All three let out a laugh. "Did she say when she needed the tiara or the money for that matter?"

"Only that her and her mom were on route to the mall, and I should okay the purchase if I get a notification."

"Your family really spends a lot of money." Kit observed out loud. "How do you afford all this shit?"

"Yea, how do you afford all of this shit?" Zack now leaned into the back seat. As if on que, Maxi opened the door and hopped back in her seat.

"Let's roll," she said. Pete caught a quick wink in his direction as Zack finessed the SUV back onto the road.

MAXI

The unspoken dialog between her brother and husband bothered Maxi at one time. Now she just saw it as a method to communicate when there were strangers present. When Kit Sellers revealed that Donald Atwood had specified that they head to the barn, yet neither her brother nor Zack received that confirmation, she knew something was up.

Zack telling her she had to pee was another clue.

Maxi went inside the house, cellphone in her jacket pocket and immediately phoned Donald Atwood.

"Hello Maxi," he answered on the first ring. "I know this isn't a social call so please be detailed." Maxi relayed the conversation from the car along with a few other details she thought important. "Jerry growled, you say."

"Yes, sir. And you know my dog, heck he worked for you! Jerry only growls when there is a danger close by."

"Got it. And Maxi, how long does it take you to urinate?"

Maxi laughed at the question. "Donald, I am a woman. What we do in the bathroom shall remain a mystery. And besides, Zack is not going anywhere without me."

Now it was Donald Atwood's turn to laugh, then his voice got serious. "Maxi, these are ruthless people. Promise me you will be careful."

"As soon as I find Ric, I will be vigilant, but until then..."

"Gotcha. I texted both Zack and Pete with instructions. I hope you find Ric soon."

"Thank you, Donald. And I hope that you can prosecute these bastards to the full extent that the law allows." Maxi hit the end button then decided to use the bathroom. "What's a few more minutes."

Opening the car door, she could feel the tension from inside. The quick wink from her brother confirmed that they received the updated text. She also noted something about his daughter and a tiara.

The second part made no sense.

L.M. Pampuro

RIC

What was it with buildings exploding around me?
Ric huddled behind the sturdy trunk of an old pine tree,
one that in the winter he would sway to avoid with his
skis. A rush of hot air followed by particles of debris "I
didn't know this would be survival camp," he muttered.

Peeking around the trunk, he saw the garage in
flames. Above him, headlights flickered as bodies
moved in and out of its illumination. He could hear a
laugh his roommate would say sounded more like a
wounded chicken than an actual human.

The thought of his college roommates, sitting in
the common room making fun of the stoned girl across
the hall's laugh brought a sad smile to his face. After this
summer, college would be a breeze, that is if crazy
mama didn't put him in a locked room or worst yet,
make him have a bodyguard.

There was a girl in one of his classes' freshman
years who was some sort of princess, or at least
pretended to be. She never spoke yet the big guy who
followed her around could answer all the professor's
questions. Man, that prof was a ball buster. He actually
asked the big guy who was taking the course, him or the
young lady.

That got a laugh from the entire class.

Ric's eyes burned from the crap now floating in the
air. He sat on the ground, protected from the flames by
the tree trunk that kept his body in the shadows.

The voices above jumped in and out of clarity.
Clear comprehension coming as the words "Zack Brady"
struck a nerve along with, "we can take care of that one

if needed later." Ric wasn't sure what "that one" was. "I need to find Zack," he whispered, as if putting the thought into the wind could make that happen.

Something about "the old barn" brought slamming doors and fading headlights. Ric crawled back to the trail. The flames still reached high into the sky from the garage. "You were my friend 'til the end, Vittles," he shielded his eyes from the brightness, "May you jam with Jerry now and forever. Rest in peace, brother."

He walked over to the abandon lodge, the door already open. Once inside the dark room, Ric went into the back office. He piled boxes on the side of the flimsy wood door and propped the window open about two inches.

This would be high enough for his fingers to slip underneath for a fast getaway, yet low enough to not look open from the trail. The smell of weed on his clothes and hands had faded a bit, yet the remaining aroma or the events of the days took their toll. Ric found a corner to sink down into and closed his eyes.

ZACK

Kit Sellers's constant babbling was starting to wear on Zack. His jaw twitched with every observation coming from the back seat. If Zack had his way, he would have just knocked the asshole out and moved on, but Atwood's instructions were clear, *Use* Sellers *as a lead to the rest of the compromised agents.*

In normal circumstances Zack would be happy to do just that, but today wasn't normal. These bastards messed with his family, and deep down he knew the Senator would get off clean, politicians always do. Even if they manage to get an indictment, his cronies in the Senate will give a stern lecture to behave while the cameras are rolling and as soon as the press leaves, they will be sharing cigars and whiskey.

Zack saw this scene playing out too many times in Washington D.C. His goal for this investigation was to take out as many as possible from the Senator's minions and hope that at least this one Senator will be too old to start over and he'll just take the money and run.

Zack qualified this current situation as gang activity. Shaking down parents by arresting their kids on false charges, running a drug lab, extortion! This would be much easier if he was dealing with the mob – they had morals compared to these jerks.

The distraction of Maxi's leg shaking indicated the high stakes game he was now playing. She didn't deserve this mess, heck, he didn't deserve this mess – no one did.

"You need to turn up here," Kit interrupted Zack's thoughts.

"What?"

"I said you need to turn up here. Change of orders, remember. We are going to the old barn. The one by the burnt marijuana field."

"Oh yeah, right," Zack said. He turned in the opposite direction.

Kit remained silent at the move as Zack followed an old fire road. The smoldering remains of the garage filled the sky. Zack moved the SUV to the same spot where the headlights had appeared the evening prior. The light from sunrise started to bring about a new day.

Maxi pushed her door open and started to walk near the smoke pile. Kit jumped out right behind.

"Did you look in the bag?" Zack asked Pete, his gaze focused on Sellers walking just behind his wife.

He heard rustling coming from the backseat. "A laptop, a second gun, and holy crap." Zack's attention moved to the back seat. Pete held up two hand grenades. "And I bet that bulge in her coat pocket is a third."

"Oh fuck!" Zack, Sig Saur in his right hand, opened the door the same moment Kit turned Maxi back in his direction.

"Leave the gun, take the cannoli," Kit said with a laugh. Her gun now visibly against Maxi's side. His wife didn't look scared, just pissed. Zack scowled in the general direction.

"Zackary Darcy Brady," Maxi started. "Ow! What the—"

"You need to shut up," Kit pushed the gun into her side with a bit more force. "Now all of us are going to head into that building there," she pointed with her free hand, "to wait for my associates."

"You do know that it is three against one," Zack said.

"Yeah, and I got the one here you care about the most. Make a move and BOOM, she dies." Kit jabbed Maxi's side again for emphasis.

"But so do you," Zack said.

"Life doesn't matter to me. You think you got problems," Kit directed her nod at Pete. "Buy the fuckin' tiara. Who gives a shit. What's a few bucks here or there, right? I'll play along for now."

"Play along?" Zack mumbled.

"What problems could you possibly have?" Great, now Maxi is getting into the conversation. Zack glared in his wife's direction, trying to catch her eye and give a signal to shut up.

"What problems could I have? What you think cause your kid's missing that you got the only problem in the world?" Kit twirled the gun. "I got more family problems than you can imagine," she said in a whiny voice. "I might as well share because," Kit pointed again towards the lodge, "Once my guys get here, well you all..."

"We all what?" Maxi stopped walking. As Kit turned her attention to Maxi, Pete moved behind the SUV.

Kit didn't notice and just kept talking. The gun in her hand started to shake as she spoke. "Everyone thinks that my uncle is a great guy, doing great things, yet I know the truth about him. He's the worst. And you know what, Marjorie knows this too, but mama tells her to—"

"Wait Marjorie Lofsmen's uncle - the Senator?" Zack asked.

"Who the hell else do you think I am talking about? He's not too bright. You must be the brains of this operation." Maxi winced with the gun hitting her hip again.

"You know, Kit, if you help us with your uncle, we could get you into witness protection—"

"Witness protection? Been there done that. How the hell do you think I got this gig? Idiots. Anyway, do you really think that will stop these guys? Not that it matters now because my people should be here any minute, this goes so far above all of our pay grades—"

"How far?"

"Let's just say that the Senator owes a lot of people."

Zack muttered "crap" under his breath. They stood for a moment, the only sound being the low growl of both dogs. Just behind both women, out of their sight line, Pete moved along the edge of the trees.

"Wait, where's tiara boy," Kit jammed the gun into Maxi as she looked around the area. "Come out or you have one less Christmas present to buy!" Kit moved the gun upward. Her hand twitched as she waited for a response.

Pete took a step into her blind spot. He brought his gun to Kit's temple. "I wouldn't do that," his voice breaking the silence.

L.M. Pampuro

MAXI

Maxi kneed Kit Sellers right between the legs. Sellers' gun flew from her hands as she hit the ground. Maxi kicked the firearm under the SUV.

Pete raised his free hand to give a quick fist pump. "Nice work, sis."

"Can we look for Ric now," Maxi said as she landed another kick to Sellers hip. Both dogs ran to her side as she saw Zack closing the hatchback.

"Come on, Bobby," Zack waved the Lab over. "Jerry will stay here with you while Pete and I look around." Zack handed her a small gun. "If she moves, shoot her in the leg as we want this one alive." He brought his attention to Kit. "We thought you were a friend. Atwood brought you to our team."

"Ha – Donald Atwood. He still thinks that his department is ethical, yet maybe not cause if it was on the up and up, you two wouldn't have jobs. Anyway, I'm not friends with losers," Kit responded. "Wait 'til my boys get here. You people are—" Maxi's foot came about swiftly to connect with her shoulder."

"Hey sis," Pete said, "We try not to leave marks. Marks might constitute brutality or excessive force in a court of law."

"Fuck the court of law. Can you clowns find my kid now? Please." Maxi sucked in a huge breath and let out a scream. "RIC!" The rest stood in silence waiting for an answer.

"Okay, so that didn't work," Zack held one of Ric's shirts that Maxi had packed, in front of Bobby's nose. "Alright Bob, time to do your job." The dog took off running in circles, the circumference growing with each loop.

Maxi kept one eye on Kit Sellers while the rest of her focus stayed with Bobby. The lab ran off the trail into the woods and from Maxi's position, she could see through the trees that the dog had stopped and sat.

She started to move in the dog's direction. Zack pulled her back. "Hey love, please keep an eye on this gal—"

"I will, love," she had an edge to her voice, "if you'd follow Bobby and see why he's stopped. Or I can if you want to—"

"Max, I would really like you to stay here." Zack's voice grated on Maxi's last nerve. She tapped her foot, drowning out Bobby's howls.

"Then freakin' go see what the dog—"

Pete called back from the woods, "He's just sitting, sniffing, and giving off a whiny sound."

"Pat him on the head and tell him to go," Zack instructed.

Bobby shot out of the woods, past the group to head in the direction of both the abandoned lodge and smoldering garage. "Please go towards the lodge," Maxi whispered.

Her brother climbed back on the trail, a little short of breath. "Don't worry," he huffed out, "I'll follow the dang dog." Just as Pete finished speaking, Bobby looped around the lodge, disappeared over the ridge, and returned smelling like a campfire.

L.M. Pampuro

Maxi brought her heel down on Kit's thigh. She watched the pain spread across Kit's face as the tears moved down her own.

RIC

"I must be hallucinating," Ric said as he could have sworn, he heard his mother scream. "Crazy mama now entering my thoughts." He pushed himself off the floor to peek out the office window.

The garage still smoked and so far, no one had come to investigate the fire. It appeared that he remained the only human in the area. More weirdness to go with the rest of his life.

Ric started to rise as shrieking sounds of metal on cement sent him back into the corner. The boxes were still stacked against the office door. He turned to the wall to press his fingers under the small opening on the windowsill. Whoever was inside the main room sounded like they were destroying the place.

Something kept hitting the metal counters while several items fell against the linoleum floor. Ric pressed further into the corner as the thing that was causing the ruckus scratched the office door.

The scratching noise moved into howls. Ric climbed out of his hiding place to press the window fully open. "Fuck, fuck, fuck," he swore as he squeezed his legs over the ledge.

The door on the other side of the room hit the wall – Ric let go and fell to the ground. As he started to right himself, a big black ball of fur fell on top of him. He scratched his arms and legs as he tried to squirm away from the animal.

A wet tongue lapped at his cheek. Ric turned his head and looked into the animal's big brown eyes. "Bobby?"

Bobby jumped off Ric's body and started to dance around and bark. Ric grabbed onto the dog's neck to hug him tight. He looked up at the window to see his stepfather's face.

"Please tell me you aren't a hallucination," Ric called.

Zack answered, "Back at ya."

MAXI

When Bobby's barks reached back to where Maxi stood, she gave Kit one more kick then took off running in the direction of the noise. Her eyes focused on the area of smoke; she almost missed her son on the ground hugging the dog.

"RIC," she screamed as she fell next to him, pushing Bobby aside to hold her child tight. "Oh my god. Oh my god. Oh my god." Maxi's whole body shook as her face became damp with tears. She wrapped both arms around Ric's shoulders, holding on with so much force, her biceps ached.

Ric whispered into her neck, "I knew that you'd get here eventually." He tightened his grip. "Know why?"

"Don't say it," Maxi warned, although both began to laugh.

"So happy crazy mama rules my world!" Ric grinned. He kissed his mother on her wet cheek. "How did you find me?"

Maxi loosened her grip to give her son a quick once over. He looked dirty and reeked like he was sprayed by a skunk. Her eyes grew wide. "Better yet, how did you get here and why do you stink like weed?"

Both started to push off the ground. "Ah, mom, how do you know what weed smells like?"

"It doesn't matter, does it?" Maxi grabbed Ric back into a hug. "I—"

BOOM!

PETE

"Leave it to my sister to leave a criminal by herself." Pete got as far as the lodge door when Maxi tore down the hill. He started to follow her yet remembered that Kit Sellers was last sitting on the ground under her watch.

Pete moved fast up the hill, but not fast enough. As he approached the car, he heard the unmistakable sound of a bullet entering the chamber. Crouched down next to the driver's side door, Kit Sellers now had the barrel of a gun aimed in his direction.

"If I were you, I wouldn't move," she said, "Just come around over here," she pointed to an area of about five yards in front of the SUV, "and we will wait for your friends to get back. That kid has been a pain in our ass."

Pete took slow steps headed towards where she had pointed. "I still don't understand why you are doing this," Pete said.

"Money."

"Why you have daughters?"

"No and neither do you. How stupid do you think I am?" Kit's eyes met Pete's while the gun shook in her hand.

"I don't think that you are stupid at all," Pete answered. "Just don't understand why anyone would—"

"Do something for money? Okay, then how about I am doing this for revenge. To get back at my power-hungry uncle for killing my dad. My dad wanted to put a stop on the illegal stuff, you know, split the firm, but my uncle, that greedy bastard murdered my dad instead.

Can you now understand why I want him dead and discredited?"

"That I can understand but you don't have to get revenge this way. Couldn't you just turn in evidence to get the Senator—"

"Dude, do you live in the real world? The Senator is a pawn. The people who manipulate that blow hard are tired of his shit. I'm just speeding up his demise."

"Why?"

"Why what?"

"Wait - Majorie is his niece, so you two are sisters?"

Pete hit a nerve. Kit moved from behind the car door to give Pete a glare down. The gun level with Pete's chest did not move.

"Marjorie likes money more than family. She is also a screw up – she tried at what ten colleges? But me," Kit fired a bullet three feet to Pete's side. "I took care of myself and kept my mother safe, especially when that prick of an uncle–"

She pulled the grenade out of her pocket, "screw this - time is up for your team," she pulled the pin and cocked her arm to throw. As her arm stretched back, Jerry laid his teeth into her ass. Kit Sellers arm went down to hit the dog. Pete dived into the frenzy.

The grenade rolled about five feet away from the lodge.

A gun fired.

L.M. Pampuro

ZACK

The sound of gunfire split the air. Zack sprinted towards it. He rounded the corner in time to see Jerry running down the hill. Past him, Pete and Kit lay by an open car door. "Oh crap," he whispered. Moving his head in the opposite direction, Zack followed Jerry's focus to the grenade, seven feet away from where the dog stood.

"Jerry!" he shrieked. The volume echoed off the building. The dog growled as it moved in the direction of the grenade. Maxi and Ric were almost at his side. "Jerry!" he yelled again; this time louder than the last. Zack moved Maxi in the direction of the woods.

Zack's strength pushed his wife's back so hard she started to fall. He just caught her before she hit the ground. With a single focus, he carried Maxi and pushed Ric to move. "Hurry into the trees." Bobby ran back up the hill to Pete.

Unexpectedly, all four paws of Jerry's paws hit Zack's back. "DOWN!" he yelled as he fell forward to take Maxi and Ric to the ground.

The explosion shook the earth. Heated debris flew over their bodies to singe Zack's hair and clothing. In the silence that followed, all froze in place.

RIC

His mother's bulk pushed his face and hands onto the ground, and something warm sat on top of his head. The ground shook more than when the garage blew up though the blast wasn't as loud. "What the—" Ric mumbled into the dirt.

When the weight above him shifted, a wet tongue gave a quick lick of his face. "Jerry?" Ric said as the dog kept tasting his forehead.

His mother shifted her body over to one side. "You, okay?" she said. Ric just nodded back. Up at the top of the hill his stepfather stood over two bodies. One looked to be moving while the other lay still.

"Why does this keep happening to us?" He turned to ask his mom.

"Love," she said. Ric nodded his head as if he understood his mother.

The entrance to the lodge now lay in a pile of rocks that Bobby circled and sniffed. A crater now where the door once stood.

Ric felt each muscle in his leg tense and relax as he went to stand. He extended his hand to help pull his mother up. Both surveyed the activity up by the car.

His mother showed more juice than he did as she led the way upward. Breathing heavy, they reached the front bumper in time for Zack to cut both off. "Take your mother over there," he pointed at the trees.

"I—"

"He will do no such thing," Maxi said. Toe tapping as loud as her voice. "Let me see Pete."

L.M. Pampuro

"Uncle Pete is over there," Ric tried to look beyond Zack.

"Ric, I really wish you would—"

"Is Uncle Pete dead?" Both his parents now stood open mouthed.

"No, Uncle Pete is not dead," his uncle's voice stretched over the car. "Nor is this slime bag. We are trying to figure out how to transport both of us to a medic."

"Although we only give a rat's ass about one."

His mom's face turned bright red. "Put my brother in the backseat with the dogs. Put the bitch in the hatchback. Ric and I will sit in front."

"Or," his stepdad countered, "You drive. Ric and the dogs sit in the passenger's seat. I put Pete in the back where I can monitor him, and we leave the other to rot."

"Cold," Ric said, "can we just get out of here because that Sheriff may come back and two explosions plus a shootout is my daily limit."

"Let your mom climb through the passenger's seat, please." The SUV shifted a bit and Uncle Pete let out a few howls that put Bobby to shame. Mom kept her gaze straight ahead up until Uncle Pete got loaded in.

Ric pulled down the sun visor to meet his uncle's scrutiny in the mirror. "No more camp for you kid," Pete said offering both a grin and a wink.

"Maybe I'll come intern with you next summer," Ric replied as both Maxi and Zack screamed "NO!" in harmony.

ZACK

The challenge of the old fire roads is to try to miss the ruts created by years of snow and the potholes from years of ski equipment being dragged along the route.

The Sheriff's car passed going in the opposite direction once they hit Amity's main drag. Maxi turned her attention to the side mirror to see if he'd turn around and follow. The universe gave them a solid.

Zack had wrapped Pete's arm in his shirt along with tying a rag halfway down his bicep. His friend needed a doctor, and they needed to go somewhere trustworthy.

"Where am I going?" Maxi interrupted Zack's thoughts.

"Let's see," Zack responded as a ringtone came from the radio speakers. Donald Atwood's voice boomed inside.

"Situation," he barked.

"Better," Zack said, and he heard Maxi agree. "We have Ric—"

"Hello Mr. Atwood," Ric chimed in.

"Well, hello young man. How are you feeling?"

"I am okay, but Uncle Pete is not."

"What happened to Malone, Brady?" Atwood's voice softened.

"Reader's digest version, your gal, Kit Sellers, is a vindictive bitch, a snake, and a traitor. I thought you vetted these people."

"And there is another Majorie connection," Maxi added.

"Are you—" Atwood stopped mid-sentence to redirect his thought. "Is Kit Sellers still alive."

"Barely," Zack stated. "We need a hospital without worries and an update from the DC team."

"Take them both to Niza General. I will have a few team members standing by."

"No."

"Brady, what do you mean, no?" Atwood's voice went an octave lower.

"No team members. I will guard both."

"Zack, I understand that you are upset—"

"Upset? I am livid! How did these people get through the vetting process?" Silence now filled the air. Maxi shifted in her seat to point to the highway. Zack motioned for her to head towards Niza.

"Zack, bring both men to Niza General and I will have team members meet you. You can't do this alone."

"Or anymore. As of today, I quit. You'll get my letter as soon as this is settled." He clicked the call end button before Atwood could comment and dialed another number. "Harper, you still west of D.C.?"

"Yeah. Hey, I saw a lot of activity down by the old lodge. You all okay?"

"We are my friend. I got one of the gals that your team will want with a gunshot wound in my backseat."

"Where are you?"

"Heading into Niza from the foothills." Zack shared his location with the push of a button.

"Take the first hospital exit and dump Ms. Sellers into the ER. No worries as I will have Elma head over to babysit."

"Gotcha. Thank both of you, Harper. I will be in touch."

"What's the plan, love?" Maxi's voice cut into Zack's internal review of available options.

"Get off at the first hospital sign you see. Elma Harper is heading there to deal with Sellers so we can just dump the bitch at the ER. I will make a phone call for a transport East."

"Wait – is Elma the little dudes mother?" Ric cut in.

"Yeah, I think she has a son about eight, why?"

"I read to him when I was in prison. I wish I knew."

"Sometimes we don't know who to trust. Zach turned his attention to Pete. "Hang in there, buddy. I gotcha."

MAXI

Elma Harper pulled up in a black Escalade at the same moment as Maxi and took total charge of the situation. They were heading towards Fremont Springs within twenty minutes.

She gave a quick nod to Ric and started to apologize to Maxi. "I couldn't blow my cover yet my heart ached for you."

Maxi gave Elma a hug, "Thank you," was her only reply. Now was not the time for an emotional confrontation.

Although she'd never admit it, her husband often left her in awe. At the Airforce base a transport waited for their departure, along with a doctor. The plane needed to be back in DC at some general's request so instead of sitting against a wall in big tube, Maxi leaned back in a leather seat that could lounged back into a prone position for sleeping.

She rested one hand on Ric's arm while the other held Zack's hand tight. The vibrations of the engine combined with her emotional drain, took a toll on her body and mind.

The nightmare wasn't completely over, yet the end seemed close.

Across the aisle, Bobby rested his chin on her brother's sedated chest. Both moved with the rhythm of Pete's breath. The doctor wandered up and down the aisle, checking vitals each time he passed.

Once Pete got settled, the doctor turned towards Zack and Maxi relaying specifics about his condition. "Your brother has a serious gunshot wound yet with a bit of physical therapy; he will be fine." From there all those awake got a stern lecture about how to treat the wounded. "You all were lucky this time. I cannot say this enough, you passed six trauma facilities on the way here and actually stopped at one to drop off the other victim. Yet did not admit your brother. This decision could have turned..." He stopped to let his words sink in

The doctor continued on about gunshot wounds and blood loss. Maxi started to doze. Medical facilities were mentioned several times.

"Will this really end," she whispered to Zack.

"For us it will. I just sent my resignation letter—"

"You wrote it that quick?"

"Awe love," Zack brushed Maxi's knuckles with his lips. "This baby has been written and waiting for the last year." He lowered his voice so only Maxi could hear. "After all those congressional hearings, I saw that nothing would change, no matter what truths I found. It's time, love. I can't not have faith in the system and still do my job. I don't operate that way."

He kissed her temple. "What about our life? Are we—"

"Safe?" Zack finished her sentence. "Yeah, we should be. I sent the Senator a copy of my resignation and said I was done. He wished us all a happy retirement and added that he might join our ranks in the future."

"I don't understand."

"You don't have to understand any of this, just know that we can move out of Vermont and go wherever you want."

"Just not Saratoga," Ric cut in. "You can visit but I need my space, at school, right Zack?" The kid's eyes couldn't plead any more.

"You be you," Zack answered while he reached over Maxi to give Ric a fist pump.

Epilogue

The fax came in from an unknown number and simply read *Congratulations on your Retirement. May we never cross paths again.* Zack laughed as he read out loud. "Come on Max, this is funny. At least he wishes us well."

She didn't think it was so funny. The Senator's arrogance bothered her from the moment she had watched her husband on TV during the Senator's inquiry sessions.

Politics sucked yet at least their part in it was over for now.

She started down the steps that led to the back patio. A bowl of tortilla chips balanced in one hand. The scene in front of her was something out of her dreams. The only missing item, a big banner that read *Happy Retirement,* Zack had nixed. *He nixes the banner but wanted the Senator's fax on the fridge.*

Sometimes her husband was a mystery.

Gathered amongst the vegetation in her backyard were some of the people in her and Zack's life. Over in one corner the two Senators from Vermont talked with a couple of Ric's friends from college who hoped to get into politics one day.

She saw Rain and Skye conversing with the drug enforcement agents that had been friends of Zack's for decades. "Oh, to be a spectator in that conversation," she mumbled to herself.

Next to a makeshift stage, Ric and his buddies fiddled with a borrowed public address system as they set up the band, or as Ric liked to say, the band of friends who will soon fill the space with music. Elma's son sat just on the edge of all the commotion.

The smell of spaghetti sauce combined with meat from a smoker brought her back to the task at hand. Maxi placed the bowl onto the food table and did a quick rearrangement of the snacks. She had cooked for two days to make this event happen in a style her parents would have been proud of. She had a lot of company and so much food they will be eating leftovers for weeks.

Out of the corner of her eye Maxi caught Donald Atwood shaking Harper's hand and turning in her direction. His long pants were in the minority on this beautiful Vermont summer's day and the manner that he tucked in his polo shirt brought him a sense of authority even in casual clothes. He stopped by a table that included his wife, along with several women who Maxi did not know, to give a quick kiss on the cheek.

Maxi noted that the center of the table had several empty bottles of wine. This prompted a quick check of the cooler to make sure there would be plenty of drinks.

"This is a wonderful event. Wonderful event," Donald greeted.

"Thank you, Donald I'm doing my best to give Zack a good send off."

"Maxi, this is wonderful." He repeated, adding, "Think about it, if all of this trouble hadn't started in Fremont, and if you hadn't got involved, even though I didn't approve of that," he gave her a look, "I don't know if we would be as far along as we are and, in the position, we're in."

Maxi held up her hand to stop him. "Donald, my son being kidnapped was not cool." She had a tight smile pasted on her face. "I never ever want to experience this again."

"I don't think you will, Max, unless Ric decides to come work for us."

Maxi let out a laugh that drew attention from some of those nearby. "Ric is not going to work for you, Donald."

"He'd be a perfect addition to our team, especially with his computer skills."

"No, Donald. My life was screwed up enough with Zack working for you. I can't imagine—"

Maxi felt a pair of arms encircle her body from behind. Zack's voice came loud and clear interrupting the conversation. "Imagine what?" he gave her a squeeze.

"Imagine Ric working for Donald." She turned her body so she could see Zack's face.

"Ric working for Donald—that would be—"

"Bad. That would be bad."

"Listen folks, all I did was suggest in passing that Ric would be a good addition to our team after he graduates. Heck, he could do freelance stuff—"

"No." Maxi's face tightened as she now stood arms crossed between Donald Atwood and her husband.

Zack began to speak in a hushed tone. "Listen, Max, I am certain that Donald was just thinking out loud," he nodded towards his old boss who returned the gesture, "and is not offering Ric a job at the agency or a freelance opportunity at this time."

"Or ever," Maxi injected.

"Or ever," Zack repeated. All three stood in uncomfortable silence for a beat. "Maxi, Donald here is going to be lonely."

"Lonely?" Donald huffed.

"Yes, because as my work partner, I am divorcing you in retirement." An uncomfortable laugh followed. "Donald, behave yourself," Zack instructed as he

pulled Maxi into the house. They faced each other inside the busy kitchen. "Maxi, Donald would not start recruiting Ric without giving me a courtesy call."

"And after you would tell me?"

"Of course, I would tell you," Zack leaned in for a kiss, yet Maxi arched her face just out of reach. "Darling, after today, you and I have the rest of our lives to be in each other's way, to share stories and find out more about each other." Zack watched his wife's shoulders relax a little. "And we can live anywhere—"

"Stop distracting me with adventures. I mean really, who would want the fortress?"

"The man who we just walked away from to start. Just say the word. The world is our playground–let's choose a swing set."

Maxi giggled. "When did you become so poetic?"

"When I married you." Zack turned Maxi towards the back door and pushed her back into the party just as Ric started to play the beginning notes of The Grateful Dead's *U.S. Blues*.

Maxi let out a deep sigh as Zack lifted her arm to twirl her around. The two began to dance, surrounded by their past, their present, and the anticipation of their next chapters.

Maximum Panic

L.M. Pampuro

Maximum Panic

Thankful & Grateful

There are so many people to thank that were part of making this story happen.

Eileen Waldman who after *Maximum Mayhem* and *Maximum Trouble* told me that I had another Maxi and Zack book to write.

Robert Calegari, my beta reader extraordinaire and maybe my biggest fan along with my E-Book tech expert, Rita Cabata.

Gina Troisi, Sonja Mongar, and A.B. Westrick – my dream mentor team at Western Connecticut State University, whose suggestions and overall feedback pushed me to write one of my bests.

Let's be real - everyone I encountered within the Western Connecticut State University MFA program taught me something – I appreciate the time and energy my mentors and peers gave to this project. (An older version served as my MFA thesis).

And then there are my past mentors – the ones who set the stage to get me here today. Christine Archer, Kay Janney, and Jamie Cat Callan will always be part of my writers' journey, each as primary mentors at the perfect time.

I surround myself with fellow creatives. Some compose music, others write books while others create visual works of art through mixed mediums- Thank you Terri Meigs, Renee Stevens, Faith Campbell-Powers, Terri Coe, Carrie Lombardi, and all of those who push me to be a better version of myself.

Special thanks to my mom and dad, and my husband and son, for their love and support ☺

Yet without my readers, booksellers, and everyone who is part of this craziness, none of this would be possible. Thank you for reading my books and helping to support my dream.

Read a book and go on an adventure!

Peace.

Get Social to Stay Updated:
instagram.com/lmpampuro
Pampuro.com
lmpampuro.substack.com

9 798988 417132